MIXED UP WITH A MARINE

A SMALL TOWN SECOND CHANCE MILITARY ROMANCE

KAIT NOLAN

TAKE THE LEAP PUBLISHING

A LETTER TO READERS

Dear Reader,

Before I get to my usual warning, I want to make sure you're notified that the prequel story, *Rescued By a Bad Boy,* which I've included in this print edition, deals with some sensitive topics. **Those triggered by issues around sexual assault are cautioned before reading.**

This stories contain swearing and pre-marital sex between the lead couple, as those things are part of the realistic lives of characters of this generation, and of many of my readers.

If either of these things are not your cup of tea, please consider that you may not be the right audience for this book. There are scores of other books out there that are written with you in mind. In fact, I've got a list of some of my favorite authors who write on the sweeter side on my website at https://kaitnolan.com/on-the-sweeter-side/

If you choose to stick with me, I hope you enjoy!

Happy reading!

Kait

RESCUED BY A BAD BOY

A BAD BOY BAKERS PREQUEL

What's a little marriage between friends?

Mia has been Braxton's best friend for years. Even when they no longer lived in the same foster family, even after he'd aged out of the system, he'd continued look out for the one person who got under his skin and made him care.

For the last six years, Mia's been keeping her head down, putting one foot in front of the other, unable to trust anyone with her secrets—including the foster brother who's been the one bright spot in her life, as well as her secret crush.

Just one more day until Mia turns eighteen—a legal adult. Brax doesn't trust her foster father and wants her out of that house. Is proposing a marriage of convenience to your best friend a little drastic? Maybe so. But what Brax feels is so far beyond friendship. Is it possible Mia feels it, too?

CHAPTER 1

Mia Torres snapped from sleep to wakefulness in a heartbeat, ears straining to analyze for threat before she opened her eyes or moved a muscle. A faint *scritch scritch* sounded at the window as the overgrown black hawthorn bush outside nodded in the wind. The clatter of breakfast dishes sounded from elsewhere in the house, but there was no squeak of floorboards, no sense of movement nearby. She cracked her eyes open and spotted her desk chair still wedged under the doorknob, exactly where she'd left it last night. Her paltry wooden sentry had done its job. Beneath the pillow, her hand relaxed, releasing the scissors she slept with. Flexing stiff fingers, she sat up and stretched. Her spine and shoulders popped.

One more day.

Less than twenty-four hours until she turned eighteen. They couldn't hold her after today. In truth, she really needed to make it through the end of the semester until graduation, but if worse came to worst and she ever had to use those scissors, she could leave tomorrow. The idea of it terrified her, but she'd figure it out. She was so over the foster system. It was supposed to keep her safe. For nearly six years, she'd bought into that, done everything she was told, kept her head down, stayed invisible. She was very, very good at being invisible. But this last placement had her questioning all the well-meaning adults who'd put her in this position, claiming it was for the best.

It hadn't been so bad when Lainey and Max had been here. But Lainey had been busted for drugs at Halloween, and Max was doing a stint in juvie for boosting some rich guy's sports car for a joy ride. For the past two months, it had been only Mia. Her foster mom, Darlene, wasn't so bad. She wasn't a warm woman, but she appreciated hard work and manners, something Mia's real mother had drilled into her from a young age. She'd held onto them after her mom died, feeling like it was a small way to honor her. But Darlene's husband, Wayne, made Mia nervous. He hadn't ever laid a hand on her, hadn't said anything outright threatening. He just watched her. Long, assessing gazes with those flat, watery blue eyes that Mia wasn't sure how to read. She didn't know if he'd stay content with only looking, and she wasn't taking any chances.

The oversized flannel shirt she dragged on over her henley hid the shape of her body. It was probably poor camouflage for the curves that had sprung up against all her hopes two years ago, but it made her feel more at ease. She'd use whatever flimsy armor she could manage. Working her long, thick sable hair into a braid, she peeked out the window at the gray January day. Freezing and gross but not actively snowing. It was as much of a win as she could expect in this part of Washington. She'd take it.

A glance at the clock told her she needed to get a move on, or she'd be late for school. The lace-up boots she'd found at a second-hand store for ten bucks would do good to make it the rest of the winter. Maybe she could shore up the inside seams with duct tape. Later. She added a second pair of socks before slipping them on and shrugging into her coat. Out of long-ingrained habit, she hauled the duffel bag out from under the bed and did a quick inventory of its contents. A few changes of clothes. Basic toiletries. The little Lego knight she'd been gifted in her first foster home by the boy who'd become her best friend. The sketch pad where she captured the dreams she didn't dare tell anyone about. A picture of her mother. The things she couldn't live without if she had to run. Satisfied all was as it should be, she shoved the go bag back in place and stuffed the last of her schoolbooks in her backpack. There'd be a quiz in U.S. Government today, and she'd been up too late preparing. Quick and quiet, she removed the chair from beneath the knob, sliding it back in place beneath the boards laid over two battered file cabinets that served as her desk. One last look to make sure everything was in place.

The scissors. Pulling them out from beneath the pillow, she hid them under the mattress.

Time to go.

Wayne was at the kitchen table, lingering over a cup of coffee. A too large figure in a quilted flannel jacket, he seemed to take up half the room just by breathing. Mia's step hitched a fraction of a second at the sight of him. He'd normally be gone to his job at the steel mill by now. Ducking her head to avoid eye contact, she made a beeline for the cabinet to grab a pack of Pop Tarts for the walk to school.

"No greeting this morning?" His voice held a smoker's rasp and something slick and oily in the tone that automatically put her back up.

Smoothing her features, Mia turned in his direction and muttered, "Morning." Then she couldn't stop herself from asking, "Aren't you late?" She regretted the words as soon as they were out. They opened the door for conversation, which was the last thing she wanted.

"It's a service day. Line's down for repair."

She grunted an acknowledgment and headed for the door.

"In a hurry?"

Without looking back, she reached for the door. "I have a test this morning."

"Have a good day at school."

Uncertain what to do with that, she just kept going, straight out into the cold. The whip of winter wind helped clear her head. Her boots crunched on old snow as she strode down the driveway to the sidewalk. A figure melted out of the trees up near the corner. Stubble darkened the cheeks of the tall, rangy boy who was well on his way to manhood. At the sight of him, Mia felt the tension in her shoulders dissolve and her heart kick into high gear.

Braxton Whitmore was her lifeline. A former foster sibling, he'd made the past six years tolerable. He'd befriended her when she'd had no one. Taught her how to fight, what to watch for. Kept her safe. And even though he'd aged out of the system last year, he was still looking out for her.

Was it any wonder she was in love with him?

Determined not to betray herself, Mia worked to control her features and hurried to meet him.

BRAX HUNCHED into the shearling-lined denim of his jacket, keeping his eyes on the house instead of the girl who'd done everything in her limited power to hide the fact that she was a woman. He'd had a lot of practice at trying not to notice those failed efforts. The baggy, shapeless clothes couldn't fully conceal that hourglass figure his fingers itched to touch. The total lack of makeup only served to draw attention to those striking, long-lashed coffee-colored eyes he wanted to drown in. As she neared, those unpainted lips curved into one of the hard-won smiles that fueled his days.

"Morning." Her breath puffed out in a cloud with the greeting.

Brax grunted an acknowledgement, his gaze shifting back to the single-story ranch where the blinds in one of the front windows twitched, as if someone were watching her. His eyes narrowed. "Wayne still home?"

"The line is down for repair, apparently."

This close, Brax could see the faint shadows beneath her eyes. "You didn't sleep well. Problem?" His gut tightened at the thought of everything that could happen to her in the night without him being there to stop it. He'd done his best to prepare her, but nothing changed the fact that she was small, and her foster father was a big son of a bitch, who could've played defensive line for the Seahawks.

Her shoulders jerked in a shrug, but she didn't avoid eye contact. "No more than usual. I'm just edgy."

So was Brax. "You're taking precautions?"

"Always."

Satisfied with her answer, he let the tension release and fell into step beside her for the trek to school, as he did every day, come rain, snow, or shine, before he went to the first of two jobs. What would she say if she knew he organized his entire work schedule around being able to see her to and from school? She'd probably be horrified by how many decisions he'd made with her in mind. He hadn't planned it that way. For so long, his focus had been on his own survival.

He'd been on the streets for nearly a year after his mother had ODed. A skinny, half-starved ten-year-old, who'd had more in common with the stray mongrels he'd sometimes emulated than the kids his age he'd seen in public. The restaurant owner who'd caught him foraging in the trash for food had lured him in with a hot meal while he called the cops who'd ultimately connected Brax with social services. It hadn't taken them long to figure out that he had no family and dumped him into the system. That had just been trading one kind of survival for another. He'd trusted no one and bounced through so many placements by the time he was thirteen, he'd earned the "problem child" label. He'd still been one step from feral when he'd landed in Mia's first foster home.

She'd been shell-shocked and so damned scared. When he'd heard her crying that first night, he'd sneaked into her room and curled up on the floor by her bed, close enough to reach up and brush her hand. It had been the first deliberate human contact he'd attempted. When she'd latched on, that little hand squeezing his, he hadn't pulled away. Thus had begun their unlikely friendship.

In her, he'd sensed the kind of gentleness that would get slaughtered by the harsh realities of the world they lived in. Some instinct he hadn't recognized had driven him to protect her. Maybe because he'd seen too much goodness broken to be able to stand by and watch as it happened to her. So he'd shaped up, because he'd known they'd ship him off somewhere else if he didn't. The social worker had been so impressed with his turnaround, she'd made sure he and Mia stayed together. At least until he'd aged out a little over a year ago. It was a minor miracle. The only good thing either of them had gotten out of foster care.

"You're thinking deep thoughts this morning." Her voice brought him back from his musings.

"Just thinking about tomorrow. It's the big one-eight."

Mia blew out a breath. "Yep."

They both knew the implications of this birthday.

"You given any more thought to what you wanna do?" He kept his voice easy, no pressure.

"Yeah. I'm gonna try to stick it out 'til graduation. If I go out on my own, I'd probably have to drop out to work enough to support myself. And even then, it probably wouldn't be enough to make it on my own."

Brax got that. He worked his ass off at two jobs so that he didn't have to depend on anyone else, and so he could put a little bit by each pay period in case of... In case. He wanted to tell her she wouldn't have to do it on her own. That she'd have him. But something held him back. Would she see the offer as friendship or a request for more? God knew he wanted more with her, but he'd never do anything to pressure her or risk destroying the trust she had in him. She was too important.

"Makes sense," he agreed equably. But he couldn't get the image of those blinds out of his mind. He wanted her out of that house, and he'd been considering extreme measures to accomplish it.

She opened a pack of Pop Tarts, passing him one, as she always did, for the last chunk of the walk. "One of these days, I'll be able to afford real pastries, like they have in the window of the bakery downtown. They always look so shiny and beautiful."

Understanding she wanted easier conversation, he followed her lead. "And what kind would you get?"

"Something raspberry. Maybe one of those tart things with all the pretty designs made out of dough. Or the pinwheels. Oh! Or those sort of swirly ones—what are they called?—palmiers."

"Why raspberry?"

"They were my mom's favorite. I don't think I've had one since she died."

Brax decided he'd move heaven and earth to get this girl something raspberry for her birthday.

At the dog groomer's across the street from the school grounds, they stopped, watching other students flowing into the two-story brick building.

"I gotta go. Test this morning."

Much as he'd hated everything about the restrictions of school, he wished he was going in there with her. He wasn't ready to walk away from her yet. He suspected he never would be. "You have time to come by my place after school?"

Her brows drew together. "Don't you have to work tonight?"

"Not until tomorrow night." He'd talk Jerry into trading shifts with him. "I have a surprise for your birthday." Or he would by the end of the day.

Her face twisted somewhere between suspicion and excitement. "Early?"

"Yes, early. I can't wait."

That earned him another of those smiles that warmed him up inside. "Then I can't either. See you after school!"

As he always did, Brax waited for her to get inside the building. The jingle of the shop bell behind him told him someone was coming out. He was unsurprised when Valentina, the tatted-up owner of Mudpuppies, strode out. She wore a hot pink bandana over her spiral curls and a smirk on her warm brown face as she looked across the school grounds. "When you gonna lock that down?"

"It's not like that, V."

"The hell it isn't. I been watching you walk her to and from school every day for the past... how many years? You are totally gone over that girl."

That was completely beside the point.

"I'm just looking out for her."

"Mmmhmm."

Brax met her skeptical gaze. "She's not ready for anything else."

Valentina crossed her arms and arched a perfectly manicured brow. "You actually asked her?" When he kept his mouth shut, she just shook her head. "That's what I thought. Boy, you're loyal as the day is long, but you sure are blind. She's crazy about you."

As the bell rang for the start of the school day, Brax glanced back at the school. Was she right? Did Mia feel more than he thought she did? Like most foster kids he knew, they both habitually played things close to the vest, masking their emotions because, in their world, feelings were weaknesses to be exploited. Was it worth the risk of finding out?

"Her birthday's tomorrow. Eighteen." He didn't know why he said it, except that it had been on his mind for weeks.

"That what you've been waiting for?"

Was it? Maybe on some level. He'd been very aware of their year and change age difference since he'd left the system, not wanting to do anything to rock the boat and put her at risk or give anyone ammunition to keep them apart.

But at eighteen, she got to make her own decisions. She'd have to fight for them, but she'd be a legal adult.

Maybe he'd talk to her about it. But he'd see how the birthday surprise went first.

"I gotta go. Lots to do today to surprise her."

Valentina grinned. "Good for you, honey."

CHAPTER 2

Damn Brax and his surprise. The wondering about it consumed Mia all day, distracting her from the class discussion on *Heart of Darkness*. She couldn't even pay attention in physics—her favorite class. She enjoyed understanding how things worked in the physical world, and on a normal day, she could lose herself in the predictability of calculations. But today wasn't normal. It crawled by with minutes that stretched like hours. Once or twice, she would have sworn the clock actually moved backward just to spite her.

What did he have planned? Neither of them had much money to speak of, and all of his needed to go to rent and bills and keeping him fed. Not that lack of funds had ever stopped him from making her birthday memorable. He always managed to come up with something that hit her right in the feels and made her feel seen. For a girl whose life had necessarily depended on invisibility, his thoughtful gestures were intoxicating. That he put forth the effort for no one but her made Mia dream of more. Of everything.

But he'd never given any sign he saw her as something other than a friend. He'd long told her he wasn't capable of attachment, despite the fact that his actions toward her said otherwise. He believed that lie about himself because he needed to. Letting himself care about someone else opened him to loss, and he'd had so very much of it. Mia understood that, so she wouldn't ask him for more than he was prepared to give.

No matter how much time she'd spent fantasizing about that arrogantly sensual mouth of his.

"Miss Torres!"

Mia blinked. Her trigonometry teacher, Mrs. Moody, came into focus, wearing a pinched expression that suggested this wasn't the first time she'd called Mia's name. "Ma'am?"

"You're being summoned to the office. Take your things."

That was when Mia noticed the perky blonde office aid waiting to escort her.

All her lovely birthday fantasies dried up, replaced by a kernel of lead in her stomach. Without fuss, she packed up her bag and left the classroom. The kernel grew with every step, every swing of that golden ponytail, as she took what felt like a gallows walk down to the first-floor office.

Her mind spun.

What could this be about? She'd done nothing wrong, so surely this wasn't a disciplinary meeting. There'd been no sightings of drug dogs doing locker checks—not that there'd have been anything for them to find, unless someone had planted something in her locker. It happened.

Maybe Curt was here with news of her father.

The momentary excitement at that thought died a rapid death. What was the likelihood any such news was good? If the Marshal was here, it likely meant one thing—that she needed to move again because someone had gotten too close. He'd prepared her for that eventuality for years, ever since he'd embedded her into the foster system.

A cold sweat broke out down her spine. She couldn't leave

now. Not without Brax. He didn't know her history. Couldn't know, per Curt's strict edict. And he'd never be allowed to come with her, even if he wanted to.

Please don't be Curt. Please don't be Curt. Please don't be Curt.

It wasn't the man who'd been both savior and jailer waiting for her in the principal's office. Fresh anxiety spun the bowling ball lodged in her gut as Wayne rose from a chair. A trucker hat with beer logo covered his head, and all she could think was *Hats aren't allowed.*

"Let's go." His tone was clipped.

Her fingers tightened on the strap of her backpack as she shot a glance at the principal. "What's going on?"

Dr. Gleason, a bookish Black man with short salt-and-pepper hair and wire-rimmed glasses he was always cleaning on the edge of his sweater vests, offered a sad smile. "I'm so sorry for your loss."

Mia swallowed, her throat threatening to close up. "Who... who died?" Oh God. Was *that* the news about her father?

"Darlene's mama. She's already headed over to Ellensburg to start making arrangements."

The stranglehold loosened. No one she knew.

But were they really expecting her to go to the funeral? She hadn't met Darlene's mother, so it wasn't as if this woman was some kind of pseudo-grandmother. Yet why else would Wayne be here to check her out of school early?

Uncomfortable with the situation, but seeing no alternatives, Mia followed her foster father out to his beat-up Chevy pickup.

Crap. How was she going to get a message to Brax? He'd be expecting to meet her in a little over an hour.

Wayne slammed the driver's side door, and Mia caught a whiff of something sharp beneath the overpowering mint of mouthwash. Had he been drinking?

Keeping a firm hold on her backpack, she curled her hand

around the door handle, prepared to leap and make a run for it. But he made it the couple miles to the house with only a little weaving. As soon as he pulled into the driveway, she was out of the truck in a flash, already heading for the house.

Could she get a message to Brax at work? Maybe while Wayne was packing, she could make the call. Or maybe she could convince Wayne to leave her here. She was more than old enough to be left on her own for a few days.

He followed her inside, shutting the door behind them. Something about that sound made the hair on the back of her neck stand up. She couldn't be trapped in a vehicle with him for three hours.

"When's the funeral?" She began to formulate her argument based on a handful of his possible answers.

"Few days. They're aiming for the weekend so the rest of the family can get there."

"I'm sure Darlene wants your support. Neither of you needs to worry about me. I'm fine here on my own, and that way I won't miss school."

Those flat eyes stared at her from across the room, and Mia instinctively curled her hands around the back of a kitchen chair.

"You ain't stayin' here on your own."

She calculated the odds of winning an argument about this at next to zero. Darlene was the one who could have been convinced, and she was already gone. But Mia tried again. "I don't have any clothes that are appropriate for a funeral."

"That don't matter."

Pick your battles.

"How many days should I pack for?" She had a black sweater. Maybe with her best pair of jeans, it would be okay.

"Don't need to pack."

Mia frowned. "But you said we'd be gone for a few days."

Wayne's lips curved into a chilling smile. "Never said we'd

be going anywhere. You and me are gonna spend some quality time together while Darlene's out of town."

He reached out and threw the deadbolt on the kitchen door. The snick of the lock echoed like a bullet in the small room.

Mia bolted, toppling the chair in hopes it would slow him down. His cocky laughter trailed her down the hall, preceding the thud of his booted feet. She scrambled for the front door, but the key that always stayed in the lock had been removed. She lost precious seconds trying the knob anyway before accepting it was locked and he'd planned this.

On a sob, she spun, darting toward her bedroom. If she could get inside, throw the lock, shove the chair under the knob, it might buy her just enough time to get to the scissors.

He charged her like a bull, his bulk slamming her into the wall and driving the breath from her lungs. Blindly, she reached out, closing her hand around the first object she touched and slamming it against his head.

Something shattered, and Wayne roared. But his grip loosened just enough she slid away, running again.

"Bitch! You'll pay for that, you ungrateful cunt."

The hallway seemed to elongate like something out of a horror movie. The doorway to her room stood ajar at the end of it. She poured on a burst of panicked speed.

Five steps. Four. Three. Two.

A massive hand clamped around her wrist like a vise, yanking her backward. Mia cried out, automatically bringing her other arm up to protect her face.

Brax's voice rang out in her head. *Fight. Bring up your knees. Kick. Bite. Never stop moving.*

As momentum propelled her into Wayne, she brought up her knee, aiming for his crotch. But he twisted away, spinning her until her back was pressed to his chest and her shoulder screamed. The pain caused her vision to flash white. His hand tightened on her wrist until the bones rubbed together, and he bent his head, his damp breath against her ear making her shudder.

"It's time you pay for everything we've given you."

BRAX WAS PROBABLY GOING to regret some of the work schedule trades he'd sorted out in order to free up his time today and tomorrow. But it would be worth it to see the look on Mia's face when he presented her with the contents of that bakery box. He'd made a foray to the high-end bakery downtown and picked up the fanciest raspberry pastry they had. He couldn't even remember what it was called, but she'd probably know. With luck, she wouldn't be expected home any time soon, so he'd get to watch her enjoy it. And if he got up the balls to have the conversation he wanted, they'd need tomorrow to get her moved. Maybe.

He wasn't sure if he was going there and didn't know what her answer would be if he did. But if his life had taught him anything, it was the value of being prepared.

Restlessness drove him to the school early. He didn't much want to stand in the cold, but Valentina might have a dog he could help with while he waited for the end of the school day. If she insisted on paying him, this time he might accept and put it toward dinner. With a little extra cash, he could pick up a pizza from Treviano's. Mia loved their wood-fired crust.

Cheered by the thought, he swung through the door of Mudpuppies.

Valentina looked up from the labradoodle she was trimming. "What are you doing back here?"

"I'm off work early. School's not out yet, so I thought I'd see if I could give you a hand while I wait."

She frowned, setting her clippers aside. "Mia already left school."

"What?" Mia never left school. Was she sick?

"Big burly guy picked her up earlier. Only reason I noticed is I was helping load up a buck wild Husky in the parking lot. I saw her get into the truck."

Wayne.

Brax felt his blood run cold. "When?"

"About a half hour ago."

Half an hour. Wayne was off work today. Alone so far as Brax knew. There was no good reason for him to take Mia out of school early. A lot could happen in thirty minutes. With the image of those blinds in his head, Brax tore out of the shop and took off at a dead run for her house.

The frigid air burned his lungs as his long legs ate up the distance. Drivers stared as he sprinted past. Of course there were no cops around when they were needed, and Brax wouldn't have stopped to explain anyway, because it would take time he didn't have. With every step, his mind supplied fresh horrors as old memories of things he'd seen and experienced far too young rose to the surface. Unwanted touches and unwashed bodies. With it came long buried panic and rage. So he didn't stop to think when he saw Wayne's truck in the drive. He went straight for the door, slamming his booted foot against it until the door frame splintered and the door swung inward with a crash.

A woman's scream echoed from down the hall, followed by the sound of flesh striking flesh. Vision hazing with red, Brax charged toward the sound, bursting into a bedroom.

In half a heartbeat, he took in Wayne, holding Mia against the wall by her throat. Her shirt was ripped, exposing one shoulder and the swell of her breast in a plain cotton bra. She writhed in his grip, kicking, flailing, clawing at the hand around her throat as he worked at her belt with the other.

Brax leapt over a fallen chair, landing on Wayne's back and cranking his arm tight around the other man's neck. Wayne dropped Mia and stumbled back, crashing into the opposite wall. Brax barely felt the impact. Mia had fallen to her knees, gasping.

"Run!" he shouted.

But she didn't run, and Brax had lost whatever advantage he'd had with surprise. Wayne drove an elbow back, catching Brax in the kidney. The shock of the pain loosened his grip enough for Wayne to throw him off. He crashed into Mia's desk. Wood splintered beneath him, but he scrambled up, dodging Wayne's meaty fists and diving for his middle. Wayne toppled like a tree. Brax rode him down to the floor, punching at that outraged face with everything he had. The impact of it sang up his arm. He threw another and another, a steady barrage of blows. Punishment for every minute he'd had his hands on Mia.

"Stop! Brax, stop! You'll kill him." Her panicked voice broke through the haze of blood lust.

Mia caught his arm long enough for Brax to register that Wayne lay still beneath him, his face so much bruised meat. It wasn't enough. Not nearly enough for what the asshole had been trying to do to her. But Brax couldn't protect her if he got sent to prison.

He rose on unsteady legs and reached for her. "How bad did he hurt you?"

She didn't answer, just buried her face against his chest, her body shaking against his. Brax wanted to crush her to him, but he didn't want to hurt her and didn't know the full extent of her injuries. He didn't have the capacity to triage just now, and this wasn't the place.

Just take the next step.

"We have to get out of here. Where's your go bag?"

She sucked in a shuddering breath and released him, kneeling by the bed to drag out the duffel bag. In seconds, she'd grabbed more clothes from the dresser drawers and shoved them inside. "That's it."

So little was coming with her. He knew what that was like. Understood having all his possessions fit into a single garbage bag. He hoped she'd leave behind the shit memories with whatever things she hadn't deemed worth bringing.

Brax checked Wayne's pulse. He had one. That was good enough. He wouldn't be going away for murder, no matter how much the bastard deserved it. "Let's go."

Mia hesitated at the door, then turned back, striding over to plant a brutal kick between Wayne's legs. He groaned but didn't regain consciousness.

Brax shot her a grim smile. "He'll be feeling that into next week. Come on."

She took the hand he offered, squeezing as if she was afraid he'd disappear. He couldn't stop himself from running gentle fingers across the angry red mark on her cheek that would turn into a bruise in a matter of hours. "I've got you, baby. Let's get out of here."

CHAPTER 3

Mia felt outside herself. As if the only thing tethering her to her own body was the firm grip of Brax's hand around hers. Her mind was nothing but static, like in a movie, after a bomb goes off. It wouldn't stay that way. She understood that, so she held on to Brax and held on to the numb as he led her back to his place, taking back roads and cutting through yards and patches of woods. Once they were inside the little one-room studio apartment, he shut the door and threw the locks. One. Two. Three.

She flinched at the sound, her mind pitching her back into the kitchen with Wayne. To the moment she'd understood that her time had run out.

"Mia."

She sucked in a breath, and Brax came into focus, gray eyes dark with worry.

"You can let go now."

She realized he was trying to slip her bag off her shoulder. The one she'd stubbornly clung to the whole way because it was everything she cared about, other than him. One by one, her fingers released. He eased the bag off her shoulder and set it to one side, tugging her over to the futon that served as both sofa and bed.

"Will you sit? I'm going to get the first aid kit."

She willed her hand to release his, but her fingers wouldn't cooperate. Baffled and feeling a little helpless, she stared at their connection. "I... can't."

"Okay." He let her trail him like a train car, retrieving the kit from a shelf in the tiny kitchen and leading her back to sit. Only then did she catch the angry red split of his knuckles.

"Oh my God." She reached for his other hand. "Brax, you're hurt."

"I'm fine. Let's get you checked out."

"Those could get infected." To settle the matter, she opened the plastic box herself and dug out disinfectant.

"Mia." He didn't quite manage to hide the exasperation in his tone.

She lifted her gaze to his. "Please. I need to do this."

He released a slow breath and nodded.

Soaking a cotton pad with antiseptic, she lifted his hand and gently dabbed at the split skin. His sharp inhale was the only sign it pained him. She blew on the cuts to ease the sting, not quite meeting his eyes. "You saved my life."

He'd saved more than that, and they both knew it. But Mia wasn't ready to let go of the numb. Not yet.

His eyes traced over her face, his intensity an almost physical caress. "I should have gotten there sooner."

"How did you even know where I was?"

She hadn't thought to question it at the time. He'd simply burst in like an avenging angel, as if summoned by her need alone.

"Valentina saw you leave with him. I was way early to pick you up and stopped in to see her. She told me. I had a bad feeling this morning, so I came as fast as I could." He reached out to cup her uninjured cheek. "I just wish I'd been faster."

Mia tipped her face into the warmth of his palm, not over-thinking the fact that this was the most he'd ever voluntarily touched her. Right now, he was the only thing keeping the cold and the fear at bay. "You came. That's what matters."

They stayed that way for a long moment, staring at each other, until at last his gaze dropped to her cheek where a bruise was surely forming. Storms boiled up in his eyes. "He hit you."

"I hit him back. And bit and kicked. Just like you taught me."

"Good girl."

It hadn't been enough. Wouldn't have been enough, if Brax hadn't shown up. That was both lowering and terrifying to admit. So she set it aside as something to deal with later, when she could actually handle it.

His fingers skimmed gently down her cheek, tipping her head back so he could get a look at her throat. "This will probably be another bruise."

When he dropped his hand, she felt bereft and shaky.

"Where else?"

With trembling fingers, she tried to unbutton the cuff of her shirt. When she couldn't, Brax took over, carefully pushing back the sleeve to reveal the livid bruising beneath in the clear pattern of fingers.

In an alarmingly calm tone, he muttered a vicious string of curses.

"I... I don't think it's broken." She rotated it, bending this way and that. It hurt, but not as she imagined a fracture would.

"It should be in a brace, either way. I don't have one here, but I've got some elastic bandages. Do you want to change... or... clean up or... something... first?"

And then she remembered the torn shirt beneath the jacket Brax had wrapped her in before they'd left the house, and the grasping, groping hands that had caused it. She swallowed against the thickness in her throat and managed a nod. "A shower would be good."

"Okay. Towels are on the shelf in the bathroom. Fair warning, the hot water gives out in about five minutes."

Five minutes wasn't nearly long enough to wash off the horror of the day.

"I'll make it work." Shoving up on shaking legs, she edged past him.

"Mia?"

She turned back, watched him swallow.

"Did he... do we need to get a rape kit done?"

And there was that word. The ugly, harsh reality of almost. What would have happened without Brax.

The numbness faded, leaving her with a bone-deep chill. She began to tremble, but she shook her head. "He didn't get that far." And she was never ever going anywhere without wearing a belt. It had slowed him down just enough.

"Okay."

On another shaky inhale, she headed toward the bathroom. But with every step, she just shook harder.

"Brax?" she whispered.

"Yeah?"

"Could you... come with me?"

There was a long beat of silence. "Into the shower?"

"Outside. I just... don't want to be alone." If he left her alone, she was deathly afraid she'd break, and she didn't know if he'd be able to put her back together again.

Another long beat passed. "Okay. I'll keep my eyes closed."

"Thank you."

He followed her into the tiny bathroom, nudging her down onto the closed seat of the toilet so he could kneel and remove her boots. It was a weirdly intimate gesture, one that settled her speeding heart a few beats. He had her. No matter what came next, he had her.

Reaching up, he tugged the elastic from her hair and gently combed out the remains of her braid. His touch was soothing, his warm, solid presence an anchor in the storm that wanted to pull her under.

He tugged back the curtain and took both her hands, raising her to her feet. "In you go. You can undress back there for some privacy."

"Thanks."

She stepped into the tub.

With a brisk nod, he shut the curtain. "I'll be right here."

As Mia began stripping off her clothes behind the flimsy barrier of the barely opaque dollar store shower curtain, Brax turned his back and scrubbed both hands down his face. He could do this. He could be the support she needed.

The curtain rustled, and fabric dropped to the floor behind him. The shirt. Her jeans. Her underwear. He darted a glance at the mirror over the sink and caught the silhouette of her curves as she bent to turn on the water. His body stirred.

Horrified, he slammed his eyes shut. She'd just been assaulted. What the hell kind of perv was he, noticing her body right now?

The stingy spray of water wasn't enough to hide the hitch in her breath or the sob she tried to hold back. The sound of it flayed him. In all the years he'd known her, he'd never seen her break. Not after that first night. But she broke now, huge racking sobs that sounded as if they were ripping her apart. Maybe they were.

He'd sworn he'd keep her safe, and he'd failed.

Brax didn't know how to make up for that. He didn't even know if he could. But he'd do whatever he had to, whatever she needed to feel safe. Even if it meant standing here doing nothing while the grief spilled out of her like so much blood.

Minutes dragged on to what felt like hours, well past the capacity of his shit water heater.

"Mia. Baby." He didn't know where the endearment came from. They weren't like that with each other. But now wasn't the time to question it.

When she didn't respond, he carefully reached an arm past the curtain to check the water temperature. It was icy. Muffling a curse, he fumbled the knobs off. Her ragged weeping filled the space, tearing at his heart. He could just make out the shape of her huddled in the back of the tub, knees drawn up to her chest. His crappy towels wouldn't be big enough to cover her fully. Moving fast, he yanked a sheet from the hamper of clean laundry he had yet to put away. Back in the bathroom, he hesitated. He didn't want to do anything to make her feel more violated than she already was.

"Baby, you need to get dry and warm."

No reply.

"I'm gonna pull back the curtain and help you out. I'm not looking."

Still no sign that she'd heard him over her own sobs.

Eyes on the ceiling, he opened the curtain and held the sheet wide. A darted glance down showed her still curled into a ball, her head bent over her knees, her hair falling forward to shield her face. All the essentials were hidden, so he crouched down, wrapping her in the sheet. She turned immediately into him, pressing her face to his shoulder, a sign of trust he didn't deserve.

"It's okay. I've got you."

It took some maneuvering to get her out of the tub without flashing anything, but he managed, carrying her back to the futon. Her teeth chattered, her body shaking hard against his, so he dragged the blanket off the back and wrapped them both.

He locked his arms around her, willing warmth and comfort into her frigid limbs, wondering if he could possibly warm her in the deep places he knew from experience would be filled with ice.

"I've got you. I've got you." He chanted it, as much to convince himself as her.

Eventually, her arms snaked out of the sheet burrito and wrapped around him, her hands fisting in the back of his shirt as if her grip alone could keep him from disappearing.

"It's okay, I'm here."

Brax had no idea if it was okay or if his presence was the comfort it used to be. Her continued tears had panic jittering in his belly. How was she not completely dehydrated yet? What if she didn't stop? She'd make herself sick, and then where would they be? He wasn't equipped to handle this. But she had no one else, so he'd damned well figure it out.

By the time she lifted her head from his shoulder, Brax was ready to make a deal with the devil himself, just so she'd stop crying.

He carefully wiped at the tears still streaming down her flushed cheeks. "Please don't cry, baby," he rasped.

Mia stared up at him with those big, liquid eyes full of so much pain. All he wanted was to make it stop for her. To make the hurt go away. Driven to comfort, he pressed his brow to hers, breathing the air she breathed, as if, by proximity alone, he could share her burden, lessen the load. Her arms tightened around him, and he tipped forward, closing the distance between them.

On a gasp, her cold lips parted under his, and Brax realized what he'd done.

He jerked back. "Oh God. I'm sorry."

If she hadn't still been clinging to him like a limpet, he'd have tossed her on the futon and bolted away. As it was, he could only stare at her in horror and shame. "I'm so sorry. I didn't mean... I wasn't trying to take advantage. I swear. I'd never—" Brax cut himself off as one hand released the death grip on his shirt. He braced himself for a well-deserved slap.

Instead, she cupped his cheek. "Brax, look at me."

That was infinitely worse, because she'd shredded any defenses he had, and he didn't know what she'd see in his face. But he did as she asked, wondering if he'd just inadvertently destroyed the best thing in his life.

Those eyes he loved seemed to search down to his very soul before her gaze dropped, impossibly, to his mouth. On the barest of sighs, she leaned in, brushing her lips against his. A question. An exploration.

"Please." Her voice was barely above a whisper, her breath feathering across his mouth in a temptation he didn't dare believe.

His body shuddered as she came back with another hesitant brush, this one a plea he didn't have the strength to ignore.

CHAPTER 4

Mia's heart hammered, dread and embarrassment filtering in when Brax didn't respond. For a few delicious moments, he'd made the horror go away, and she'd thought maybe something good would come out of this awful day. But he stayed frozen.

She was a teary mess. Of course, he didn't want her. Shame flushed her skin as she pulled back, abruptly realizing she was naked beneath the sheet. "I'm sorry. I thought—"

"Mia." His voice was unbearably gentle.

She couldn't look at him. Couldn't bear to see pity or apology in his eyes.

But one of his long-fingered hands skimmed up her back, under the fall of her hair, to gently curve around her nape. The touch grounded her, even as she shut her eyes to close in the mortification. His lips brushed her brow, her temple. Chaste, affectionate gestures meant to comfort. Her heart stuttered at the first kiss to her cheek, then picked up as he followed the trail of her tears down one side. By the time he made it to the other, she hardly dared to breathe.

He whispered her name again. Somehow, she scraped

together the courage to open her eyes. This wasn't the carefully guarded boy she'd known for years. His gaze stayed steady on her face, full of an unmistakable heat and something that might've been wonder. But it was the tenderness that stole what was left of her breath. And this time, when he pressed his lips to hers, she thought she'd drown in the sweetness of it.

Oh. This. He'd been hiding *this* behind that tough facade? How had she not known? Not sensed *something*?

He took her deeper by slow degrees, showing a patience she hadn't expected. Her body went warm and loose. She wrapped her arms around him, wanting closer to his warmth, needing to feel more than his hands on her back and neck. A rumble sounded in his chest, part frustration, part arousal, as the sheet slipped from her shoulder. He tugged it back, never taking his mouth from hers.

"Brax."

He hummed a question against her lips.

"I want more." It terrified her to admit it, but if not now, then when? Life was short, and if today had proved anything at all, it was often brutal. This was something else. She needed the something else.

He stopped, those storm-dark eyes searching hers. "Baby, after what you've been through—"

She refused to think about that, not when her focus was so full of him and how good he made her feel. "I don't want to let the dark back in." She nipped at his bottom lip. "Help me forget."

At his uncertainty, she shrugged, letting the sheet fall, exposing her breasts. She'd never been naked with anyone, but the hard bob of his Adam's apple made her bold. Grabbing one of his hands, she brought it to her breast. "Touch me. Please."

On a ragged inhale, he cupped her, the roughness of his callused fingers a delicious friction on her sensitive skin. She pressed into the touch, loving how full and heavy she felt in his palm.

"So pretty." His thumb circled, teasing her nipple to a peak. When he bent to take it into his mouth, she gasped, spearing her fingers in his hair. As he sucked, heat built low in her belly. Restless, she shifted in his lap, somehow wanting to both escape and find more. When he tipped her back on the futon, she went willingly. And oh, this was better. His hands could move more freely now, stroking, exploring, down her torso, along the outside of her thigh. With each new sensation of pleasure, she sighed, but it wasn't enough to ease the tension humming through her.

"Brax. I need more." More of what exactly she wasn't sure, but she trusted he could give it to her.

"I've got you." One of his big, warm hands slid between her thighs, and she gasped, arching hard into the touch.

Taking her mouth again, he began to rub. Mia's legs fell open, her hips circling of their own volition. His fingers traced the wetness there, sending her pulse into triple time as something deep inside wound tighter. She whimpered.

His rhythm faltered. "You okay?"

"Oh God, don't stop. I need... I need..." She felt as if he'd opened a black hole inside her, one that sucked in sensation and pleasure, but could never be satisfied.

"I've got you," he repeated and slid one finger inside her.

She barely had time to gasp before he eased in another, filling that ache he'd built. Her hips rose and fell, and she couldn't even be embarrassed about the sounds she made as he pumped his fingers in time with her rhythm. When he pressed his thumb to the bundle of nerves at the apex of her thighs, she all but levitated off the futon, screaming as her body clamped around him, as all that vibrating tension let loose.

Dizzy, gasping, Mia struggled to focus on Brax leaning anxiously over her. "Okay?"

Was he kidding? Couldn't he tell he'd just literally blown her mind? She'd had orgasms before, on her own, in the privacy of her shower. But they'd been nothing like this. "I think... I just... had an out-of-body experience."

One corner of his mouth quirked with the trace of the arrogance she secretly found sexy. "Better?"

Fisting a hand in his shirt, she drew his mouth back to hers. "It's a start."

His huff of laughter cut off when she shoved the shirt up.

"Mia. We shouldn't."

"We absolutely should." If his fingers felt that good, what would it be like to have the rest of him?

"You're not thinking clearly. And you're injured."

She shifted her hands to his belt, then lower, finding the bulge of his arousal. "I'm thinking perfectly clearly. I want you. You want me. Easy math. And I swear to you, I'm not feeling any pain." There was no room for it amid all the sensation he aroused.

"It's too fast."

"For who?"

"You." He choked the syllable out as she stroked him. "Christ, I'm trying to be a good guy here."

"Brax, you're the best guy. You always have been. I want to be with you. I always have."

On a curse, he dropped his head to his shoulder. "Baby, this isn't something we can take back."

"I know. I don't want to take it back." She kissed him again, long and slow, making an effort to seduce him this time. "Be with me. Give me something beautiful to remember." She wasn't fighting fair. But fairness had no place in reality. She needed him, and she desperately wanted him to need her back.

On a long sigh, he pressed his brow to hers, then dragged his shirt over his head. "If you change your mind at any point, just say the word. It's okay."

She wouldn't change her mind. Especially not when he slipped out of his jeans and boxers, and she saw how much he wanted her. Her fingers itched to touch, to explore the shape of him, but when she reached to do just that, he twisted away.

"I won't last if you get your hands on me. Just let me take care of you."

"Okay." She settled back, watching him pull a condom from his wallet and set it in easy reach.

This was happening. She was about to have sex with her best friend. Finally.

He stretched out over her, and the feel of his naked body against hers was a whole other glory of sensation. He was all lean muscles and gentle hands as he aroused her again with more of those drugging kisses. She arched against him, feeling the prod of his erection against her leg. She wanted to feel it at her center, against that bundle of delicious nerves.

As if reading her mind, he shifted himself so the length of him slid through the gathering wetness, just over her clit.

"Oh, God yes. Now."

"Patience. You need to be ready." He kept up a torturous rhythm until she thought she'd go mad from wanting.

"Please. Now. Please."

He rolled away, just far enough to sheath himself. Then he was back, settling where she needed him most, the blunt head of him nudging her entrance. "Be sure, baby."

Eyes on his, she bucked, taking the first little bit of him inside her. "I am."

"I'll go slow."

Setting his jaw, he pressed inside with short, shallow thrusts. Sweat broke out on his brow as he worked himself deeper, millimeter by millimeter, and oh, this was so much more than his fingers. He stopped and started several times, holding perfectly still, giving her body a chance to relax and adjust before resuming those short, shallow thrusts until he was all the way inside, and she couldn't feel anything but the heat of him. The sensation of fullness stole her breath.

He was with her. Inside her. There wasn't room for anything but the love welling up in her heart. The words wanted to spill out, but she had just enough sense left to know they'd freak him out. The first time she told him wasn't going to be when she was high on endorphins, wasn't going to be under any circumstances he could dismiss. So she'd show him instead.

Framing his face in both hands, she kissed him. "Thank you."

His mouth lingered on hers as he began to move, and she lost herself to the rhythmic push and pull of their bodies. That glorious tension built again, and this time she could feel the rise of it in the tightening of his body over and inside her. His pace quickened, his body driving into hers, banishing all the shadows, until he reached between them, pushing her over the edge into a glorious freefall, and leapt off the cliff behind her.

THE ONLY REASON Brax was pretty sure he wasn't dead was the feel of full breasts pressed to his chest, and the fluttering heat around his cock that was the closest thing he'd ever experienced to heaven. As there wasn't a chance he'd earned a spot past the pearly gates, he concluded he was still alive. Still alive, and very naked with his best friend.

Holy. Shit.

He'd sworn he wouldn't touch her. Would never push for anything she didn't want to give. She'd just given him everything mere hours after she'd been assaulted. That clinched it. He was totally going to the special hell.

"You're thinking too loud." Her sleepy voice had him cracking open his eyes.

Mia lay beneath him, eyes closed, tracing lazy patterns

down his back, one leg still hooked behind his knee. She looked blissed out and exhausted, and so beautiful he ached from it. And there were finger-shaped bruises around her throat.

Fuck. What have I done?

"I'm crushing you." He pushed up, using the excuse of watching as he carefully gripped the condom and pulled out to avoid meeting her gaze. "Let me just take care of this." And maybe when he was done in the bathroom, he'd find more than two brain cells to rub together to process what had just happened.

He cleaned up and splashed some icy water on his face. "Get it the fuck together, Whitmore."

The face looking back at him in the mirror was shell-shocked. He'd had sex with Mia. And now they had to figure out what came next.

What if it was just a onetime thing? Something to help her get through today's trauma? He'd never begrudge her that. But he could never unknow what she felt like beneath his hands, how her skin tasted. It was one thing to picture her naked. It was entirely another to know exactly how she looked, flushed with arousal. He'd never stop wanting her, and he had no idea if he could keep being just her friend after this.

But she'd said she'd wanted to be with him. That she always had. Was that the lust talking, or did she mean it? Could she feel as much for him as he did for her? Did he have the guts to ask her? And hell, was now even the time to talk about this? There were several major issues hanging over their heads that they'd effectively put off with sex. Really amazing sex.

With no idea what to say, he opened the door.

"What is this?"

At some point during his freak out, Mia had dug out one of his T-shirts. It fell to mid-thigh, looking a thousand times better on her than it ever had on him. Because his brain immediately began fantasizing about stripping her out of it, it took Brax several seconds to register that she held the bakery box. In all the chaos, he'd forgotten about it. He couldn't read her expression, except that she definitely wasn't happy.

He rubbed the back of his neck and wished he wasn't buck naked. "Did you open it?"

She nodded. Her palm flattened on the top of the box. "This is basically the Cadillac of French pastries. They only make them at that fancy bakery downtown, and they cost the earth."

Shit. Maybe he'd gotten the wrong thing.

"It was supposed to be a surprise for your birthday. You said you wanted something raspberry." The explanation felt lame, but it was all he could think to say without understanding why she was upset.

Mia's throat worked, and fresh tears glimmered in those big brown eyes.

"Oh shit. Please don't cry." He absolutely could not handle more tears. "You don't have to eat it. We can throw it out."

"No!" She clutched the box to her chest like a treasure. "This is why."

He was so damned confused. "Why what?"

"Why I love you. Because you thought to do this. Because you *did* do this, even though you totally shouldn't have spent the money."

From somewhere in the back of his brain, Brax wanted to retort that it was his money, but he was too busy staring at her, his heart galloping. "You love me?"

Her brows drew together. "Of course I do. It's always been you. I wouldn't have basically jumped you if I didn't. You weren't just a convenient warm body to lose myself in." As he continued to stare at her, she set the box on the futon and crossed over, worry radiating off her. "Christ, Brax, tell me you know I wasn't using you. You're my best friend. Tell me I didn't just ruin that by pushing you to cross this line."

She loved him. And that changed everything. The roiling fear inside him eased.

He brushed the hair back from her face. "I can't stay friends." As the blood drained out of her cheeks, he rushed to finish. "Not when I want so much more."

Uncertainty flickered in her eyes. "To clarify, you want more with me?"

He tipped her face up. "I want everything with you."

Her smile bloomed like a sunrise. She threw her arms around him and fused her mouth with his. In only a moment, it became rapidly apparent that she was still naked beneath that shirt, and his body had plenty of ideas about what to do with that information. Before the blood drained back out of his head, he set her back a few inches.

"Baby, stop. There are things we need to talk about."

"Like what?"

Brax absolutely hated to do this to her, but they couldn't just fall back into bed. There was big shit they needed to handle. "Like what we're going to tell the police."

The light of her joy winked out, and he felt like the world's biggest dick.

She closed her eyes. "I know I have to. If for no other reason than so no one else gets placed in their home."

"And just in case he's reported me."

Her eyes snapped open, bright with fresh fear. "You were protecting me."

"That won't be the story he tells."

"We'll document my injuries. They have to believe us."

"I don't think that'll be a problem." Brax had no idea whether that was actually true, but she needed the confidence. "Is Patricia still your caseworker?"

"Yeah. The moment this gets reported, she'll be trying to put me somewhere else. I can't go through that again."

It was what he'd needed to hear. Linking their hands, he tugged her close. "Stay with me."

Regret twisted his features. "They're not gonna let me do that."

"You turn eighteen tomorrow. We should get married."

Her mouth fell open. "I'm sorry, what?"

"Okay, I know this isn't the most romantic proposal, but think about it. They can't split us up if we're married. And at eighteen, they'd have a hard time placing you, anyway. There's no support there. We can support each other, like we always have. We'd just have some actual protections under the law this way. We could drive over the state line into Idaho tomorrow. There's no waiting period there."

Sheer disbelief was probably not a good sign.

"How do you even know that?"

"I... might have been thinking about this for a while. I wanted a way to get you out of that house, so I could better protect you. I'd have suggested it anyway, as a marriage of convenience, but now..." He took a breath. "I know we're young, and I know it won't be easy. But I'm in love with you. I think I always have been. So marry me, Mia. Let me give you the protection of my name and my body."

She stared at him for long enough that nerves began to jitter. It was too much, too fast. She wasn't ready. But he'd thought this would be the right thing for them both.

"I'm sorry. I'm getting ahead of things. I—"

"Yes."

His brain stopped the hamster wheel worrying. "Really?"

Her arms slid around him. "You're my person. You've been my family for years when I had none. I'd love nothing more than to make that official."

Her person. Damn, but he liked the sound of that. And he loved the idea of her being his.

Grinning, he scooped her up for another kiss. "I'll make arrangements to borrow a car."

She lifted her legs and wrapped them around his hips. "Brax?"

"Yeah?"

"How do you feel about eating pastry naked to celebrate?"

"Happy birthday to you."

CHAPTER 5

"Are you nervous?"

Mia glanced at Valentina. "Do I look nervous?"

The older woman nodded toward the hands Mia had knotted at her waist.

She blew out a breath, consciously releasing the death grip she had on her own fingers. "Okay, yeah, I guess I am nervous."

They hadn't gone to Idaho. In her haste to get the hell away from Wayne, Mia hadn't remembered all the documents that proved her identity. Those were, unfortunately, necessary when applying for a marriage license. So she'd had to suck it up and make the report on Wayne's assault sooner rather than later. The whole thing had caused more than a few waves. Between worry that Brax would get into trouble, and anxiety over the fact that she was breaking the rules about lying low, Mia had been a wreck.

But the police had believed her. The livid bruising on her throat and wrist, in the perfect shape of Wayne's hand, had helped with that. He was arrested. No charges were being brought against Brax, and Patricia had helped her get the last of her things from the house. It wasn't much. In the middle of all that, she and Brax had applied for their marriage license and scheduled the first available appointment with a justice of the peace.

Now here she was on the cusp of marrying her best friend. If he showed.

He's going to show.

The worry was absolutely stupid. Mia knew that. Brax loved her. She didn't doubt that. But it hadn't stopped the anxiety dreams that he'd up and changed his mind and high-tailed it out of town. The fact that he'd asked her to meet him at the courthouse, instead of coming together, hadn't helped, but he'd insisted he had something he needed to do alone and had sent Valentina to watch over her in the meantime.

"You wishing for the big white wedding?"

"No." And thank God for that. In her deep purple sweater and best jeans, she definitely looked nothing like a bride today. Her clothing choices had been driven by what would hide the bruising. "It's just my first time being away from him since the attack. I know Wayne's behind bars, but I can't shake this anxiety that I'm not safe anywhere Brax isn't."

Valentina wrapped an arm around her shoulders. "Oh, sweetie, it'll take time. And that's okay."

After a moment's hesitation, Mia leaned into the embrace. How long had it been since she'd had true comfort from a woman? Had there been anyone since her mother died?

"I know I have to get over it and get out there sometime, especially since he'll be back to work tomorrow, and I'll have to go back to school." She shook her head. "I can't fathom going back to school after all this, but Brax is insistent that we can make it until I graduate, without my having to quit to find full-time work." But how much of that was the truth and how much was because he knew she wanted to officially graduate?

"Would it make you feel better to have a part-time job?"

"Absolutely. But I don't know what I can find that will allow me to work around my school schedule and doesn't require transportation. We certainly can't afford a car."

"I could use somebody at the shop. Phones and scheduling to start, while that wrist heals up, and if you do well with the dogs, we can move you on into grooming. I can work around school, and you can pick up some weekend hours to round it out."

Mia gaped at her. "Are you serious?"

Valentina nodded, her springy curls bouncing. "It won't make you rich, but it'll help keep you in ramen and eggs. That's what I lived on when I started out."

"Oh my God, that's amazing. Yes! I would love that."

"You and Brax are good kids. I want to make sure y'all start off on the right foot. You can come on by the shop after school tomorrow, and we'll sort out a schedule."

"Thank you!" She squeezed Valentina in a hug and glanced at the big clock on the wall in the courthouse entryway. "Our appointment's in ten minutes." Where the hell was her groom?

The door swung open, and Brax hustled inside, fresh snow dusting his dark brown hair.

Mia rushed toward him. "There you are!"

"Sorry I took so long. But I had a couple of important stops."

Mia stared at the cluster of pink, purple, and white blooms he held out.

"I wanted you to have some flowers to carry for today."

Her throat went thick. "Brax." She took the bouquet, burying her face in them. They didn't have much scent, but that hardly mattered. No one had ever given her flowers, and he'd made sure she had some on their wedding day. She beamed up at him. "Is there a secret romantic hiding behind that bad boy exterior of yours?"

He pokered up, shifting on his feet. "I don't know what you're talking about."

"Smooth move, Whitmore." Valentina nodded in approval.

Mia smiled, feeling all the fear and tension melt away. He was here. He hadn't changed his mind. "What was the other stop?"

Digging into his coat pocket, he pulled out a small velvet pouch, upending the contents into his broad palm. A pair of plain silver bands caught the light.

"They aren't fancy. I'll get you something better later, but this is important. You're important. And I admit, I'm caveman enough to want you to wear something marking you as mine."

This man, who'd come up through hell and found his way to her, had such unexpected depths. Today they'd claim each other and each wear a symbol for the world to see. She rose to her toes, brushing her lips over his. "They're perfect."

"Y'all should probably start heading toward the judge's chambers. Your appointment is in just a few minutes," Valentina reminded them.

Mia's belly gave a nervous jump. "I'm just gonna run to the bathroom. I'll be two minutes."

The bathrooms were tucked around the corner, at the end of a long, shadowy hallway. Several of the fluorescent bulbs in the overhead lights had gone out, and the ones remaining flickered like something out of a horror movie. Nervous again, she ducked into the empty women's room and did her business as quickly as possible. The judge would be ready for them any minute, and then they'd get this show on the road. She'd feel better when it was done.

Hurrying now, she stepped back into the hall and felt her heart stop as she spotted the tall, hulking shape in the shadows. Terror exploded through her, turning her limbs to jelly. She opened her mouth to scream when he stepped into the light.

"Hello, Mia."

Relief had her sagging against the wall. "What the hell is

wrong with you? You don't lurk in dark hallways to surprise women coming out of the bathroom."

"Sorry." Curt's lined face twisted in chagrin. "But you've been hard to get near the past few days. You've been drawing attention to yourself."

Scowling, Mia looked up and down the hall to make sure they were still alone before dragging down the turtleneck on her sweater to show her throat. "I was sexually assaulted by my foster father and would have been raped or worse if Brax hadn't shown up. What the fuck was I supposed to do? This whole setup was supposed to keep me safe. You promised me, and you promised my mother."

He closed his eyes and swore. "I'm sorry. Shit, I'm so sorry. I don't have nearly the control over this situation as I would if you were fully in the program."

"Which you can't do, so there's no point bringing it up."

"I can still help. Get you out of here. Set you up somewhere else."

The mere suggestion of it had fresh fear spinning through her. Mia shook her head. "No. I'm not going anywhere. I'm marrying Brax." She braced herself for a fight, for all the well-meaning, I-know-better-than-you arguments about how getting married at eighteen was a terrible idea.

Curt studied her for a long moment, his blue eyes inscrutable. "It's a good idea."

She blinked, thrown by his ready acceptance. "You're not going to try to talk me out of it?"

"He's been by your side for six years. He'll keep you safe, and this is another way for you to disappear. But Mia, he can't know. For his own safety, he has to be kept in the dark about who you really are."

She shut down the twinge of worry at that. "I'm so far down this rabbit hole that girl doesn't exist anymore."

Curt nodded. "Good. Now get a move on. Your groom is waiting."

She'd already turned toward the front of the courthouse when he called her name again. She glanced back. "What?"

"Congratulations."

EPILOGUE

NEARLY THREE YEARS LATER

Mia held on as Brax tried to roll out of bed.

"Baby, I've got to get ready for work."

She groaned in protest and nipped at his bare shoulder. "Stupid bills. I'd so much rather start my day with you than coffee."

He hauled her against his morning wood. "If we hadn't already definitively proved we can't keep track of time in the shower, I'd indulge you. But I can't afford to be late again." With a deep, lingering kiss that had her sinking into sleepy pleasure, he pulled away and climbed out of bed, tucking the covers around her. "You've got twenty more minutes before you have to be up. Doze a little."

She watched him stride naked to the bathroom, admiring his leanly muscled backside before scooting over into the warm spot he'd vacated. The pipes thumped and clunked as he turned on the shower, and she let herself drift and dream.

They'd come a long way since they'd gotten married. They both had good, steady work, had finally secured a reliable car, and were on their way to saving for a bigger place. One where they could hopefully, finally get the dog she'd been wanting forever. This studio apartment was a few steps up from the one they'd shared in the beginning. The water heater capacity alone had been worth the increase in rent when they'd moved to Spokane. Through some lucky dumpster diving at semester's end at the local universities, they'd managed to furnish the place in cozy enough fashion, with a real bed and a second-hand sofa that was a considerable step up from that old futon.

She still sometimes missed that old futon.

The edge of the bed dipped as Brax sat down, pressing a kiss to her brow. "Time to get up, Sleeping Beauty. Your turn to get ready for work."

"I'm up," she promised.

"I need to see those pretty eyes open and your ass actually out of bed."

Mia wanted to object, but she had to admit there was sufficient evidence that she could sleep through alarms and snooze buttons. On another groan, she threw back the covers and slid out of bed, wincing as her feet hit the cold floor. "I'm really up now."

Brax grinned and pulled her in, stroking a hand down her bare back. "How about I make it up to you tonight? You, me, that box of brownie mix you think I don't know is in the back of the cabinet. Clothing optional."

She hooked her fingers in his belt loops. "Promise?"

Humor and heat lit those beloved gray eyes. "Absolutely. I love you."

"I love you, too."

He lowered his head for one more kiss before copping a friendly feel of her ass and backing away. "See you tonight."

"Have a good day at work."

Once the door shut behind him, Mia made a beeline for the shower herself, lingering in the hot water as long as she dared. If she missed the bus, she'd be hoofing it in the cold to get to the alternative pickup spot and still might not make it to work on time.

Her phone was ringing when she shut off the water. On a curse, she snagged a towel and dashed to answer, dripping all over the floor.

"Hello?"

"Maria?"

Mia felt all the blood drain out of her head at the sound of the voice she hadn't heard since she was six years old. "Daddy?"

"Hey, baby girl."

A thousand questions clogged in her throat. How he'd found her. How he was doing. Had he missed her? But before she could find voice for a single one, he was speaking again.

"I need to see you."

"What? Where? I don't—"

"I can't explain over the phone. I need to see you in person. Today. Come to this address." He reeled the location off.

"That's four hours away."

"It's important, baby girl. And God, I want to see you so bad."

She couldn't see him. That was Rule 1. Even talking to him right now was violating a half dozen of Curt's other rules. But fifteen years of questions boiled up inside her. This might be her only chance to ask. "I'll be there."

"Come alone. Don't tell anybody. I'll explain everything when I see you."

"Okay."

"See you soon." He hung up before she could say another word.

Mia stood for a long moment, still dripping from her shower as she stared at the phone in her hand. She should tell Brax. Except there was no way to explain part without explaining all, and Curt had been clear that it was safest if Brax knew nothing. She was no longer sure that was true, but she needed to know what her father had to say. Needed to look him in the eye to ask if whatever he'd gotten involved in had been worth losing his family.

She'd be home by tonight, and she could figure out what to tell Brax then.

Moving fast, she dried off and dressed. She took the time to call in to work, citing an emergency, then looked up the bus schedule for how she could get to Seattle. It would be tight, but if she hurried, she'd just make it. And surely, he'd wait for her if she was a little late.

At the door, she hesitated, years of training and instinct sending her back to the bed to haul out the go bag she hadn't touched since they'd moved in. It was probably overkill, but just in case.

Bag over her shoulder, she locked the apartment door behind her and headed out to finally get some answers.

PLEASE KEEP READING for the conclusion of Brax and Mia's story in *Mixed Up with a Marine.*

MIXED UP WITH A MARINE

BAD BOY BAKERS BOOK 1

Can a Marine turned baker and a jaded contractor find their way to a second chance?

Braxton Whitmore needs a change. After leaving the Marines, he's free to build a new life. But is he gonna be a baker? *Really?* When his buddy inherits a decrepit bar and proposes they partner up to turn it into a bakery, Brax figures why not? Until his ex comes walking in.

Mia Whitmore has built a new life for herself, far from the heartbreak and secrets that tore her marriage apart. The last thing she expects is for her estranged husband to be business partners with her latest client. Or for Brax to think they're already divorced.

As they're forced into proximity on the renovation, truths come to light, and Brax and Mia get a second chance. But when past secrets become present danger, Brax puts everything on the line to protect the woman who's always held his heart.

Braxton Whitmore had never seen so many bras in one place in his life. And he'd been to Victoria's Secret a time or two. His gaze snagged on one particularly heinous neon orange brassiere, one of many being used as ornamentation along the perimeter of the dingy cinder block walls. Its cups were large enough to fit his entire head. In a combat helmet.

"You have got to be shitting me. *This* is your inheritance?"

Jonah Ferguson moved past Brax into the bar proper. "In all its horrifying glory. Told y'all you had to see it to believe it."

Holt Steele, the remaining member of their trio, crossed thick arms over his chest. "I see it, but I'm not sure I believe it. Your dad actually owned this place?"

"For near to twenty years. Picked it over my mama, my sister, and me." If that still bothered Jonah, his matter-of-fact tone didn't betray it. "Don't know why the hell he left it to us when he couldn't be bothered to give a shit while he was living, but Sam and Griff are being all newlywed and getting ready for the baby, and she doesn't want anything to do with the place. She'd happily burn it to the ground."

"I'm not sure she's got the wrong idea," Brax muttered, moving further into the dimly lit bar. Were the windows actually spray painted? The whole effect made him feel like he was back in a war zone, but he shuddered to think what direct sunlight might reveal about the place.

"It's an eyesore for sure, but if we can clean it up, make it less terrifying, we'd get more profit off the sale. And be more likely to actually find a buyer."

Brax took another disgusted look around, noting the designations carved directly into the door frames above the restrooms—Poles and Holes. Classy. "Didn't realize you were that much of an optimist."

"You gotta have some imagination," Jonah insisted. "Look past the filth. Basically, everything in here can go. We strip out the gross, do some demolition, clean everything that needs cleaning, that gives us a blank canvas."

Holt arched a skeptical brow. "You got a dump truck load of fairy dust out back? Because it's gonna take more than demo and cleaning to make this a blank canvas worth a damn."

Tuning out Jonah's retort, Brax mentally stripped the place down. New flooring, sheetrock walls over the cinderblock, new ceiling, and better lighting would go a long way to improving the place. But that was all window dressing. No way in hell was that the extent of necessary renovations. He strode across the cracked concrete floors, deliberately not giving consideration to what the stains might be. A quick peek into the men's room showed a trough and a single stall housing an avocado green toilet. An outdoor water spigot served as a faucet over a cracked and rusty sink. The women's side was hardly better.

"Bathrooms need total gutting." And possibly dynamite.

He headed behind the long, scarred bar and through the swinging door into what passed for the kitchen. The space was long and narrow—a health code violation from one end to the other. A door to one side opened into what had probably been a storage room. A few empty liquor boxes lay abandoned in a corner beside another door that led, presumably, to the delivery entrance. The actual cooking area was made up of a range so caked in grease it would likely go up in flames if anybody dared to turn it on. Beside that stretched a single, warped steel table, garnished with a few dead roach carcasses and rat droppings. A deep commercial sink sat next to that, adjacent to a dishwasher Brax recognized as a model that had been ancient back when he'd done his stint as a busboy in high school.

He shoved back out into the main bar. "Kitchen needs gutting, too. Jesus, how long has it been since the place closed down?"

"Lonnie died eight months ago. We let his bartender keep running it for another six before pulling the plug."

"Ten bucks says somebody was paying off a health inspector. That's way more than two months' worth of nasty back there."

Jonah started to take down one of the rickety chairs stacked on tables, then evidently thought better of it. "Look, it's a shithole. I know it. I just want to make it less of one. If that's just cleaning and fresh paint, fine. But it's a project. We need a project, at least while we figure out what we all want to do now we're done up in Syracuse."

They lapsed into silence, considering.

Even before he'd joined the Marine Corps, Brax hadn't been a guy to just sit. He'd spent most of the year since he separated from the military at an experimental therapy program working through PTSD and anxiety. It was where he'd met Jonah, a former SEAL, and Holt, an Army Ranger. They'd all worked through their shit and been trained as master bakers in the process. Who knew baking worked as therapy? Dr. Audrey Graham, apparently. She was the genius behind the program, of which the three of them were part of the first group of graduates.

Brax enjoyed baking—which had been a hell of a surprise to him—but, at the end of the day, he was still a Marine. He was used to being extremely physical. This place was going to take a fuckton of work, one way or the other. Hard, disgusting work. He wasn't under any delusion that they'd turn a sow's ear into a silk purse, but there was something appealing about the prospect of doing something visibly productive. Maybe spending a few weeks working on this place was exactly what they all needed while they figured out what the hell they wanted to do with their lives now that they were all civilians again.

He shrugged. "Hell, why not? It's not like I've got anything better to be doing right now. Holt?"

"Long as I get to swing a sledgehammer."

Jonah grinned. "I expect that can be arranged. C'mon. Let's head on over to my mom's place. She's so excited I brought you along with me, she's beside herself. Prepare to be spoiled."

Holt headed for the door. "I could go for some spoiling."

Brax didn't even know what to do with that. Of the three of them, he was the most alone. Jonah had his mom and sister, and a brother-in-law Brax had served with in the Marines. Holt had a sister somewhere or other. Brax had no one. No family. No wife. Not anymore.

As he trailed his friends out of the bar, temper kindled. Why the hell was he even thinking of Mia? It had been nearly ten years. She'd left. She'd made her choice. He'd moved on with his life. So why the hell couldn't he get her out of his head?

It was Griff's fault. The two of them had bonded in the field over their complicated feelings about their ex-wives. But unlike Brax, Griff had been the one to end things with Sam after they'd impulsively married in Vegas at twenty-two. He'd always planned to go back for her, after turning himself into the man he thought she deserved. Brax had stood up for Griff as informal best man at their second Vegas wedding a few months back.

And damn if it hadn't stirred up all the old feelings. He'd become a Marine to escape all that shit. The betrayal and, damn it, the longing. Because he'd never been able to get over Mia. For so many years, she'd been his everything. And then she'd left, with no explanation. Bailing on their marriage. On him. There was no reason to think that just because his friend had found a second chance, there was the remotest of possibilities for one of his own.

He didn't want a second chance. He didn't want a woman, period. After Mia, he'd basically sworn off relationships or any sort of entanglement, keeping himself in one war zone after another so he didn't have to think about the life he'd never have. Without that outlet, he needed a new distraction.

Maybe a few weeks of hard, sweaty labor would be just enough to clear this shit out of his head so he could figure out what came next.

"Are you sure you want to take on this train wreck?"

Mia Whitmore ignored the skepticism from her best friend and stroked a hand along the stone that made up one wall of the kitchen. It had been part of the original cabin that had stood on the site, and she appreciated its inclusion into the design of the overall house. Even if the designer had been drunk or high. She hadn't been able to decide which. "Too late for regrets now. I already closed on the property."

Luca Gallo blew out a breath. "Well, I guess it's not the hardest flip we've ever done."

"Nothing will ever top that crack house you talked me into

helping you convert right after we met." They'd redone the two-bedroom bungalow he'd gotten for pennies on the dollar from rafters to floor joists. She'd loved nearly every minute.

"Hey, we made a tidy profit on that house when the neighborhood gentrified. And you fell into a career you loved."

"For which I thank you, oh wise one."

"Still, I see now why you wanted me to come out to Tennessee. You're gonna need all the help you can get with this thing."

She nudged his shoulder with her own. "I wanted you to come out because I miss your ugly face and because you needed a change, not because I wanted free labor."

In truth, this house wasn't a flip. It would be a labor of love; one she didn't want anyone else's hands on. At least not more than strictly necessary for the elements that would require more than her two hands. With this purchase, she was taking ownership of a dream that had once been shared. One she'd held onto for far too long.

Almost ten years. After all this time, she had to admit her estranged husband was never coming back to her. She knew what he believed, and he hadn't been interested in explanations. She'd long ago given up trying. Leaving Washington to start over here in Eden's Ridge had been her first step in trying to move on with her life. In the past two years, she'd begun putting down true roots in Tennessee. She was half owner in a business she loved and, in the friends she'd made here, she'd begun to build the kind of family she hadn't had.

But she hadn't given up on Brax, hadn't relinquished that last kernel of hope that maybe... *maybe* there was some circumstance where they could find their way back to each other. And it was time to move on. Deep down, she knew that. So, when she'd found the house, so much what they'd dreamed of in all its mismatched, rambling glory, set into the side of the mountain, she'd taken the plunge.

By the time she finished the renovation, maybe she'd be able to finally let him go. To exorcise the ghost of him in the manifestation of the dream they'd once spoken of in intimate whispers, curled up in bed in their cramped, drafty studio apartment. Then she'd decide whether to live here, turn it into one of her vacation rentals, or straight up sell it. Either way, the renovation would take months in her off time from Mountainview Construction. She was okay with that. Therapy took time.

"I missed your face, too, Mia."

Luca's uncharacteristically serious tone set off alarm bells, reminding her of one of the other reasons she'd left Washington. She'd begun to suspect that her best friend might harbor more than just platonic feelings for her. Mia couldn't go there with him. Couldn't go there with anyone. She wasn't free to pursue a relationship, even if she'd wanted to. Which she didn't. She'd come to Tennessee hoping that the distance would give her some clarity, and she'd convinced herself that she'd imagined the whole thing and balked at nothing. Especially when he'd begun seriously dating and gotten engaged about six months after she'd left.

She'd missed Luca. Missed having someone who understood her. Someone who shared a common language built on years of friendship. So, when his fiancée had broken things off three months before their planned wedding, leaving him high and dry for an investment banker who was more champagne and caviar than beer and nachos, she'd invited him to come east for a while and work for her, trying the area on for size. She hoped like hell she hadn't made a mistake because, as much progress as she'd made, she didn't have the bandwidth to cope with feelings she couldn't return.

Flashing a smile in his direction, she meandered toward the living room. "Well, I say we celebrate your new residency in Eden's Ridge with a night out at Elvira's Tavern so I can prove I'm still the world's best wingwoman. January's slower for the tourist trade, but there will be some, and I can think of a handful of locals who are going to be all over that blond Italian hotness."

He trotted after her. "Is that your plan, then? Entangle me with a local, so I move here permanently?"

"You know me so well." She stopped in front of a 1970s brick monstrosity of a fireplace. "Now, put your professional hat on. Imagine ripping out this horrifying excuse for a fireplace and replacing it with river rock going all the way up. I'd vault the ceiling here to give it some loft. Put up a big, live-edge beam across just there for a mantle and build out the hearth."

Luca nodded, his brown eyes sparkling as his interest piqued. "Now you're talking." He pivoted to the wall across from the fireplace, where a row of three small double-paned windows showed signs of moisture between the glass. "You could knock those out and put in a big picture window to take advantage of that view."

"I'm doing one better. Opening the whole space with accordion doors that will lead out to a big ass deck and entertainment space. It'll be a bit of a tricky build, with the slope the way it is, but it's doable, and that view can't be beat."

"Will the higher humidity here be an issue for those doors?"

They lost themselves in the familiar banter of the work they both loved as they wandered through the house, discussing possibilities. She enjoyed sharing her vision with someone who could see and appreciate it before the first hammer was swung, and she liked the additional considerations he brought up. It would be her house, not a perfect execution of that long ago dream. She could consider other suggestions. Not to mention, she knew a hell of a lot more now as a professional contractor than she had at nineteen. She'd improve on the vision, work with what was here, excise what didn't fit. It was what she was doing with her life, after all.

As they completed their tour back in the kitchen, Luca

slumped back against the counter and crossed his arms. "Well, I still think you're crazy. It'll be a ton of work. But it'll be a helluva property when you're through."

"That's the idea. Now, how are you feeling about pizza and beer? Elvira's is the best around."

"Isn't it also the only pizza around?"

"I mean, yeah." Eden's Ridge only had a year-round resident population of only a little under three thousand people. "But that doesn't mean it isn't good."

"Fair point. I'm amenable. I haven't hit up that food group today."

"Then let's get a move on. I—" The opening bars of Metallica's "Enter Sandman" blared from Mia's back pocket. "Hang on. This might be related to work." She dug out her phone. "Hello?"

"Mia Whitmore?"

Something in the man's flat, formal delivery had more of those inner alarm bells ringing. Whatever this was, it wasn't work.

"Speaking."

"I'm calling on behalf of a mutual friend."

She froze, recognizing the long-ago established code. "We haven't been in touch in quite some time."

"I understand. I'm sorry to say, our mutual friend is dead."

Mia's breath wheezed out like air from a punctured tire, and she wilted back against the nearest wall. "When?"

"Last week. Heart attack. We're closing out his... projects and thought you'd want to know."

Projects. Plural. So maybe she hadn't been the only one.

Aware of Luca's concerned gaze, she locked down the spiral of automatic anxiety and questions. "Yes, I appreciate you letting me know."

"To be clear, we consider those projects wrapped."

Translation: *If anything happens, you're on your own.*

Well, she'd effectively been on her own for almost a decade, so nothing much would change there.

"Understood."

"Goodbye, Mrs. Whitmore." The caller hung up before she could reply.

Mia lowered the phone. "I'm gonna have to cancel on dinner."

"Miss Rebecca, this is the best meatloaf I've ever eaten in my life." Holt pressed a hand to his heart, his face beaming with sincerity. "Will you marry me?"

Brax snorted into his mashed potatoes as Jonah's mom laughed, a full, rich peal of sound that echoed through the kitchen.

"Broadway, quit hitting on my mama."

"Sorry, dude. The maker of this meatloaf deserves to be worshipped."

Rebecca's cheeks pinked, the laugh lines around the green eyes she'd passed on to her son deepening. Brax had no trouble believing she'd been a former pageant queen. She had a magnetism that was utterly irresistible. And the meatloaf really was awesome.

"I'm glad you like it. There's plenty more where that came from. Jonah's always been able to eat like a lumberjack. I figured you and Brax would be the same."

"Yes, ma'am, you figured right."

Grinning, she served them all another slice before passing the bowls of potatoes and roasted brussels sprouts.

Brax took more of all of it. "I didn't know brussels sprouts could actually taste *good.*"

"Bacon makes everything better," Rebecca pronounced.

"True story. I just never thought to add it to baby cabbages."

Jonah waved a fork in his direction. "This is Tennessee, son. Bacon is its own food group here."

"And for a long time, it was the only way I could get this one to eat his vegetables."

"Hey! I resemble that remark."

Rebecca leaned over and pressed a smacking kiss to Jonah's cheek. "It's good to have you home."

"Good to be home."

Brax wondered what it must've been like to have a mom like this. One who looked out for you and made sure you ate your vegetables. Hell, one who made sure you ate at all. One who showered you with open affection, instead of back hands when you didn't scramble out of the way fast enough. He had few memories of the junkie who'd birthed him, and the ones he had, he wished he didn't. After she'd died, he'd been on his own, living on the streets for nearly a year before he'd been scooped up and into the foster system. None of the foster parents he'd been saddled with had been worth much, either. Certainly, none of them had been like Rebecca. This house, covered in family photos of the three of them, where the love had practically soaked into the walls, felt like a whole other planet. He'd only ever felt so at peace and accepted with one person. And in the grand scheme of things, his marriage to Mia had been barely more than a blink. Then again, she'd been his person years before they'd said, "I do."

Christ, why was he thinking of her again?

Hearing his name, Brax blinked, tuning back into the conversation. "Ma'am?"

Rebecca flashed a smile. "I asked if you'd like pie."

That perked him up. "There's pie, too?"

"Apple. With vanilla ice cream. It might not be quite up to what the three of you can whip out now, but it's always been pretty good."

"Pretty good," as it turned out, was an understatement. As the buttery, flaky pastry melted on his tongue and melded with the cinnamon and apples, Brax couldn't stop a moan of appreciation. "Holt, move over. You've got competition. I've got to marry her for this pie."

Delighted, Rebecca laughed again. "Jonah, you should bring your friends home more often. It's fantastic for my ego."

"We can all agree that my mom can cook circles around a lot of people, but I sure as hell am not gonna be calling either of you two assholes 'Daddy,' so lay off."

The laughter and camaraderie lasted through the rest of the meal. Afterward, they overruled Rebecca's attempts to do the dishes.

"It's the least we can do for you, putting us up and feeding us," Holt insisted.

With a satisfied smile, she popped up on her toes to press a kiss to each of their cheeks. "Y'all are good boys. I'm gonna go read for a while. The latest Paisley Parish book is out."

She walked out of the room, humming.

Brax moved over to the sink and turned on the water. "Dude, I hope you know how incredibly lucky you are."

"Seriously," Holt agreed. "Your mom is a treasure. I don't think I realized moms like that actually existed."

Jonah opened a drawer, pulling out dish towels. "I am a shameless mama's boy. She made sure Sam and I never felt a lack from having a single parent."

Holt took a towel. "Did she ever try dating anybody else?"

"Nope. Lonnie did a number on her. Far as I know, she's never had a single date."

Yeah, Brax understood what that was like. Sometimes things ended so badly, it wasn't worth trying again. He plunged his hands into the soapy water and attacked the meatloaf pan as Jonah started loading the dishwasher.

"Either way, she'll totally adopt you two. A bunch of my friends growing up considered her a second mom. A bunch of Sam's too. She's always liked having a houseful."

"I'm completely down for that. She just might permanently change my standards for what I want in a woman," Holt announced.

Brax passed him the pan. "I'd love that, too. But is she really gonna be okay with having three grown men underfoot for however long this clean-up takes?"

"Well, there are some options there that I wanted to discuss with y'all."

Brax and Holt exchanged a look. "That sounds ominous."

"Not ominous. Let's finish these up and grab a beer. I've got an idea to tell you about."

Once the dishes were put away and the counters wiped down, the three of them settled in the living room. Brax sprawled in the overstuffed chair by the little fireplace, propping one foot on his knee. "Okay, out with it, Ferguson. I recognize that scheming light in your eye."

"So, we all went into Dr. Graham's program because we had shit to work out. Coming out the other side with a certified civilian skill was a bonus rather than the end game. And now, we're all wondering what the hell we're gonna do next." Jonah tipped back his beer. "She made it clear that we're going to need the kind of community that we can become a part of, make a difference in. We can do that here."

Holt rubbed absently at his knee, where his prosthetic attached. "By doing what, exactly?"

"Exactly what we were trained to do. We're damned good bakers. Sure, not a one of us expected to be good at it or even to like it. None of us thought that's what we'd be doing when we grew up. But we have an opportunity here that we're not likely to have somewhere else."

Brax stared him down. "You want to open a bakery in the bar."

Jonah tipped his bottle in Brax's direction. "Got it in one. I own the building free and clear. Or Sam and I do, and I've already run the idea by her. Not having rent or a mortgage lowers the overhead of getting a business started."

"Were you in the same building we were yesterday?" Holt demanded. "It's not like we can just clean up and slap some paint on the place and it suddenly look inviting. We're talking about major renovation. And that's on top of buying all the necessary equipment. We'd need ovens, display cases, a proper walk-in cooler, better seating. *And* that's assuming there are no structural issues with the building itself. We don't have the skills to do all that, which means hiring out, which means even more costs."

Brax picked up the thread. "There's also the question of whether a town this size can generate enough revenue to support all three of us. Eden's Ridge is a small town. Hell, the entire population of Stone County can't be more than—what? —fifteen thousand?"

"Bit over twenty. I don't dispute there'd be a lot of moving parts, and if we decide to do it, then we can cross all those bridges, ask all those questions. The one that needs answering more immediately is whether this is something either of you would want at all. I'm not gonna be offended if you say no, and I'm not expecting an answer right this second. I just wanted to present the option. Y'all have become some of my closest friends this past year, and if I was gonna go into business for myself, actually gonna open a bakery, I'd want to do it with y'all."

Brax grinned. "Awww, you like us."

Holt clinked his bottle to Jonah's. "We love you, too, brother."

"You've got time to think about it. But I did set up an appointment tomorrow with a contractor. Buddy of mine from high school has his own construction company, and he's gonna come out to give us an estimate on what we might be looking at. It may be that it'll be too much, and that'll put an end to the whole idea. But then at least we'll know."

Brax took a pull on his beer and sat with the idea. Jonah's proposal would mean putting down real roots. He'd never really felt the urge. Not since his marriage imploded. But maybe it was time. He certainly hadn't grown up as part of a community. Neither had Holt.

What would it be like to live in a place like this? Where undoubtedly everybody more or less knew everybody and was probably all up in each other's business. That was how it was supposed to work in small towns, right? But it would also mean setting himself up in a place where people would give a damn about him. Brax had finally reached a point in his life where he believed he actually deserved that. Most of the time.

"I assume, if we did this, we'd be looking for a more permanent place to live. Your mother's cooking aside, it's not practical for us to stay here long term."

"There are rental options. Both vacation rentals we could nab for a few weeks if we stick to the original plan, or regular rentals if we opt to open the bakery. Porter—that's my buddy— also has some properties. We can talk to him about those tomorrow, too, because I doubt any of us are gonna want to sleep on the couch for more than a few nights."

Holt leaned forward, setting his beer on the coffee table. "Speaking of which, we gotta figure out who has the short straw. Put 'em in, fellas."

Brax and Jonah likewise sat forward, each with a fist in their palms for the time-honored tradition of rock-paper-scissors.

"On three."

By the time she made it home, Mia couldn't even remember the excuse she'd given Luca for why she had to bail on dinner. Certainly not the truth. Prevarication on this particular subject was so ingrained, so rote after nearly twenty years, she hadn't even considered bringing him into her confidence. She'd been taught for so long that bringing anyone in on the truth would put them in danger, and she'd taken that lesson to heart, never even telling Brax.

Now the man who'd issued that edict was dead, and she didn't know how to feel about it. Her entire life had changed because of Curt Savage. He'd saved her life. Twice. And ruined it. Which wasn't exactly a fair assessment. If she'd made different choices, the second time wouldn't have been necessary, and she wouldn't have lost the one person in her life who mattered most.

Wrestling with a boatload of conflicting emotions, she opened the door to the world's most perfect distraction. Leno, her beloved buckskin pit bull, bounced and leaped, doing a full-body wriggle of joy as she came inside. As always, his broad doggie grin coaxed a smile out of her as she crouched to love on her baby.

"Hey buddy. How's my best boy? Have you been good since lunch?"

Leno barked and bounced in a circle.

"Okay, okay. I know you're ready." In accordance with their daily routine, she grabbed the harness and leash off a hook by the back door. "Stand still, you goober. This goes faster that way."

Leno bounced another circle and slurped a kiss up Mia's

cheek. Cringing and laughing, she swiped her face and finally got the harness clipped.

"Let's go."

Her enthusiastic pup towed her out the door and down the driveway, immediately veering left, his tail wagging ninety to nothing as he searched for Suzy, the Black lab next door who was the love of his life. He dragged Mia off the street to walk the fence line, the metronome swish of his tail slowing when no Suzy appeared.

"Doesn't look like she's out tonight, pal. It's pretty cold. Let's get moving."

Leno whined but returned to the street to continue their walk. Moving was good. It kept Mia's brain from spinning too far out of control pondering the consequences of Curt's death. Would there even *be* consequences? She hadn't been in willing, direct contact with him in nearly a decade, not since she'd told him to go to hell. But she knew he'd kept tabs and watched out for her anyway, because of the deathbed promise he'd made to her mother. Now there'd be no one keeping tabs, no one making sure she wasn't in danger.

Nothing had happened. Not in all these years since she'd last seen him. Mia didn't know whether that was because she hadn't been the target they'd thought she might be, or because she'd done exactly as she'd been told and stayed hidden. Maybe it didn't matter in the end. She wasn't the girl she'd been, and it wasn't like she'd be fool enough to try to connect to her old life again. No one was left from that life to connect to. In all likelihood, she was safe.

"Leno! Leno!"

At the bright little-girl squee, Leno made a beeline to the other side of the road. A pajama-clad Maddie Black came barreling down the front walk, arms spread wide. Bracing herself for the familiar bittersweet interaction, Mia took a firmer grip on the leash so Leno couldn't accidentally knock the child down.

"Maddie, slow down! Remember, gentle hands!" Cayla, Maddie's harried mom, came hurrying out the front door of their little house, pulling on a sweater.

Drawing a curtain on her dark thoughts, Mia prepared to be neighborly for a few minutes, while Leno and Maddie engaged in their ritual love fest. The two collided with joy on both sides, Leno bathing Maddie's face in kisses, Maddie giggling madly as she went to her knees to hug him. Mia's heart pinched at the child's unabashed delight. Once upon a time, she'd thought she'd have a child of her own. That maybe she could give the kind of childhood she and Brax hadn't had. Now she contented herself with her dog and being on the periphery of other children's lives.

Cayla made it down to the edge of the street. "We thought you might not be walking tonight. Maddie's been camped at the front window since dinner."

Mia found a smile for the pair of them. "I'm running a little behind. My friend Luca just moved to town, and I was giving him a tour of the new property I bought to renovate."

Cayla studied her face, a crease forming between her blonde brows. "Everything okay? You look... I don't know. Off somehow."

It was proof of how much her life had shifted that she hadn't been able to completely blank her face. "It's fine. I just found out someone I used to know passed away."

Cayla instantly reached out to lay a hand on Mia's arm. "Oh, I'm so sorry for your loss. Do you want to come in for a glass of wine?"

The last thing she needed was to hang out with this kind single mom, lest she be tempted to reveal something in the name of sorting out her own thoughts. "No, I'm good. But thank you. Have you had any more problems with that bathroom faucet dripping?"

"Not a one. Whatever seal you replaced did the trick. Thank you again for helping out."

"Of course. Glad to. No reason to call out a plumber for a little thing like that. How's the search for office space going?"

A few years before, Cayla had started an event planning business. Up to now she'd been working from home, meeting prospective clients at their homes or businesses, but she'd finally gained enough traction to look at getting her own separate office space.

"Well, I might have found something. You know Willie Thompson's garage across from The Right Attitude?"

"Sure."

"Well, Mick Routledge—he's one of the mechanics there. We went to high school together forever ago—Anyway, Mick told me Willie owns that little house right next door. 'House' is probably a generous description. It's more like a converted one-room shack with a bathroom. Willie's been wanting to rent it for a while, but nobody wanted to be that close to the bar. Now that it's closed down, depending on what goes in there, it might be worth looking at again. The price is right, and a bunch of paint would cover up a multitude of cosmetic deficiencies."

Mia wrestled with whether to intervene or leave it be. She didn't have a stake in this, and Cayla had every right to make her own decision. But she was a sweet woman without a lot of money to waste. Mia couldn't watch her make a potential mistake. "Maybe hold off on signing anything until I can take a look? I don't want to get all up in your business, but it can't hurt to have a professional evaluation of the structure, just to make sure everything's sound before putting pen to paper."

"Oh, would you? That would be great! And no, I wasn't planning on anything until we find out whether there's just going to be another bar going in."

"Well, I might be able to help on that front, too. Porter and I have a meeting tomorrow with the new owner to discuss renovations. I don't know yet if he's wanting to renovate to sell, or to turn it into something else."

"I'd love to be a fly on the wall for that conversation. Jonah was a little ahead of me in school, but I had some classes with his sister. They never had anything to do with their daddy, and there was definitely no love lost for the business. I'd be surprised if they didn't want to just do what needs doing to wash their hands of it."

"Guess we'll see. I need to be getting on. Leno here will be wanting some dinner."

"Of course. Maddie, say goodnight to Leno and Mia."

The little girl squeezed Leno and pressed a noisy kiss to his head. "Bye Leno! Bye Miss Mia!"

"Night, kiddo. We'll see you both later." With one last wave, she watched the two disappear into the house and made her way back to her own.

After filling Leno's bowl with kibble, she poured herself a tumbler of bourbon and dropped onto the sofa in her Spartan living room. After two years of living here, she'd done little more than grab a few flea market pieces she'd have no trouble walking away from. She was still living as if she had to be ready to pick up and go at a moment's notice.

Now that Curt was dead, there was no one and nothing left to upset the life she was building. She'd bought into her business and begun setting down roots on that side. Maybe it really was time to make a home and a life meant to last.

"Jonah, it's so good to have you back! Y'all enjoy your breakfast now and thank you for your service."

As the comfortably curvy woman who owned Crystal's Diner—Crystal, Brax presumed—strode away, the three of them tucked into the morning's special of eggs, bacon, biscuits, and grits. She was the fourth person to welcome Jonah home since they'd sat down. Did his buddy appreciate being seen as a hometown hero? Would he, in Jonah's shoes? Brax didn't know. As far as he could tell, everything about Eden's Ridge was about as far from where he'd come from as it was possible to be. He didn't know if those differences were something he could get used to or not.

"Does everybody know you here?" Brax asked.

"Not everybody. But since Mama owns the salon in town, everybody does know her, so by proxy, they've kept up with me all these years."

Holt split a biscuit and started layering on bacon and eggs. "That's nice. Makes you feel like people give a shit."

"It is nice. Most of the time. It was hell as a teenager any time my friends and I got into shit because, nine times out of ten, somebody had notified our parents before we got home. But there's comfort in that, too. It was a good place to grow up. I don't think I appreciated that at the time, and I didn't know I'd want to come back. Then again, I never figured on retiring from the Navy this early."

The head injury that had damaged Jonah's hearing and left him with a prolonged case of post-concussion syndrome had seen to that. Though his brain had healed, Brax knew his buddy was still working through some emotional fallout about the premature termination of his career. They all had their issues around leaving military service.

"So, what's the plan today?" Brax was itching to *do* something.

"Meeting with Porter at ten. Until then, we'll work on tossing what can be tossed. Starting with the questionable lingerie border."

Holt made a face. "I don't think what's hanging on those walls can be called lingerie. That implies a level of class that just isn't there."

"Ferguson, I'm gonna have to issue you a citation for not letting me know you were back in town."

They all looked up at the guy with the badge who'd stopped by their table, a to-go cup of coffee in hand.

Jonah's face split into a grin. "Xander." He slid out of the booth and embraced the other man in a back-slapping hug.

"How the hell are you, man?"

"I'm good. We just got in yesterday." He nodded in their direction. "Meet Brax Whitmore and Holt Steele. They're friends of mine from Syracuse who came down to help me with the cleanup. Y'all, this is Sheriff Xander Kincaid, one of my good buddies from high school."

"Nice to meet y'all. I heard you might be doing more than just cleanup."

"Maybe. Porter's been talking, huh?"

"He mentioned it at family breakfast at the inn this morning."

"We'll see what he says after he gets a good look at the place."

"Be awesome if that 'maybe' means you're coming home for good."

"We'll see."

As the two of them continued the small-town catch up, Brax leaned a little closer to Holt and murmured. "Does this feel like another planet to you?"

"Yup. I think I like it, though."

"You thinking about taking his offer?"

"Haven't decided yet, but leaning toward yes. No other options on the table at the moment, and I'm not sure I've got a good reason to say no. You?"

"Jury's still out." But the overwhelming friendliness of the town was a weight on the side of staying. The truth was, he didn't have a weight on the side of *going* anywhere else. Maybe that was a sign unto itself.

The radio on Xander's duty belt crackled. He fiddled with a knob. "That's my cue. I gotta get on. But we need to get together while you're here. Kennedy will want to have you out to dinner, and Caroline needs to meet her Uncle Jonah."

"Wouldn't miss it."

"I'll be in touch. Brax, Holt, welcome to Eden's Ridge."

There were at least three more interruptions by the time they'd finished breakfast, and two more on the way to where they'd parked. By the time they made it to the bar, it was already past nine.

Jonah wedged a busted chunk of cinderblock against the heavy black door. "We might ought to prop open the pass through and the back door, too. See if we can't get some cross ventilation going to air the place out. The cold's gotta be better than the smell."

"Meanwhile, did you pack some hazmat suits?" Brax asked.

"Got gloves and industrial-size garbage bags. That'll get us started."

They went to work, pulling down bras and tossing them in the big garbage cans. As they stripped the walls, Brax examined the building with fresh eyes.

"You know, if that wall dividing the kitchen from the front isn't load bearing, it could be ripped out and moved further forward to enlarge the kitchen. That'd leave room for all the extra ovens and cooling racks we'd need."

"If the business was set up to be mostly a pick-up and carryout situation, there wouldn't be need for anywhere near this level of seating," Holt mused. "Maybe just a half-dozen tabletops."

Jonah flashed a grin. "Admit it. Y'all are intrigued by the idea."

"Thinking about it," Brax conceded. "Don't know what it'd cost, but ripping off the current roof and going up so we could vault the ceiling would significantly change the profile of the building and make it feel more open. Maybe add some beams and skylights."

"Skylights, he says," Holt scoffed.

Brax shrugged and tossed another bra into the can. "If we're gonna dream, why not dream big?"

"It's worth asking Porter about," Jonah agreed. "Though that kind of massive structural change would significantly increase renovation costs."

"Might be worth it to truly change the face of the place. I get the impression people's memories here will run long. If we truly wanted to start a new business here, seems like it would be important to make this place look as little like the original structure as possible."

Holt pulled down the last bra. "You make a good point. But there's got to be stuff that can be done that's more budget friendly. I know we've all got money put back that we can invest, but we need to be smart about it."

"Hence today's consultation," Jonah reminded them. "Which is about to begin. I think I hear a truck."

A rangy blond guy strode in a minute later, travel mug in hand. His eyes widened as he took in the initial changes. "Well, that's already a drastic improvement in decorating."

"We figured it was the best place to start. How you doing, man?" Jonah offered his hand and got pulled in for another of those back-slapping hugs.

"Good. Faith is teething, so nobody's sleeping, but everybody's healthy, so we sure can't complain."

"Great to hear. Porter, this is Holt and Brax, my prospective business partners."

Something flickered over Porter's face before he seemed to shrug it off. "Good to meet you."

Brax wondered what that was about.

"Jonah mentioned one of you was Army?"

Holt nodded. "Rangers."

"I was Reserves for about eight years. There are actually several Rangers here in the area. Buddies of mine from back in the day at Fort Benning. One of them—Sebastian Donnelly—opened an equine therapy center here. And then Harrison Wilkes and Ty Brooks both settled here with their wives."

Holt brightened. "Harrison's here? We went through Ranger school together. I haven't met the other two, but I know them by reputation."

"I'll put you in touch," Porter promised.

"Are we ready to get this show on the road?" Jonah asked.

"In just a bit. I'm waiting for my business partner. She had to stop by the office to pick something up but was more or less right behind me."

The crunch of tires on gravel announced her arrival.

"That'll be her now. She's really the one you'll want to talk to. She's got a lot more experience with commercial renovations than I do."

A minute later, a woman strode through the door, clipboard under one arm, a phone pressed to her ear. She hesitated in the shadowy entryway. "No, we need that order for the Saint James' house."

Everything in Brax went on high alert at the sound of that voice.

"I've got to go. I have a consultation. Yeah. Yeah. Thanks, Marty. You're a jewel." She hung up the phone, shoving it into her back pocket as she stepped into the bar. "Sorry I'm late. I—"

Her eyes met his, and the clipboard clattered to the floor, all the blood draining out of those all-too-familiar golden-toned cheeks.

"Brax."

~

HIS NAME CAME out in a whisper because Mia couldn't breathe for the elephant that had just dropped down on her chest.

The husband she'd lost all those years ago—the man she'd thought never to see again—was right here. Bigger, broader, and bearded, but she'd know those storm-dark gray eyes anywhere. No one else's gaze had ever felt like a physical touch.

He was *here*, in Eden's Ridge, in the flesh. And it was more than apparent he hadn't come in search of her, as those arrogantly sensual lips went from an O of shock to pressing into a thin line.

One of the other two men with him glanced between them. "Uh, you two know each other?"

She couldn't process fast enough to actually respond. How could she even answer that question in a way that wouldn't necessitate lengthy explanations?

Brax sucked in a slow breath through his nose, not taking his eyes off her as he crossed his arms. "We used to. Mia's my ex-wife."

Oh, like that.

His words slid swift and vicious into her heart, and it took everything she had not to fall to her knees as the hope that he'd ever want her back, that there was ever a way to fix what she'd broken, simply died. Grief rose like a tidal wave, crashing against the shock of seeing him again. Curling her hands in on themselves, she pushed back at them both. If all she had left were the scraps of her pride, by God, she'd cling to them like a life raft to keep from falling apart in front of him and everyone else. She was a fucking professional.

"If that's your end goal, then we can deal with that while you're here." Her voice came out admirably steady, considering she felt as if she was bleeding out from some mortal wound.

His brows drew together. "Excuse me?"

She managed to take in another breath, to keep speaking in a calm fashion. "A divorce. It's probably long overdue, considering." Just saying it hurt. But if it was what he wanted, she had no right to hold him back.

Brax stared at her as if she'd sprouted a second head. "We were divorced nearly ten years ago."

It was her turn to stare as she turned over what he'd said. But no matter which way she looked at it, she couldn't make sense of the statement. "What are you talking about? I've never seen any divorce papers, Brax."

Those muscled arms dropped, and he took half a step toward her before he stopped himself. "What the hell?"

Porter spoke up. "Um, maybe we should give y'all some time to... uh... talk."

The other men filed out, clearly wanting to avoid the impending drama. And then she was alone in this defunct, skeezy bar, with the man she'd been in love with most of her life.

Because she understood that this might well be the last time she ever laid eyes on him, Mia let herself drink him in, cataloging the changes. He'd added a good thirty or forty pounds of muscle to that tall, lean frame. The curve of well-toned muscle strained the fabric of his long-sleeved t-shirt. His hair was shorter than it had been, no doubt a remnant of his years in the Marines. That stubborn, square jaw she'd once been free to trace with her hands was edged in a close-cropped beard. But he still had that wary, watchful gaze he'd always had. Here was the adult version of the near-feral boy who'd befriended her all those years ago in her first foster placement. Full of suspicion and certain of betrayal.

She knew him, knew he believed she'd abandoned him. Even if it had been only a suspicion before, she could see it in the barely leashed rage bubbling beneath the surface. Somehow, confirmation of what she'd always known was another blow. He truly thought the very worst of her. And if he believed that, had he ever really known her at all?

Of course, he hadn't. She'd never told him who she was. Never been allowed to. She'd deluded herself into believing it was to keep him safe. She'd shared all the parts that mattered with him. Her hopes. Her dreams. Her heart. At the end of the day, it hadn't been enough.

What the hell was she supposed to say now? There was no explanation that would make him forgive her. If he'd been willing to listen, he'd have opened one of her letters at some point, instead of sending them all back. He had no interest in answers, no intention of forgiving her. Even if he had, the only man who knew the truth, who could have backed her actions up, was dead now. Brax had no reason to listen to her.

He was still staring at her, and he'd locked down whatever he was feeling, other than anger. She couldn't read him, and that was another blow. She'd once known every nuance of his face, the meaning of every shift in posture. But it had been so very long. Of course, he'd changed. Hadn't she? That was life, wasn't it? And maybe there truly wasn't anything left for him but fury.

The idea of that hurt her heart. That he'd hardened himself, closed himself off again because of her, was a tough truth to accept. She hadn't just broken them. In a sense, she'd broken him. Unintended consequence or not, it was her worst fear realized, and she'd have to learn to live with the guilt of that.

I'm sorry. I'm so damned sorry.

The words hovered at the tip of her tongue. But she couldn't say them. They were paltry and empty after this long, and nothing in his body language said he'd be willing to hear an apology of any kind. So, she swallowed and said the one true thing she didn't have to think about. "It's good to see you."

He just looked at her, nostrils flaring, hands flexing and straightening, before turning his back on her and walking out.

B rax hung up the phone, wondering how the hell his life had gotten so fucked up.

The state of Washington had no record of his divorce ever being filed. He and Mia were still legally married.

Holy shit.

Jonah came into the living room, a bottle of Jack Daniels dangling from his hand. "I'm gonna guess, from the look on your face, that the news is not what you were hoping."

Brax scrubbed a hand down his face. "We're still married."

Holt set down a trio of glasses. "Well, that's a hell of a thing. Didn't you ever think to check on it before? To make sure it went through?"

"It hasn't come up." Relationships of any kind weren't something he'd sought out. After Mia, he hadn't been interested in risking that again.

Jonah poured them all a healthy two fingers of whiskey. "What happened with you two, anyway? I mean, I know you said she left a long time ago, but what really happened?"

Brax had less than zero interest in getting into this, but as his mess was impacting his friends, he recognized he owed them some kind of explanation.

Accepting a glass, and figuring it was five o'clock some-where, he sank back into his chair. "We got married right after she turned eighteen."

"Damn, that's young," Holt observed.

"We met in the foster system when we were kids. Were best friends for years. Neither of us had anybody else. I'd been plan-ning on asking her as a sort of platonic marriage of conve-nience, just so we'd have each other when she aged out, too. But then her foster father assaulted her." His hand tightened on the glass as he remembered, with vivid clarity, seeing the bastard holding Mia to a wall by her throat. "I nearly killed him. Probably would have if she hadn't stopped me. But I had to get her out and away."

Jonah sucked in a breath. "Shit."

Brax tipped back the whiskey, wishing the burn of it would wipe out the memories of what had come next. "Major shit like that has a way of bringing things to light. Like the fact that we were in love with each other. So, we got married for real, so they couldn't try to put her anywhere else and I could keep her safe. And it was good. I mean, we were poor as dirt, and we worked our asses off, living paycheck-to-paycheck, but we were together. And then one day she was gone."

Jonah splashed more whiskey into Brax's empty glass. "That was just it?"

That definitely hadn't been just it.

"I didn't realize anything was wrong until she didn't come home after work. Then I contacted her boss, who said she hadn't been in at all that day. I checked with all our friends, called all the area hospitals. Nobody could find her. I was totally losing my shit by the time I contacted the police to report her missing. We all spent weeks searching. I went everywhere I could think to go. Put up posters. The whole shebang. And then I realized her go bag was missing."

Holt frowned. "She kept a go bag?"

"For as long as I'd known her. I never thought it was odd because we got moved so often, and frequently on short notice, in the foster system. It was a big deal when she stopped checking it every day after we got married. And I guess I just forgot about it until then. When I reported that fact to the police, the detective on the case said I needed to accept that maybe she didn't want to be found. I didn't want to listen, but when there was no sign after more than a month—" Brax shrugged. "I couldn't stay in our apartment after that. I was so pissed. So hurt. I needed somewhere to put all that rage, so I divorced her—thought I divorced her, via mail—and enlisted."

"Divorce by mail is a thing?" Jonah asked.

"It is in Washington."

"Huh."

Holt set his glass aside. "Given the issues with the postal service, the idea of divorce by mail seems kind of risky."

"I was twenty-two and one step above broke. It was what I could afford." And it had been the easiest way to dissolve things. No judges. No lawyers. No having to admit to anyone, face-to-face, that the woman he'd loved had left him without a word.

Easing back on the sofa, Holt began massaging his knee. "And you never heard from her again, until today?"

Brax hesitated. "She wrote me for the first few years I was in the Marines."

"Wait, wait. She wrote you?" Jonah demanded. "How did she even know where to find you?"

"I'd left the details with our landlord in the event she came back. I guess she did at some point."

"So, what did she say?"

"I don't know. I never read any of the letters. Just marked them return to sender."

Jonah slapped his glass down on the coffee table. "Dude, seriously? Didn't you wonder?"

He had wondered. There were times when the wondering had eaten him alive. But he didn't want to hear how she'd been unhappy, and he hadn't even seen. How he hadn't been enough for her. How the life they were living didn't work for her anymore.

"We were over. What did it matter?"

"Except you're not over," Holt challenged.

"Evidently not." But they'd fix that. Once and for all, they'd take advantage of this awkward-as-hell reunion and get a damned divorce.

Bracing his elbows on his knees, Jonah leaned forward. "Look, man, I know you weren't expecting any of this. I'll understand if you want to bail on this project. Being in the same town as your ex is not what you signed on for."

He'd given it some thought. A part of him wanted to get the hell out of Eden's Ridge and away from the woman who'd stirred far too much when she'd appeared today. But that smacked of cowardice. "No. I said I'd do it. And it makes sense that we need to interact on some level to get this divorce sorted."

"All right. Are you going to be able to work with her on the renovation if we go that route?"

Shit. Brax hadn't considered that. Porter had said this was Mia's area of expertise. Not that they'd gotten through the consultation at all after the surprise reunion. But he didn't want to ruin Jonah and Holt's opportunity by letting this shit run his life.

"We can keep out of each other's way." And he was grown-up enough not to spout all the petty, spiteful things he'd thought to say to her over the years. At least not in front of others.

Holt frowned, his brows drawn together in a thoughtful expression.

"What?" Brax prompted.

"There's one question—well, there are about a hundred questions I'd want answered. But the biggest one I'd want to know the answer to... If she left you the way you think, why didn't *she* seek a divorce in all these years? Wouldn't she want to be able to move on with her life?"

Brax wanted to believe that didn't matter. He wanted to hang on to the version of events that had been his constant companion for the past decade. But the same question had been niggling at him. Because it was weird.

Then again, nothing about her defection had been normal. Who the hell knew what had been in her head or why she hadn't done the logical thing? At this point, he didn't care. He just wanted to be done with her so he could finally get on with his own life.

"I'M NOT sure that could have gone much worse." Mia dropped her head to Porter's kitchen counter.

"The fact that you kept your shit together through the rest of the workday was impressive and, I feel compelled to say, was wholly unnecessary. I'd have understood if you needed a day off."

"And have the rest of the day to stew in my juices? No, thank you." She looked up as Porter set a beer down in front of her. "I'm not sure this is sufficient for unexpectedly running into my estranged husband, who has evidently thought we were divorced for the past decade."

"I've got you, girl." Porter's wife, Maggie, set a shot of tequila beside the beer. "We're out of limes, but I figure it's an emergency."

"I love you." Mia tossed back the shot, wincing as the alcohol burned down to her gut. "Thank God Luca was down at the Ganaway job with Brick today. The last thing I need is to deal with his thoughts on this whole thing."

"Does he know Brax?" Maggie asked.

"No. He knows the aftermath of Brax. Which was… bad. So, he's always quietly hated him. He doesn't understand my allegiance, and I don't have the bandwidth to have that argument with him again right now. I know it's coming because there's not going to be any keeping this a secret. Of course, that's assuming my very presence here doesn't torpedo our shot at getting this gig. I'm really sorry if this costs us the job."

Porter slid onto the stool beside her and gave her shoulder a brotherly squeeze. It was a mark of how much she'd settled in here that she didn't shy away from the touch.

"Screw the job. We've got plenty of work to keep the company occupied well into summer. I'm worried about you. I saw the look on your face. If he'd stabbed you in the gut, I don't think you'd have been any more shocked."

"Sounds about right." She scrubbed both hands over her face. "I've imagined seeing him again so many times, and I never knew what to say. And then today, finding out he's thought we were divorced all this time was just—I guess part of why I held on to hope for so long is because we weren't divorced. I thought there was a chance, however remote, that someday we'd come back to each other. Which is stupid. I know what he thinks I did, and I have no defense for it."

"What he *thinks* you did?" Leave it to Maggie, the attorney, to zero in on the discrepancy.

Even now, the truth clogged in Mia's throat. She poured herself another shot of tequila. "It's complicated. There are reasons I couldn't tell him, and I can't tell you."

"Fair enough. I know something about that." The NDA Maggie had signed years before had nearly derailed her relationship with Porter before the truth had come out from an entirely different quarter. "Are you still bound by those reasons?"

Was she? Curt was dead. All the players she'd been connected to were dead, too, as far as she knew. Was nearly twenty years enough time to keep a secret? What would Brax do if she told him everything? Not just what had happened ten years ago, but who she really was. Why she'd been foster care to begin with. Would it change how he saw her? Make him revise his bad opinion?

But that was pipe dream thinking. He'd never give her the chance to give that explanation. And even if he did, the truth sounded like some kind of fiction. A wild tale she'd concocted to justify the unforgivable.

"It doesn't matter. He wants a divorce. I won't fight him on it. He has a right to move on with his life, and maybe, if we do this, I'll be able to move on with mine."

But she didn't know how. She'd learned how to live in limbo during these years without him. She'd learned how to live in fear in the years before him. But she had no idea how to function in a world where even the possibility of a connection to him was no longer a reality.

Porter studied her. Mia knew he saw more than she wanted, but she didn't have it in her to hide her roiling emotions. Not now.

"You don't want to let him go."

"No." She didn't want to give up. And that just made her ten kinds of fool because the angry man she'd seen today wasn't her Brax. He wasn't the guy who'd saved her life. Wasn't the guy who'd gone out of his way to make sure she had flowers to carry on their unconventional wedding day. Wasn't the guy who'd walked her to and from school every single day after he'd aged out of the system himself, just to make sure she was safe.

The realization that her Brax might well no longer exist absolutely broke her heart. Mia hadn't realized her capacity for grief could get any bigger. But she knew better than most that people could learn to survive far more than they realized.

Porter's voice was gentle. "Isn't it worth trying to talk to him about this, now that you're in the same place?"

"He sent back over a hundred letters unopened before I gave up trying. I don't expect him to be any more interested in an explanation now than he was then." Because she couldn't stand the look of sympathy on Porter's face, she tossed back the second shot and turned her attention to Maggie. "So, what's involved with filing for divorce in Tennessee?"

An abrupt wail sounded from down the hall.

"Hold that thought. Her Fussiness has awakened from her nap."

Porter slid off the stool. "I've got her. Y'all go ahead."

They both watched him go.

Maggie lowered her voice. "Okay, I don't know if there's anything you want or need to say that he shouldn't hear, and you aren't obligated to tell me a damned thing. But if any of this involves some kind of legal entanglement beyond a divorce, you can count on my discretion if you need a sounding board. I know what it's like to get in over your head."

Mia's throat went thick. None of what she was dealing with fell under a true legal entanglement. That would've been so much simpler than the reality and would've provided her with far more protections. But it was a lovely reminder that she had friends here, and even if her marriage was over for good, she wasn't alone.

"Thanks, Maggie. I really appreciate it."

Porter came back, his sixteen-month-old daughter in his arms. The sight of those sleepy eyes and that downy blonde hair sticking up in every direction as she snuggled against her father's shoulder was an extra bittersweet punch today. Yeah, she needed to wrap this up and get home to Leno, where she could lick her wounds in peace.

"So... the filing?"

Maggie leveled her with a look but didn't press. "The paperwork itself isn't complicated. You've both had entirely separate residences for years, so unless he decides to come after the assets you've accrued since then—"

"Unlikely."

"Then it would be uncontested. Once the initial request is filed, Tennessee requires a sixty-day cooling-off period for couples with no offspring."

Mia struggled to ignore the phantom pain in her side. "Well, we don't have any of those." And never would.

"Then the two of you can sort out the details yourselves, in terms of division of assets and the like, and submit the appropriate paperwork to the court clerk. It's pretty simple at that point."

Simple. As if the dismantling of a marriage was an easy thing.

"One other thing," Maggie added. "Tennessee also requires a six-month residency before allowing someone to file, so unless he wants to file in whatever state he has residency, you're the one who will need to file."

Mia shut her eyes. She'd get through this. Somehow. "Okay, if that's what it takes, then that's what we'll do."

Needing to escape, she slid off her stool. "Thank you both for the moral support. I'm gonna get on home. Porter, maybe it's best if you're the one who calls Jonah to reschedule the consultation. Assuming he even still wants one."

"Sure. I'll do that. You sure you're okay?"

"Not even a little bit. But that's never stopped me before. I'll see you tomorrow."

5

"You don't have to be here for this."

Brax leveled Jonah with a flat stare. "I'm fine."

"That why you've been pacing like a caged tiger since we got here?"

Brax stopped in the process of doing exactly that around the perimeter of the bar. He *was* fine. It was natural to feel a little dread at seeing his wife again. Christ Almighty, why should that rattle him so much? It changed nothing. It was just a formality that hadn't yet been disentangled.

And he hadn't been able to stop wondering about that since Holt had brought it up.

Now wasn't the time or place to ask her. They'd had enough delays getting this consultation meeting rescheduled. Delays that had given them enough time to attack the interior of the building with more commercial cleaners than he'd been aware existed in the world. Perhaps that had been a waste of time, if they were only going to demo the place for a renovation, but it had given them something to do. And at least he didn't feel like he'd get tetanus just from walking inside.

The sound of tires on gravel had his gut tightening. Time to put his game face on. The idea of having to use it with Mia felt unnatural. For so many years, she'd been the only one he could let his guard down around. The only one he'd been able to trust. And she'd betrayed him. He'd never imagined she could or would. Before she'd left, he would have staked his life on her loyalty. Which just went to show that he wasn't as good a judge of character as he'd believed.

She came through the door with Porter, and this time Brax let himself look, to soak in the sight of her. Her body was a compact package of lean muscle, no doubt built on the job, but she still had the curves he'd always loved. She didn't hide them now, as she had when they were teens. Then again, the oversized shirts and jackets she'd favored would likely be a danger on a construction site. She'd pulled her thick, sable hair back into a low ponytail, leaving her face unframed. Her cheeks were sharper now, and he recognized the signs of poor sleep in the shadows beneath those long-lashed eyes. It annoyed Brax that his first thought was concern.

Mia's gaze settled on him for a long moment. Assessing his mood, perhaps? He concentrated on betraying nothing, simply crossing his arms, and waiting.

She swallowed and put on her fake-it-'til-you-make-it smile. "Good morning, gentlemen. Thank you for meeting with us again. How about you tell us what it is you're thinking about doing here so we can get started?"

Straight to it, then. That was probably best, before the awkward could take over. If she was going to act like a professional, so would he.

As it was Jonah's building, they left him to answer. "Well, we're looking into what it would take to convert this place into a bakery."

"A bakery?" Mia blinked and looked over at Brax. "That is... not what I was expecting. Okay." She swung her attention back to Jonah and Holt. "Are you looking at a combination bakery and coffee shop, with a need for lots of seating or more of a carryout business model?"

It was a good question from someone not in the business. Then again, bakeries had been one of her favorite places to go on the rare occasion they could afford a treat. He supposed that hadn't changed, and she was a woman who paid attention.

"We're skewing toward more of the latter. The kitchen needs expanding, for sure, to accommodate all three of us."

Brax wasn't at all sure he'd take the offer, but now wasn't the time to mention it.

Mia darted another quick look in his direction. Curiosity. Surprise. But she held in whatever questions she had. "Let's take a look."

They all trooped back through the swinging door into the less disgusting kitchen. Brax had tackled the range himself. Without the layers of grease and grime, the unit appeared to be half decent. Likely it would do for the caramels, jams, and other fillings that needed stovetop cooking. If they could keep from having to replace it for a year or two, it would save them several thousand dollars.

Mia wandered the space, eying the location of power outlets, pipes, the drain. "I expect you'll want to put in—what? —two sets of double commercial ovens? You'll need bigger prep sinks, at least one more stainless-steel counter." She muttered to herself, making notes on the clipboard she held. "Hmm."

Giving the existing stainless counter a testing push, she smoothly hopped up onto it, reaching up to shift over one of the tiles in the drop ceiling.

"I wouldn't stick my head up there," Holt muttered.

Mia flashed a wry smile. "Part of the job." But she did tap the frame with a flashlight. When nothing moved, she rose to her toes, attempting to peer into the darkness. "Damn. Not tall enough. Porter, you want to come play ladder?"

Brax didn't know why he did it. Maybe as a challenge to

himself. But he found himself beside the table before the other man could move. "Use me."

Startled, she glanced down at him. "I don't—"

He simply made a basket with his hands and waited as questions flitted through her eyes.

After a long, long moment, she stepped into his hands and up onto his shoulders. The tread of her work boots dug into his skin, weirdly grounding. When she wobbled, he offered his hand. Her fingers closed around his, and Brax felt the fine tremors in the touch. She wasn't anywhere near as unaffected as she wanted him to believe.

And damn it, that got to him.

Mia straightened, her head and shoulders disappearing through the ceiling. She peered into the darkness, panning her light inside the hole. As she shifted, Brax wrapped his hands around her lower legs, keeping her steady. He tried not to notice the muscles of her calves and *really* tried not to think about the last time he'd been this close to her legs.

This was a terrible idea. He shouldn't have laid a hand on her. Shouldn't have let himself be reminded of the feel of her skin against his.

"Well, there's good news and bad news. Let me down."

When she would have stepped clumsily down from his shoulders, Brax simply reached up and gripped her hips, plucking her from her perch. Mia squeaked, her hands flailing for a moment before landing on his shoulders.

Oh boy. That was another terrible idea.

Those strong fingers dug in, and for a moment he thought she'd wrap around him. The fact that he wanted it so damned much had him setting her on her feet and stepping hastily back.

She swayed for a moment, eyes wide. Brax resisted the urge to swipe away the streak of dust on her cheek.

"Um. The good news is that the wall between the kitchen

and the dining space isn't load bearing. That means we can move it without a lot of fuss. The bad news is that, although nothing is moving up there right now, a colony of something has set up nests in the ceiling, so there's a good chance the wiring has been gnawed on. The entire system will need inspection to determine what may need replacement or upgrade for the heavier load the ovens will take."

She added a few more notations to her clipboard. "How set are y'all on keeping the kitchen entirely separate from the dining area?"

"What do you mean?" Holt asked.

"You could get a more open feel for the entire space if you left the kitchen in more or less plain view of the dining area. People could watch you work. It could be a nice mix of functional kitchen and sort of industrial rustic. Knock out that wall there, move it out about fifteen feet, and case it with heavy beams. Raise the ceiling, maybe put in some skylights."

"Like that place in Spokane," Brax murmured, remembering exactly the image she was outlining. How many times had they hit up that bakery for special occasions, to indulge her sweet tooth?

Her look was hesitant. "Yeah. Exactly. Then you either leave it fully open, with counters dividing the space, or have a large pass-through, maybe with a rolling garage door sort of deal, so you have the option to open or close for more privacy to work."

Brax didn't know how to feel about the fact that she was suggesting something from their past. He didn't get the sense she was trying to manipulate anything, but it felt weird to have any of their shared history coming out here. Still, it would be a solid use of the space.

They continued to discuss the options, including the prospective addition of a wrap-around porch, which would offer outdoor seating when the weather was nice and would change the face of the building without as much expense as raising the roofline. By the time they'd gone through every-thing, Brax could sense the humming excitement of his friends.

"I'll work up a quote and design by the end of the week, dividing things out by different phases," Mia promised.

"Sounds good." Jonah shook her hand. "You've got a lot of good ideas. We look forward to seeing them."

She nodded and turned to Brax. "Can I speak with you for a minute?"

After only a moment's hesitation, he followed her out to her truck, wondering if this was where the awkward would rear its ugly head. She opened the door, tossing the clipboard inside and rummaging around a bit before coming up with an envelope.

"This is what I found about divorce laws in Tennessee. Everything you need to know is inside. Unless you want to file in whatever state you have residency, I'll have to get the ball rolling here. Look it over and let me know what you want to do."

Surprised she was this on top of things, Brax took the enve-lope. "Thanks."

She shifted restlessly, as if she wanted to say something. "Well, okay then. I'll get to work on that estimate."

Brax tapped the envelope against his palm as she dragged open the driver's side door again. "Why didn't you seek this out before?"

He hadn't meant to ask, but hell, he'd resisted getting answers of any kind for years. His willpower to keep holding out was sapped.

Mia turned back, dark eyes searching his face. "Because you were deployed for most of it, and I didn't want to do anything that might distract you and get you killed. And because—" She cut herself off, looking away toward the mountains in the distance.

"Because what?"

Her hand flexed on the door. "Because I never wanted this."

Stunned, Brax could only stare as she slid into the truck and slammed the door. He was still staring as she drove away, leaving him with even more questions than he'd had before.

BY ALL RIGHTS, Mia should've been heading to a job site. They had several in various stages around the county just now. But she'd bailed, sending Porter a text to say she wanted to work on the prospective designs for the bakery. Which she would. Later. During the wee hours when she inevitably couldn't sleep because she was over-analyzing every second of her interaction with Brax today and remembering how it had felt to have his hands on her again in any capacity.

For now, she'd driven to her project house, needing some solo time to get her head on straight. If they got this job, she'd be seeing Brax on a regular basis. Hell, he could be moving here to Eden's Ridge. It wasn't a big town. She'd see him. And he wouldn't be hers.

Could she handle that? Being faced with the aftermath of her mistakes? Having a front-row seat to everything she'd lost if —*when* he moved on with someone else.

Oh Jesus, he'd thought they were divorced for the past decade. He probably had moved on. He wasn't bound up with the past like she was. What if he had a girlfriend somewhere? A whole other *life* somewhere? He'd had the time and opportunity to build one, same as she had. And with the information he'd been given, he had every right to move on. The divorce was just a formality for him. He'd let her go a long time ago. She was the only one who had to deal with this as a fresh wound.

Feeling ill, she braced herself on the kitchen island.

What the hell was she doing here? Was working on this

house, the thing the two of them used to dream of, really going to exorcise the ghost of their relationship when the man himself was here? When he wanted to end things? Wouldn't this turn out to be just another reminder?

The screen door squeaked open, and she straightened, hastily wiping at the tears she hadn't intended to shed.

"You're avoiding me, my girl." Luca's teasing voice preceded the footsteps into the kitchen. "So, I came to beard the lioness in her den and offer my back for help with whatever project you have going."

Of course, he had. Because their friendship was long-standing enough not to stand on ceremony or invitations.

The smile she'd heard in his tone faded as he circled around the counter and caught sight of her face. "Mia? What's wrong? What happened?"

He closed the distance between them and would've folded her into an embrace if she hadn't held up a hand.

She wasn't ready for this. She'd barely processed the news herself. But she had to tell him about Brax being in town before he got blindsided with it as part of the crew if they got the job. God, she didn't even want to think about the gossip that would run rampant through the crew when this came out. Her relationship status, or lack thereof, had been a major point of curiosity at Mountainview Construction. But one thing at a time. Luca was the one in front of her, so she'd deal with him first.

The long exhale did nothing to calm her racing heart. Better to spit it out quick, like ripping off a Band-aid. "Brax is in town."

Luca's hands curled into fists and fury leapt in his eyes. "What did that son of a bitch say to you? What did he do?"

That instant readiness to defend was both endearing and exhausting. Just being in the same room with his snapping temper left her even more drained than she already had been.

"Calm down. There's no reason for this over-protective routine. He didn't come here looking for me."

"Then what the hell is he doing here?"

She rubbed at the ache blooming in her temple. "Prospectively opening a bakery with a couple of military friends. Mountainview got called to work up a quote on the renovation of the building."

Luca's brows drew together. "So, it's just a fluke that he's in town?"

"Looks that way. Convenient, really, since he wants a divorce."

"Good." Luca's fierce tone had her flinching. He gentled at once. "I'm sorry, honey, but this is way overdue. I know you've had your reasons for not pursuing it, but it's long past time to press play on your life again."

Even as part of her knew he was right, she resented it. And on the heels of the resentment came guilt, because Luca had been there for her through her darkest days, and she loved him for it.

He ran a hand down her arm, and Mia fought the urge to step back, bristling like a porcupine.

"You're not gonna take the job, are you?"

"This is my business. Mountainview Construction is the best in the area, so yeah, we're gonna work up an estimate, and if they choose to hire us, we'll take it."

"Is that really a good idea?"

"I'm not letting my disaster of a personal life get in the way of a lucrative opportunity. There are too many people counting on us for a paycheck. You included. It's a matter of professional reputation."

A muscle ticked in Luca's jaw. "Is that all it is?"

"I have my pride. That may be all I have left when this is all over, but by God, I'm hanging onto it. So, if we get the job, we do the job. It's not like he's going to be underfoot while we're working. I don't even know if the rest of them will be around during the renovation. Right now, it's a bunch of blanks, and I'm not going to waste my limited energy worrying about things that haven't happened yet."

"And the divorce?"

Mia held in her wince. She'd have to get used to the word. It would apply soon enough. "We'll do what's necessary in order to finalize it. In a couple of months, it'll be resolved, and we'll be on to the next job."

He studied her in silence for a long minute before nodding. "Okay. I know you don't feel like it right now, but someday, when this is all over, you'll want to celebrate being free of this burden. When you are, I'm there. Your ride or die."

She couldn't imagine that day ever coming. But she knew Luca meant well, so she worked up a wan smile. "Thanks, pal. Don't know what I'd do without you."

He swung an arm around her shoulders. "You'd take a shit-ton longer on this flip. C'mon. Let's find something for you to demo. You'll feel better if you break something."

6

Brax's meeting with an attorney in Johnson City didn't take too long. Since he wasn't fighting for a piece of whatever she'd built in the last decade, it was clear-cut enough. With ten years of separation and no kids, the court wouldn't fight the petition. There was no sense in him filing in New York since she was willing, so he'd let her know, and they'd get the divorce process officially started. Properly this time.

He'd expected to feel some measure of relief at that fact, but he was restless. Probably he'd stay that way until everything was finalized in a couple of months. In the meantime, he had bigger decisions to make.

Jonah and Holt were in the living room when he got back, both peering at some kind of paperwork.

"She's talented. I'll give her that." Holt's tone held respect, something Brax knew took effort to earn.

Twisting open the beer he'd snagged from the fridge on his way inside, he dropped into a chair. "Who's talented?"

"Mia. She dropped by copies of the proposal while you were gone." Jonah held one out. "How'd it go?"

"It went." He took the folder and flipped through.

She'd put together multiple elevations of the building, giving several options for changing the face of it. The interior drawings considered everything they'd discussed, and then some. Detailed estimates and timelines were included with each variation. The whole package was slick and professional.

"Wow."

"I gather you didn't know she could do this?" Holt asked.

"She used to draw. Protected those sketch pads like Fort Knox. I didn't know she'd turned it into this." He traced the lines of one of the interior options. The one that resembled the bakery she'd loved in Spokane. She'd captured the feel of it perfectly, down to the hazy suggestion of customers at half the tables, an assortment of pastries, breads, and cakes on their plates.

Jonah tossed down his folder. "Okay, so let's get down to brass tacks. The numbers she's given are within the budget we all discussed, provided we're all three in. But the money isn't the only important thing here. We need to talk about whether we're really gonna do this. I, for one, believe we can make it work. I've worked up a business plan—"

"When did you find time to do that?" Brax asked.

"Rachel helped. We had a couple calls about it. She had a lot of good suggestions for how we can phase things in without overwhelming ourselves."

"Uh huh." Holt's lips twitched.

Jonah scowled. "What?"

"Nothing. Consulting with our teacher is perfectly sensible. The fact that she's single, age-appropriate, gorgeous, and you basically couldn't take your eyes off her for the past year is beside the point."

"Shut up, asshole. She's widowed and not looking."

Which, Brax reflected, wasn't at all the same thing as Jonah not being interested. But saying so would just put him in a pisser of a mood, so Brax kept his mouth shut on that point. "What exactly did she say?"

They discussed numbers. Expenditures. Income projections. Basic operational budget. Legal costs of acquiring the business license and setting up an LLC.

"At the end of the day, the numbers work," Jonah declared. "That first year is liable to be a little lean while we get established, but since we'd own the building outright, once we pay off renovation and other startup costs, we're free and clear. The more of those we pay out-of-pocket up front, the less we'll owe."

"And the less we have in reserve if something goes wrong," Holt pointed out. "What are our options for a business loan?"

"I can get an appointment down at the bank to discuss that later this week. I didn't see the sense in crossing that bridge unless we were serious. So where do you two fall? Yay or nay?"

Holt sat back, sipping at his beer. "At the risk of adding additional pressure to Brax, I'm in. I'd much rather work with you two than take my chances with total strangers somewhere else. I like the town, and I think we can build something good here." He shifted his attention to Brax. "But I know it's not that simple for you. This isn't just a business decision."

"I haven't made any decisions with Mia in mind for nearly ten years. The fact that she's here, that we're still married for a couple of months while the legalities get sorted, really shouldn't play into this." And if he kept saying it, maybe he'd believe it.

"Really think about what you're saying, man," Jonah urged. "Can you live in a town this size with the possibility of running into your ex-wife at the grocery store or the diner? Because whatever you're telling yourself, you've still got unresolved feelings for her."

Brax narrowed his eyes. "They were perfectly resolved until I found out the divorce hadn't gone through. They'll settle once the paperwork is finalized."

"Will they?" Holt asked. "Is a piece of paper going to magically make all the questions go away? Or are you going to finally take advantage of the fact that you're both in the same place for the first time in ten years so you can finally get some answers? Because you *need* answers, my brother. No matter how much you deny it. I don't think there's gonna be any moving on without that."

Sometimes Holt's keen observational skills really pissed Brax off. He'd been fine without answers all this time. Maybe they'd come naturally out of being around each other again. But he wouldn't force them. He didn't want that confrontation. Didn't want to spew all the frustration and betrayal all over her like some kind of acid. That, in itself, was progress he didn't want to undo.

"Maybe you should talk to Dr. Graham about all this," Jonah suggested.

"I don't need to talk to a therapist about it. What's going on with Mia is unusual and complicated. That doesn't mean I'm somehow unclear on what I want. And what I want is to take this leap with both of you." The certainty of it settled in his bones as he spoke the words. "I want this business. I want the community ties that we can build here."

"Good to hear. But I have to play devil's advocate," Holt admitted. "What happens if it turns out you can't handle living in the same town as your ex?"

Brax tamped down his frustration and really considered the question. They weren't asking to give him grief. "If worse comes to worst, based on these projected numbers, you could buy me out within two years. I stayed in crap deployments a lot longer than that. But I don't think it'll come to that. Mia and I are adults. We can figure out our situation without it affecting the business."

Jonah and Holt exchanged a long look, then Jonah extended his beer. "Okay then. Let's do it!"

They toasted to the decision, and Brax felt lighter for it. This was the right move. Everything else would sort itself out.

"Now, how about we discuss living arrangements?" he prompted. "Because I've drawn the short straw more than either of you two assholes, and I would really like a proper bed."

THE LAST THING Mia expected to see when she arrived at the bar for demo day was a sheriff's cruiser out front.

"That can't be good."

Throwing her truck into park and wishing she'd taken the time to drink the coffee in her travel mug, she headed for the building. The heavy black door was open, and she could see signs of the lock having been jimmied.

Shit.

The guys were inside with Xander, standing around the bar. Her gaze moved unerringly to Brax, standing shoulder to shoulder with his friends, arms crossed, glowering like a bouncer as the sheriff scribbled notes on a pad.

"What's going on?"

Jonah scowled. "Somebody broke in last night."

"Did they take anything?"

He stretched out his arms. "What the hell was there to take? We already got rid of the tables and chairs, and the VFW hauled off the pool table the other day."

She automatically glanced around, looking for other signs of vandalism, but the place was bare and clean-ish. At least compared to how it had looked on her first visit.

"Maybe somebody thought there'd be booze left and bailed when they didn't find anything," Holt suggested.

"We'll get the locks replaced ASAP." Mia turned to Xander. "We're scheduled to do demo today. Do I need to hold off my crew for you to finish whatever investigating you're gonna do?"

"I'll check the doors for prints, but with nothing missing or damaged other than the door itself, I don't expect to find much. I mean, it's a bar. There will be all kinds of prints around here."

Jonah scrubbed a hand over his head. "That doesn't seem necessary. I didn't expect you to be able to do anything. Just wanted to file the report, cross all the T's and what not."

"You'll let me know if anything else pops up?"

"Sure will. I'll walk you out."

As the two men headed outside, Mia wiped damp hands on her jeans and turned to Brax. "Talk to you a minute?"

Holt jerked a thumb toward the door. "I'll just—"

They both watched him go, Mia noting the faintest of limps in his stride.

Not knowing what else to do with her hands, she shoved them in the back pockets of her jeans, rocking back on her heels. "I wanted to let you know I filed the paperwork yesterday, like we discussed."

He blinked those unreadable gray eyes. "I appreciate that."

"I'm told that so long as we sort out our terms over the next couple of months and have them properly drafted, once the sixty days are up, we can file the agreement and be done with it."

"Okay. Sounds good."

Sounds good.

The ease of the statement hit her like a fresh knife to the gut. Nothing about this was good. Not the circumstances or the lies he'd believed or his maddening neutrality. Couldn't he betray just a flicker of regret at ending things?

"Let us know where you want us." Jonah's voice pulled Mia out of the dark spiral of her thoughts.

"Excuse me?"

"It's our building, and we want to help. Consider us part of your crew."

That was an absolutely terrible idea.

"Except you're not part of my crew, and we'd be liable if you get injured on my job site."

He shrugged. "We'll sign waivers. Fact is, we've got time and nothing else to do. We can follow orders."

She raised a brow. "From a woman?"

"Yes, ma'am."

Mia had to hand it to him. He didn't smirk or come off as condescending. She shifted to Brax. "You're okay with this? Working with me?"

He jerked a nod, no hesitancy or discomfort in his expression. Did she mean so little now that this wasn't a big deal to him?

Locking away that fresh hurt, she looked at his companions. They were formidable. Both over six feet, and well-muscled, despite however long they'd been out of the military. They certainly had the brawn to manage what she'd throw at them.

"I know Brax has done construction before. Have you?"

Holt's lips twitched. "Enough."

"I don't figure demolition is any harder than rebuilding infrastructure in war-torn countries," Jonah added.

She could tell them no. Cite liability reasons. Porter would back her up. But somehow, that felt like the coward's way out. She had to find a way to be around Brax without her heart bleeding fresh. Maybe exposure therapy was the way to go. And God willing, the job would be over before their marriage was.

"Fine. This goes against my better judgement, but it can't hurt to have extra hands. You'll all sign waivers; you do what I say, when I say it, without argument. And if I deem you're more harm than help, you're out."

"Seems fair," Jonah agreed.

She shifted her attention back to Brax. "We also have to decide what we're telling the crew about who you are."

He arched a brow. "Do we have to tell them anything?"

"Please, they gossip worse than a bunch of middle school girls."

"What do they know about... us?"

She swallowed. "Nothing. I've kept my relationship status quiet. Porter knows, obviously. And one other guy on the crew, who I worked with in Washington."

"Then let's keep it that way."

Oh, he was utterly delusional if he thought the secret of their connection was going to stay secret for longer than two point five seconds after Luca laid eyes on him. But fine. If that was the way he wanted to play it, it was his funeral. He might be a military badass, but her crew was loyal to her, and they outnumbered him. If anybody thought he was disrespecting her, they'd hand him his ass and boot him out the door.

By the time the ass-covering paperwork was signed, the dumpster had been delivered, and her crew had arrived. Luca showed up with a chip on his shoulder the size of Tennessee. She could see it in his posture the moment he slid out of his truck and stalked in her direction. He scanned the group, obviously looking for Brax. She'd have to head him off and have a word before the start of the workday. The last thing she needed was some kind of over-protective display of male dominance.

"Who pissed in your Fruit Loops this morning?" she asked.

A flicker of humor lit Luca's eyes before he continued his scan. "That him?" He jerked his chin toward where Brax stood in conversation with Holt.

Mia wrapped her hand around Luca's arm, propelling him away from listening ears. "Yes. And you will damned well remember that this is my job site, my crew, and your role here is not as my guard dog. Right now, I'm not your best friend. I'm your boss. Be the professional I know you are. They're clients. So be polite."

"I can be civil." His credibility was undermined by the fact that he growled it.

"Can you? Because I will bench your ass from this job if you don't behave. Keep your attitude to yourself."

Luca blew out a breath and relaxed his aggressive posture. "Sorry. I just don't want to see you hurt any more than you already have been."

"I appreciate that. But this is about my business, not my personal life. Don't cross the line. Okay?"

He saluted, and Mia chose not to call him out on the sarcasm of the gesture. She hadn't had enough coffee to deal with this.

Retrieving her travel mug from the truck, she let loose a whistle and called her crew together. "Let's get this show on the road!"

7

"**M**arried!" The yelped word got cut off as somebody cuffed the speaker on the back of the head.

Brax sighed. He supposed, given Mia's assessment that her crew were a bunch of gossips, a week was a solid period of peace before the news got out about their connection. They'd probably only gotten that much because she'd been working everybody ninety to nothing from the swing of the first sledgehammer.

It was weird seeing her in command like this. She ran a tight crew and worked harder than any of her men. They treated her with deference and respect, something he knew would be hard-earned by a woman in this kind of job. She dished and joked with them without tolerating any pissing around or time-wasting.

The hard work showed in the stripped-out shell of the building. Everything, including the God-awful bathrooms, had been gutted. The drop ceiling was gone, and Mia and her team were currently going over the electrical with a fine-toothed comb, upgrading and replacing wiring as necessary. The hum of a generator and air compressor underscored the thump of hammers and nail guns as others framed up new walls. The garish work lamps that had been hauled in to illuminate their progress gave the whole thing the air of a crime scene.

"I thought she was widowed."

"I always assumed she was divorced."

"She's not a lesbian?"

"No, you idiot. Just because she's good at building shit, doesn't make her a lesbian."

The whispered conversation cut off as all three men realized Brax was glaring at them.

"Looks like the cat is out of the bag," Holt murmured.

"So it seems."

"She did warn you."

"Yeah." He hadn't seen the need to address it. But that had been before the death glares from the guy who'd worked with her in Washington. At least, he assumed that's who Luca was. He was new to town, whereas Mia had been here for a couple of years. Brax had picked up that much from listening in to conversations this week.

The guy kept staring at Brax as if he had the power to incinerate him on the spot with his eyes. Just what was the nature of his relationship with Mia? And why did Brax care? They'd already sorted out their terms for the divorce agreement. Simple. Civilized. No muss, no fuss. He'd choked back all the questions he'd wanted to ask, deeming it better not to open that can of worms since they'd be working together for the next few months. She was having the formal document drawn up by her attorney. The dissolution of their marriage was a waiting game at this point. She could see whoever the hell she wanted to see.

Was that why she hadn't fought him on any of it, after not pursuing a divorce all these years? Because Luca was waiting in the wings?

It didn't matter. Divorce was what he wanted.

But he hadn't been able to forget that she'd said it wasn't what *she* wanted.

The question of what she *did* want was becoming harder and harder not to ask, because the woman he saw now bore no resemblance to the image of her he'd built up in his mind. The one he'd held on to for all these years to keep his anger alive. That anger was getting harder and harder to maintain. Maybe if she'd offered excuses or justifications. But she'd done none of that. Said nothing to defend herself. And he didn't know how to make sense of that. Then again, he hadn't given her the option.

Something clattered to the concrete floor below where Mia perched on a ladder, working on wiring above her head.

"Shit. Can somebody hand me those wire cutters?"

Brax crossed over, scooping them up before anyone else could.

She met his eyes for a charged moment before taking the tool from his hand. "Thanks."

He just nodded as she reached up and resumed her work. His gaze dropped to the swath of bare skin revealed by the rise of her shirt. He couldn't help it. Her abs were toned and tight, and a hint of ink along her side had his fingers itching to touch and explore. Not that he'd do any such thing. But old habits apparently died hard. He was about to turn away when he caught sight of an angry knot of scar tissue just above her hip. One he'd never seen before. The wheal of it twisted in a far-too-familiar pattern that made his blood run cold.

"There. The last of the damage from the rats is fixed." Mia shoved the wire cutters into her tool belt and came down the ladder. "We can finish up wiring the extra—"

Brax barely heard her. The moment her feet touched the floor, he grabbed her wrist, intending to pull her closer for a better look at the scar. "What the fuck is this?"

She exploded into motion, flowing with the momentum to drive an elbow into his gut. Brax countered the groin strike—

barely—and released her, taking two steps back, his hands held up in peace. "I'm sorry."

He had only a moment to see the pale flash of her cheeks, the curl of her fists, before Luca was in his face, pushing him back further.

"What the fuck is wrong with you, laying hands on her?"

He tried to take a swing, but Jonah intervened, hauling the other man back. "Hold up. I don't think that's what's going on."

Brax sidestepped them both, keeping his focus on Mia. "I'm sorry. I shouldn't have grabbed you. I know better."

Fuck, he did know better. The sound of her hitching breath had him cursing himself for not remembering. For not being more careful. And shit, what the hell else had happened to her in the years they were apart?

On a growl, Luca jerked away from Jonah, his demeanor softening as he put himself between them, a human shield. His tone was low and soothing. Brax noted he was very careful not to touch her, but something in the stance betrayed some sort of intimacy that had an irrational spark of jealousy flashing through him. It used to be that she'd never have trusted anyone but him like that.

Her shoulders were still jerking with unsteady breaths. Needing to make this right, Brax stepped toward her again, navigating the wall of men who'd crowded close, ready to stop him. Luca spun around, his face thunderous.

"Luca, stand down." Mia's voice wasn't loud, but it rang with authority, nonetheless.

He stopped, his hands fisted, a muscle jumping in his clenched jaw.

She stepped around him, extending a hand toward Brax. He recognized it as both a request for comfort and a message to the rest of her crew that she trusted him. That he wasn't an abusive asshole, which was probably exactly how he'd come across.

Fuck.

Moving slowly, he curled his hand around hers, pulling her into his arms for the first time in a decade. She wrapped around him, melting into him, and holding tight enough he could feel her shaking. Needing to comfort, he couldn't stop himself from pressing a kiss to her brow, inhaling the scent of her skin. "I'm sorry. Baby, I'm sorry. I know better."

She let out a slow, shuddering breath. "I'm sorry, too. Old habits."

"New training. You've picked up some new moves since I taught you."

"Seemed sensible." The *without you there to protect me* was implied.

Brax curled tighter around her, keeping his voice low, as much to hide the tremor in it as to keep from being overheard. "Why do you have a mother-fucking bullet scar?"

She hissed in a breath but said nothing.

"Am I wrong?"

Another interminable heartbeat passed. "No."

That single, soft syllable punched a hole in his anger.

She'd been shot. Somehow. Some way. And he hadn't known. Hadn't been there to stop it. Whatever it was.

And suddenly a thousand other possibilities for why she'd disappeared began unfolding in his mind, along with a montage of all those letters he'd marked returned to sender.

Guilt flooded through him.

"What happened?"

She shook her head, stepping back. "Not here."

Yeah, okay. Much as he suddenly needed the answers that he'd spent years avoiding, this wasn't the time or place. Not when they were surrounded by her crew and his friends, and everyone was staring. More than one of the Mountainview guys looked ready to dismember him and dump his body in a shallow grave under a concrete foundation if he so much as breathed wrong. Luca would clearly be leading that charge.

Brax squeezed her hands back. "Later."

With a jerky nod, she released him.

He immediately missed her touch, but he stayed where he was because he could see her trying to pull herself back together, cobbling back that professional mask.

"Okay, show's over. Everybody get back to work."

As the sounds of work slowly started again, he wished he could recover so easily.

FINISHING out the workday was a special form of torture. Mia hated what her reaction had betrayed to her crew, hated the looks of concern they'd kept shooting her way, even as she appreciated their willingness to defend. She didn't want to be seen as weak or broken. She was neither.

But she was preoccupied the rest of the day, stewing in anxiety over what to say to Brax. This was her chance to come clean. To tell him everything. But would the truth put him in danger? How could it when everyone directly involved was now dead? It wasn't as if he'd go around announcing it to the world.

If he even believed her.

She wasn't certain he would. Reality was stranger than so much fiction, and she had no idea how he'd react. She didn't dare hope that it would change anything. Never mind how he'd held her today, as if everything between them wasn't shattered. It was the first true glimpse she'd had of her Brax since he'd walked back into her life, and she'd wanted to cling to it. To him.

But she'd long ago learned to manage her expectations. The best she could hope for was closure. And maybe, if she was lucky, forgiveness. She'd have to make do with that.

Fresh nerves kindled as he pulled into the driveway behind her. He'd stayed close all afternoon, his protective instincts roused by a threat he didn't yet understand. That her crew had let him was indication enough that she'd successfully diffused their suspicion that he'd been her abuser. She'd seen that agile mind of his running through a million and one scenarios for how she'd gotten shot. None of the assumptions he'd made about why she'd left would have included that, and the truth was going to be difficult for him to handle.

"Come on in. You'll have to give me a minute to corral the dog. He's... enthusiastic."

"You always wanted a dog."

It was one of the many things they'd talked about after they'd married. Something they'd have one day, when they could afford to live somewhere that would allow it. A little house all their own and a goofy, sloppy mutt.

"He's good company." Mia opened the back door to the leaping joy of her pooch. "Hey, pal. Hey! Who's my good boy? Whoops. No. Sit. We have a visitor. Show you have some manners."

Leno barked and leaped in a circle, doing his level best to shove past her to get to Brax where he stood in the doorway.

"Holy shit. That dog has the biggest head I've ever seen on a pit bull."

"Yeah, his 'Pet me!' demands are hard to ignore. Leno, sit. Sit!"

The dog lowered his hindquarters almost to the floor, his little stub tail wagging a hundred miles an hour as he fixed glittering eyes on Brax, long pink tongue lolling.

Mia hooked her hand in his collar and motioned Brax forward. "Let him give you a sniff."

Brax crouched down and offered his knuckles. The dog snuffled and licked his hand, drawing out a reluctant smile even before he lunged forward to kiss Brax in the face. "You're just a big softie, aren't you?"

"Total marshmallow. He's a cuddler."

"Why Leno?"

She hesitated. But this was hardly the most personal thing she'd be telling him tonight. "Because he made me laugh when I thought I'd never smile again." Avoiding his eyes, she straightened. "C'mon, bud. Let's go potty. Outside."

Abandoning Brax, he bolted for the back door. Mia let him out to do his business in the fenced backyard, leaving the door ajar as she went back to the kitchen.

"You want a drink?"

"No."

"You might change your mind before the end."

She retrieved two glasses and popped up on a stool to grab the dusty bottle of Knob Creek from the cabinet over the fridge as Leno bounded back inside. This conversation called for the emergency stash.

"Have a seat. Let me just feed him."

The dog head-butted Brax's knees, earning a head scratch before racing for the garage door and nosing at his leash and harness.

"We're doing things out-of-order tonight. Dinner first. We'll do that thing later."

"That thing?"

She glanced at Brax where he leaned in the doorway. "W-A-L-K. I can't say the word, or he'll go bananas."

Once Leno was nose deep in kibble, Mia carried the glasses and booze to the living room. Brax prowled after her but didn't sit. His whole posture held a ready-for-action tension that spoke of dread. Mia could relate. Cracking the seal, she splashed a generous two fingers into one glass and lowered to the sofa, already exhausted by what was to come.

"There's so much I should have told you years ago. I want to preface all of this by saying the reasons for my silence weren't about not trusting you."

His brows drew together. "Not trusting me with what?"

"I'm getting there. It's a long story, and I'd ask that you let me get through all of it."

"Okay."

It seemed only fitting to go way back to the very beginning. "I've never told you anything about my father. I was a daddy's girl. Only child. A surprise baby that he absolutely delighted in. My earliest memory is of riding his shoulders around town." She sipped at the bourbon, wondering if it would do anything to warm her inside.

"I was six when my mother left him. It absolutely broke my heart. I cried and cried because I didn't understand why we didn't go home to Daddy. She told me he was involved with bad people, and we weren't safe there. I've never been back to New York. That's where I was born. A little suburb outside the city."

Aware Brax had heard none of this, she chanced a look in his direction. Arms crossed, he stood wide-legged and stiff, his expression dialed in somewhere between suspicion and confusion, clearly wondering where this was going.

"We moved all over. A month here. Three there. For years. Enough new places that I lost whatever semblance of an accent I had. Until we landed in Texas. Somewhere people like us could more easily blend in. Just two more Latina women in a veritable ocean of them. We stopped running then. I didn't realize it was because she was sick and couldn't run anymore. There were no doctors. No treatment. There was no money for any of it. When she realized she was dying, she contacted someone. A U.S. Marshal. I don't know how she knew Curt. But he came when she called, and she begged him to protect me. Whatever it took. She wanted him to put me into WITSEC."

Brax dropped his arms, taking two halting steps forward before he stopped himself. "Your mother was trying to put you into witness protection? What the hell was your dad into?"

"That's the million-dollar question. I don't know. And because I didn't know, I had nothing to trade, and there were no grounds for the government to pay to make me disappear. But that didn't change the fact that I could still be used as leverage against him. There's more than one way to hide someone, and Curt made her a deathbed promise to see me safe. So, he pulled some strings, got me a new name, a new state, and plugged me into the foster system."

He scrubbed a hand down his face. "Jesus."

"From the moment we left New York, I'd been taught the importance of staying hidden. Of not trying to contact anyone from my old life. My mother made me promise before she died. By that point, I'd been hiding half my life. After six years, secrecy was just a way of life. So, I kept my mouth shut, and I sucked it up and dealt. But I kept thinking Daddy would come find me, come rescue me."

How many nights had she silently cried herself to sleep, wishing and hoping her father would show up and take her away from the hell she'd landed in? More than she could count.

"Except he didn't."

"No." She tried to work up a semblance of a smile. "You did. You made all those years bearable. From that first night in my first foster home, you gave me a new family and made me feel safe for the first time since I was a child. You always made me feel safe."

His face clouded, his hands flexing and releasing. "I didn't manage to keep you that way."

"You showed up when it mattered. You got me out before he could do worse than knock me around."

This was old territory. She'd never been able to convince him he hadn't failed in not predicting when her foster father would snap. In the end, he'd saved her. And that had brought them together as more than the friends they'd always been.

"After that assault, I was terrified. That Wayne would get out and find me, but more, that all the attention from the police and the social workers would out me. I was sure Curt was going to pull me out, make me move again."

"You were still in contact with him?"

"He kept tabs on me. He was there at the courthouse the day we got married. I was all set to fight him, because the last thing I wanted was to leave you, but it turned out he was fully in favor of the marriage. It was another name change. Another layer to keep me hidden. The fact that I loved you was immaterial to him. Either way, I left the courthouse as your wife, and I hoped I'd never see him again."

"I gather that didn't happen."

If only.

This was where the story got harder. "It probably would have if I'd stuck to the rules." Needing the fortification, she drained the last of her bourbon, wincing at the burn down to her gut. Setting the empty glass on the table, she met his eyes. "My father contacted me a few months before I turned twenty-one."

Brax stared at her for a long moment before finally sinking into a chair. "Your father."

"I don't know how he tracked me down, but he wanted to see me. He told me to come alone, to tell no one. I was so well trained on that front that I didn't breathe a word to you. I didn't want to do anything to put you at risk, and I fully expected to be back that night."

His brows drew together. "You planned to come back, but you took your go bag." It was an accusation, not a question.

She nodded, knowing how that must have looked to him. "Just in case. Too many years of training and instinct."

"Where did you go? Not to Spokane or anywhere nearby. I tore that city apart looking for you. Every hospital. Every fucking alley. If you'd been there, I'd have found you."

Mia's heart squeezed. She'd never known how he'd reacted in the days immediately after her disappearance. This was what she'd expected from the husband who'd loved her. How much had it taken to break him?

"Seattle. I met him in Seattle. I didn't plan to go with him, but I needed to see him. Needed to see if he was still the man I remembered. I needed to ask him if whatever he was involved in was worth losing his family."

"What did he say?"

She swallowed hard, wishing for another drink but making no move to refill her glass. "'You look so much like your mother.' That was all he got out before the bullets started flying." She jerked her shoulders, deliberately minimizing the terror of what came after because Brax had lost all color in his face. "I guess he was followed. I don't know. I went down. So did he. I heard him stop breathing, and I thought that was the last thing I'd ever hear."

Because she was starting to shake, she sucked in a few controlled breaths. Leno leapt up onto the couch, wiggling his way under her arm and onto her lap. His warm bulk was a comfort, so she indulged his demands for attention, curling her arms around him.

"I woke up in the hospital three days later. Curt was there. My father was dead. Bled out at the scene. I should have." Guilt and grief washed through her. She couldn't get into that piece now. It would serve no purpose. "All I wanted was to go home, but they needed to keep me for longer because of complications from surgery. I knew you had to be losing your mind with worry. Curt wouldn't let me call you because he had me being treated under yet another name, so I begged him to go tell you what was happening. He said he would."

Brax shook his head, rocking slightly in his chair. "No one ever came to me. The police never told me anything."

"I didn't get out of the hospital for a while, and then I was in protective custody for about six weeks. Before he let me loose, he admitted that he'd made an executive decision to lie to you for your own protection. That he'd outright lied to your face, pretending to be lead detective on the case, and encouraging you to think that I'd left. I was free to start over yet again because, to him, my marriage to you had been nothing more than a means to an end. We fought over it, and I told him exactly what he could do with his questionable protection. But by the time I got home, you were gone."

He exploded out of the chair, pacing the room like a caged animal. "Why didn't you tell me?"

"I tried. You sent back all my letters. More than a hundred of them." She'd been furious at that and crushed at his refusal to even give her a chance to explain. But the anger had long since burned out, leaving nothing but exhaustion. "Eventually, enough time passed that I figured you were too angry to ever hear the truth, so I stopped trying."

His cheeks had gone from pale to practically gray. The muscles in his biceps bulged as he speared both hands through his hair, linking them behind his head. "I thought you left me." The admission was a choked whisper.

"I know." She said it with all the gentleness she could muster because she did know. And she knew what it was doing to him to find out he was wrong, when he'd always been her protector. "You acted based on the information you had. I never blamed you for that. I made a choice. The wrong one. And I lost everything." So much more than he knew.

Tears clogged her throat, threatening to spill over. But she fought them back, needing to get through the last of it. Sensing the rising tension in the room, Leno whined, tucking his enormous head against her shoulder.

"Look, I know this is too little, far too late, but I need you to know that I never stopped loving you. If I'd known what would happen, I'd never have gone. I would never have left you willingly. Whatever else you take away from this, whether or not you believe me about the rest, believe that."

The last of his stoic mask cracked. Anguish twisted his features as he wrestled with this earthquake to his reality. Mia wanted to go to him, to wrap him in all the love and comfort she still had to give. But that wasn't who they were to each other anymore.

So, she shifted Leno over and poured another drink instead.

"I have to—I need to—I just have to go."

"Brax."

But he was out the door before she could disentangle from the dog.

When his engine cranked, she sank back down, tossing back the drink and letting the tears come at last.

8

Everything Brax had believed was wrong.

All these years, he'd been convinced Mia had left him. Abandoned the life they'd been building because he hadn't been enough. He'd hated her for that. Hated her for reminding him of the mother who'd seen him as an inconvenient afterthought. For showing him that no matter how hard he worked, how much he loved, something else would always be more important. For his mother, it had been drugs. For Mia... He'd never known what was more important than him. And he'd spent years rejecting her overtures because he was afraid of the answer.

Now he had the truth, and he didn't know how to cope with it.

He'd left her. After all his vows to love and protect her, *he'd* left *her*.

She wasn't without fault. She should've told him all her history before. After they'd gotten married, at the very least. If he'd known, she could have told him about her dad's contact. He could've gone with her. Or stopped her.

Christ, she could have died, and he wouldn't have known.

He'd have gone the rest of this life thinking the worst of her. And here she'd accepted his hostility and refusal to listen without saying a word to defend herself. Just taking it as her due because she clearly blamed herself for all of it. He'd seen it in her face, in the simple acceptance that everything was over and broken between them.

He'd done that. Because he'd trusted what he'd been told and leaned into his own sense of betrayal instead of what he knew deep down in his gut.

It was more than he could face, so he'd bolted. Leaving her there on the verge of tears.

He was such an asshole. That was the conclusion he'd reached by the time he made it back to Jonah's mom's house hours later.

Someone had left a light on for him and the kitchen door unlocked. Brax slipped quietly inside, figuring he'd ended up with the short straw for the couch tonight, having not been around for the draw. That was fine. It wasn't like he'd be sleeping.

"Ah, you're home." Rebecca strode into the kitchen in fuzzy socks and a long flannel robe, her hair pulled back in a tail.

"I didn't mean to wake you."

"You didn't." She angled her head, giving him a long study with what he could only think of as a Mom look, though his own had never done such a thing. After a long moment, her face softened, and she closed the distance between them to fold him into a hug.

Brax didn't move. He didn't know what to do with this easily offered affection. Mia was the only one he'd ever really allowed this close. But Rebecca's soft lavender fragrance and the circle of her arms felt damned good, so he gave in and bent his head to her shoulder, awkwardly returning the hug.

She rubbed circles on his back in much the same way he

imagined she would a child. "You've been through the wringer tonight, haven't you?"

He coughed out a laugh.

Rebecca eased back, patting his cheek. "I'll make you some tea."

Brax didn't really want tea, but this whole maternal caretaking thing was new to him, so he just said, "Thanks."

As she puttered around, filling the kettle and pulling out mugs, he sank down at the kitchen table, feeling about a hundred years old.

"You don't have to tell me what's wrong. But I've got a good ear if you want to."

He thought of what Mia had said. About all the secrets that had been kept as a matter of safety. She hadn't said if those still held. Safer to assume they did. But the idea of talking this through with another woman, maybe getting some parental-type advice, was more appealing than he would have imagined.

"Did Jonah say where I was going?"

"To talk to Mia."

He scrubbed a hand over his head. "More like to listen."

Rebecca poured boiling water over the tea bags and brought the mugs to the table. "I'm guessing what she had to say was hard to hear."

"That would be an understatement." Not sure where to start, Brax restlessly turned the mug between his hands. "We married really young. She was just eighteen."

"Mmm. I understand that. I wasn't much older when I married Jonah and Sam's father. Were you high school sweethearts?"

"No. Former foster siblings. We were friends. Had each other's back in the system."

"You went through a lot together."

"Yeah." He sipped at the tea and found it not as lousy as he expected. "Things were good. Hard, but good. I'd have done anything for her."

"Jonah mentioned you'd been split for a long time. What happened?"

With a humorless laugh, he lifted the mug again. "It's complicated. But not what I thought. I've spent a decade believing something of her, being pissed and hurt about it, and it turns out I was completely wrong. I'm the bad guy."

Rebecca wrapped long-fingered hands around her own mug, peering at him over the rim. "Mmm. And that's hard because you strive to be the good guy."

"I don't know about that."

Her dimples fluttered. "I do. You're a lot like Jonah on that front."

"Don't paint me to be some kind of saint. I raised plenty of hell when I was younger, and my reasons for going into the service were a whole lot more about having somewhere to put my anger than some greater good."

"Maybe. But you're a good man, or he wouldn't be friends with you. Now whatever it is you think you did—"

"Did do. There's no 'think' about it."

"Whatever it is you did, did you do it on purpose, to hurt her?"

Brax wrapped his hands around the mug, feeling the warmth soak into his palms as he considered the question. "Yes, and no. I was reacting to what I thought she'd done. Lashing out. But I was operating on bad intel. In the normal course of things, no, I would never have set out to hurt her."

"Well, that doesn't make you a bad guy, Brax. It makes you human."

"I still feel like a total asshole."

The dimples deepened into a full smile. "Assholes are human, too. So long as you come out the other side not wanting to continue to be an asshole, you're doing okay. Does finding out the truth change anything for you about her?"

Did it?

Mia had said she'd never stopped loving him. And underneath all the hurt he'd been carting from continent to continent, war zone to war zone, he knew he still loved her. Or at least the her she used to be.

"I miss my wife." The admission hurt because he knew the lion's share of the lost years was on him. If he'd listened before, when she'd tried to tell him, instead of clinging to his hurt pride... "I don't know how we come back from this."

"Well, I expect one way or the other, the right place to start is probably an apology."

No question he owed her that.

"I'm sorry doesn't seem like enough."

"So maybe think a little bigger. What would tell her you really mean it?"

"I don't..." He trailed off, thinking way back to their beginning. It was a long shot, but maybe...

"Will it keep you awake if I use the kitchen tonight?"

"Nope." She patted his hand. "You go right ahead."

He curled his fingers around hers and squeezed. "Thanks for momming me. It's a new experience. I kinda like it."

Rebecca beamed. "Anytime, sweetheart."

Brax shoved back from the table. "Where's the nearest all-night grocery?"

FOR ALL THE years she'd worked construction, Mia had never dreaded going to work. The job had always been her salvation. A place she could go and face problems that she could actually solve with her own two hands. But in the wake of her big reveal to Brax, she considered calling in sick. She felt like warmed-over death, more from lack of sleep and too many tears than the bourbon. Last night was an end of... something. There was relief in unburdening herself of the secret she'd carried most of her life. But it was a cold comfort. At this stage, it probably changed nothing.

She'd lied to him for years. Her reasons felt valid to her, but he might not feel the same. He was her husband. He'd been her best friend. The man who was supposed to be her partner in all things. And she'd shut him out. He wouldn't forgive that easily.

She had no idea how he was going to be at the job site. If he'd be at work at all. She wouldn't blame him if he wasn't. Who knew when he'd be ready to face her again? Not to mention the inevitable questions from the crew who'd been witness to The Incident yesterday. Her certain knowledge that she needed to be there, to shut that shit down before it got out of hand, was the main thing that propelled her into her truck. If she was showing up well before her team and the clients, well, she wanted time to finish her coffee first.

She didn't expect to see Brax's truck already there. Had he come here last night instead of going back to Jonah's?

As she idled at the top of the drive, unsure what to do, he opened the driver's side and slid out some sort of package under his arm.

Well, he wasn't avoiding her. That was a positive sign. Right?

Heart knocking against her ribs, Mia pulled up beside him and got out, her work boots crunching on the gravel of the parking lot.

"Hey." His breath puffed out in a cloud in the frigid, early morning January air.

"Hey." What exactly did you say to your not-exactly-estranged-anymore-but-not-really-yours-either husband?

He dug his free hand into his coat pocket, shoulders

rounding in an uncharacteristic show of nerves. "I wanted to apologize for last night. For walking out."

An apology hadn't been on her admittedly short list of expectations. "I hit you with a lot of information. I've had years to process. You haven't."

"Still. I didn't handle it as well as I should have."

"I don't think there is a right way to handle the kind of news I dumped on you."

One corner of his mouth lifted in a shadow of his usual sardonic smile. "I guess not."

He shifted from foot to foot before finally offering the package under his arm. "I brought you this."

Mia took it automatically, carefully opening the tented foil to reveal what was inside. Her breath caught at the sight of the exquisitely braided pastry. It was a raspberry Danish. Her favorite. The thing he'd gone out of his way to procure for her eighteenth birthday, and every successive birthday thereafter until she'd left. But this was... more, somehow. The plait of the pastry was more complex and beautiful than was usual, with finely crafted pastry flowers and leaves, such that the braid itself looked like lush vines bursting with fruit. It was still warm from the oven, the scent of butter and raspberries wafting up to make her mouth water.

"Brax. It's beautiful." Where the hell had he found this? And then she realized, taking in the foil and aluminum tray beneath. He was a fully trained professional baker now. "You made this?"

He ducked his head in a nod, his shoulders hunching toward his ears. "Happy birthday."

She blinked. Birthday? He was right. Today was her birthday. For a moment, she could only stare. She'd stopped celebrating so many years ago that she'd forgotten. "I didn't even remember. I don't know what to say." Which was just as well because her throat was going thick, and her eyes began to burn with more unshed tears.

"You don't have to say anything. Just... I wanted you to know that *I* remembered. And that I'm sorry." His face spasmed. "So fucking sorry, Mia."

He'd been beating himself up all night. It was there in the hollows of his cheeks, the shadows beneath those stormy eyes. The idea of it made her heart hurt.

Needing to comfort, she dropped the tailgate of her truck and set the pastry aside, ignoring her own fear of rejection as she stepped into him, lifting her hands to frame his face. "I didn't tell you with the intention of hurting you or making you blame yourself for things outside your control. I told you because you deserved the truth."

His arms came around her, crushing her to him in a fierce hug that all but squeezed the breath out of her. Every cell in her body sighed at the sensation of his warmth curling around her. Barely suppressing a whimper, she burrowed in, tightening her own arms as if she'd never let go. God, she was so touch-starved. She needed this from him like she needed to breathe, and judging by how his fingers worked into her hair, kneading at her nape as he rocked her, so did he. At least for this moment.

How long had it been since she'd let anyone close? Even for something so simple as a hug? There'd been Luca, but by her own preference, that contact was few and far between and wasn't anything like this. And she just... didn't trust people enough to get this close.

They stood that way for a long time, breathing each other in, until the sun peeked well over the ridge and other vehicles rolled in for the day. Even as doors slammed, they didn't move. Mia felt the eyes on them and didn't care. She didn't know if she'd ever get this again, and she'd be damned if she let go first.

Dimly, she heard the door to the building being unlocked and people piling in.

From inside, someone let loose an emphatic, "Son of a bitch."

Mia held tighter, knowing this little interlude was coming to an end.

A few moments later, her foreman, Brick Hooper, cleared his throat. "Uh, boss. We got a problem."

9

"There's no sign of forced entry." Deputy Ty Brooks, one of the Rangers who'd relocated to Eden's Ridge, straightened from where he'd been examining the door. "Those minor scratches could be from a key or could be from being picked. Hard to tell. Xander said y'all were replacing the locks after the break-in a couple weeks ago. Did that happen?"

"Yeah, we did that immediately," Brax reported. "They're better locks than what was on it originally, but we didn't invest in the kind of thing that would've been impossible to pick. I mean, why would we? We weren't expecting this."

Ty rocked back on his heels. "Sorry to say, this isn't the first supply theft we've had."

"How long has this been going on?" Holt asked.

"Couple months."

"We've been hit at a few of our other sites," Mia confirmed. "Smaller thefts. Nothing to this extent."

On the surface, she looked composed, but Brax could see the tension gathering beneath. He wanted to go back to half an hour ago, when she was in his arms and his world was starting to feel in balance again. Before the crew had discovered that all the supplies and lumber laid in from yesterday, to begin the framing of the new roof and porch, had been stolen.

Jonah crossed his arms, his green eyes hard as glass. "Y'all don't have any idea who's behind it?"

"As she said, up 'til now, it's been smaller stuff. It's harder to trace a couple packs of shingles or a few dozen two-by-fours. This gives us a lot more to look for. Our Chief Investigator should be here shortly."

"Even if you're able to find everything, it means a delay." Mia turned to the three of them. "We're dead in the water until we replace what was stolen. As soon as Deputy Brooks is finished with me, I'll be headed straight to the office to file a claim with our insurance."

"How much time are we gonna lose?" Holt asked.

"Today for sure. After that, it depends. I'm going to send my people to Knoxville to see if they can replace what we lost. Short notice will come at something of a premium, but I'll do whatever I can to minimize the impact on the overall project budget."

"We'll obviously do everything we can to recover your materials," Ty assured them. "Either way, as soon as I finish speaking to the rest of the crew, I'm also headed back to the station to write up the report you'll need for insurance."

He and Mia exchanged contact information.

"If you're through with me for the moment, I'm gonna go talk to my crew."

"Go ahead. If you'll ask them to stick around so I can ask some questions, I'd appreciate it."

"You got it." Mia's gait was tight, her hands balled into fists as she strode over to where the rest of the crew was gathered.

Given the time and effort she put into her work, this had to hit hard. Brax itched to pull her back into his arms, to do what he could to soothe her. But that wasn't his role right now. For all that they'd crossed some kind of line this morning, he didn't know where they stood. Right now, this was her workplace, and she was the boss.

Still, it had felt so damned good to hold her again.

Unable to do anything else, he trailed after her.

Luca broke away from the group as she approached, reaching out to put an arm around her. Brax gritted his teeth. He didn't have any right to be jealous of whatever relationship she had with the other man. But even as he watched, she shook her head, shrugging off the touch. Was that because she was in work mode right now, or because things weren't more than friends between the two of them?

"Okay guys, listen up. There's nothing we're gonna be able to do today with our supplies missing. Deputy Brooks wants to speak to each of you, so please hang around for that. Brick, Luca, Brandon. I want the three of you to take the truck down to Knoxville. Check with all our sources there to see what you can round up as replacements for everything, so we can get back on schedule Monday. Brick, you should have the original inventory list in your email."

The foreman nodded. "Yup."

"Mia, I don't know that I—" Luca began.

"I want you in Knoxville today." Her tone brooked no argument. "Everybody else, once you've talked to Deputy Brooks, you're free to take the rest of the day off. Be sure to check your email this weekend, as I'll be changing the work schedule coming up."

As she walked away without another word, Luca pressed his lips into a thin line, shooting a fulminating glare in Brax's direction. Apparently, he'd seen Mia with him this morning and didn't approve. Shocker.

Her expression lost some of its fierceness, shifting into uncertainty as she neared him. "I'm sorry."

"Nobody's blaming you for this."

She huffed. "I'm sorry for that, too. I've got to go deal with this and update Porter, but I just wanted to say thank you again for... everything."

That felt too much like an end to something, but Brax didn't know what to say. She had business to take care of. Their personal situation would have to wait. So, he just nodded.

"See you later."

He watched as she snagged the Danish from her tailgate, climbed into her truck, and drove away, wondering what he could say or do to get things back on track. Whatever on track was.

The guys were inside with Ty.

Jonah kicked at a little chunk of two-by-four. "Well, this is some shit."

"Not Mountainview's fault," Brax pointed out.

"No, of course not. We're not blaming Mia. Where is she, anyway?"

"Headed to the office to call the insurance company and update Porter."

"Speaking of Mia... what happened last night?" Holt asked.

The entire foundation of my world got ripped out from under me. Not that he was going to make such a dramatic statement. Even if it was true. "We talked. Or rather, she talked. I listened."

"And?"

Brax jerked his shoulders, more out of discomfort than dismissal. "I was wrong." He was still figuring out how to come to terms with exactly how wrong he'd been.

Jonah went brows up. "Looked like y'all were all friendly-like when we got here this morning."

"I don't know what we are yet. But our conversation got interrupted by all this shit. I'm going after her. See if I can catch her at the Mountainview office. You guys need me for anything?"

"Nah. Go get your woman."

Brax didn't think she was his woman. But he was starting to think he might want her to be again.

Before he could make his escape, a woman stepped through the door.

"Sorry I'm late. There were... cows." She shook her head. "I still can't believe I live somewhere that's an acceptable reason for tardiness."

Ty laughed. "Your city is showing. Y'all, this is Chief Investigator Leanne Hammond, who cut her teeth in Raleigh before gracing us with her presence." He made introductions to the rest of them.

"Sorry to meet you under these circumstances, gentlemen. I'd like to ask you some questions."

AFTER MAKING the initial report of the theft to insurance, reallocation of staff and resources took longer than Mia wanted. She adjusted next week's schedule, hoping to make up for today's lost time. Of course, that entirely depended on whether her guys could get everything they needed in Knoxville. And there were other adjustments to make to the project budget, so the theft wasn't as much of a hit to the bottom line. There were lines she could tug about some reclaimed materials. She'd have to run those ideas by Brax and his friends, see what they thought about changing up some of the design. By the time she finished and had updated Porter, her mind was reeling. She made the executive decision to take the rest of the day off to decompress.

Her phone pinged with a text from Luca as she locked up the office.

We need to talk.

Mia ignored the message and climbed into her truck. She knew he was pissed she'd sent him on this errand. That she was pulling the boss card right now. But, God, she needed time to think. Alone. Too much had happened that she needed to process before confronting Luca's concerns about what he'd walked up on this morning. No doubt he had plenty.

He'd always had opinions about Brax. But he didn't *know* Brax. Didn't know the full story. He only knew the aftermath. There was no one in her life who knew everything, and a lifetime of compartmentalization had left her exhausted down to the bone.

She drove to her project house, needing to hide away for a while. The quiet of the mountain soaked into her as she carried her precious pastry inside, along with a quilt she kept in the back of the truck. If she wanted to have a foolish little picnic on the floor, there was no one here to judge or question her about it. It was her birthday, damn it, and her right.

As she spread the blanket on the hideous shag carpet in front of the hearth, she admitted the truth to herself. That she'd bought this house for the ghost of who she and Brax had once been. It had never been a reclamation, and she couldn't see it as an investment property. It was yet another sign that she refused to give up on him. On them. As were the wedding rings she still wore on a chain around her neck, resting over the heart that would always be his. Did that make her a fool? Yesterday she'd have said absolutely. But now?

She tugged out the chain, ran her fingers over the silver bands they'd exchanged so many years ago. Brax had left his behind when he'd enlisted, along with the remnants of their life. She'd been lucky the landlord hadn't tossed it all by the time she was able to get back. Probably, she should've taken that gesture as what he'd meant it to be. An end to their marriage, whether the paperwork had come with it or not. But she hadn't been able to let him go. Not when she'd lost everything else. For a long time, that foolish hope had been the only thing to keep her going, through the unfathomable grief and loneliness, until she'd found something else to live for.

But what he'd done today... She had no idea how to take it. His apology meant so much to her. That he believed her. That he didn't hate her anymore. She'd long ago given up hope of that possibility. She didn't dare let herself believe that there was any more than that for them.

But he'd made her this pastry. A throwback to when they'd first come together. The thing was almost too pretty to eat. Almost. She tore off a tiny piece and popped it into her mouth. After all the delays, it was no longer warm, but oh God. The buttery, flakey pastry melted on her tongue, melding with the tart sweet raspberry filling that was pure ecstasy for her mouth. He'd *made* this. With his own two hands. He could *bake*.

Maybe it really was just supposed to be a birthday present. An acknowledgment that he remembered it was her favorite. A simple peace offering after all the years of hostility and silence. That made the most sense. After all this time, they couldn't just pick back up where they'd left off. They were surely different people. And it wasn't as if he wanted that. Life wasn't a fairy tale, where everything sorted itself out and the truth set you free.

Tearing off another piece, she strode to the windows on the back wall, staring out at the view of the mountains beyond. She needed to be satisfied with this. With the idea of maybe, possibly, becoming friends again. That had to be enough. It was a gift she'd never expected to get. Wanting anything else was just... greedy. And she knew better than to let herself want too much. That just led to disappointment.

At a sound behind her, Mia whipped around.

Brax stood in the doorway. His gaze moved from her to take in the room. "You bought the house."

That he understood it immediately, without explanation, made her feel both seen and exposed. She'd admitted she still loved him last night, but somehow this felt bigger, more private. She froze, unable to speak or turn away as he closed the distance between them.

She wanted to ask how he'd found her, what he was doing here, but his gait hitched as he spotted the rings she hadn't remembered to tuck back into her shirt, and her tongue glued itself to the roof of her mouth. Those eyes darkened, boiling with a different kind of storm as he reached out to run his fingers along the chain.

Mia shivered as if he'd stroked her skin.

"You never gave up on us." That low, rough voice made her shudder.

Still unable to speak, she just shook her head once.

Brax threaded his fingers in her hair, bending to press his brow to hers. "I'm sorry I did."

His touch was an anchor, a balm. Mia couldn't stop herself from reaching for him, needing to feel that he was real, that he was here. That he felt the same regrets for lost time.

In the sun-dappled living room, they breathed the same air, mingling in shared pain, and she quaked because, oh God, she needed him. She'd needed him for so very long. And at the moment, she didn't care that they had no future. She didn't care that it was probably a terrible idea. She needed him. Even if only for a goodbye.

So she found her voice.

"Brax. Touch me. Please."

10

The echo of that long ago plea all but stopped Brax's breath.

Had he been thinking of their first time when he'd made that pastry? Wishing for a chance to go back and do everything over again? Maybe. He'd wanted to give her something to remind her of when things hadn't been complicated, and the only thing that had mattered was being together. He hadn't thought beyond that, and the supply theft had derailed whatever half-assed plan he might've concocted. Not that he'd had a good one after being awake all night.

He'd come out here to beg her forgiveness. To talk about what might come next. Whether she could give him another chance to prove he could be something other than a short-sighted, temperamental asshole.

But he hadn't expected this.

There was nothing on earth he wanted more than this woman in this moment. Stroking a thumb along the softness of her cheek, Brax tipped her head back and lowered his mouth to hers. Mia trembled and opened for him, her hands fisting in his shirt.

Her tongue tangled with his and the taste of her flooded into him, raspberries and sunsets and every good thing that had ever represented home. He was parched and desperate, wanting nothing more than to drown in her, to fill up this vast empty reservoir he'd been carting around for years. But he held himself back, resolved to keep things gentle, to give her some kind of tenderness, as if that could possibly make up for how much he'd hurt her. And because he wanted to savor this moment of reconnection. Savor her.

But she erupted under his hands, hauling him closer, front to front, until she pressed against the erection straining behind his fly and set fire to all his good intentions. With an impatient nip, she broke the kiss long enough to gasp, "Need you." And when she brought her mouth back to his, she tasted of delicious madness.

Riding the wave of lust, relief, and desperation, they yanked and dragged at clothes, spinning, stumbling, until she was naked beneath him on the blanket, and he could close his mouth over one tight, brown nipple. Flexing her fingers in his hair, Mia cried out, arching against him in a familiar bid for more and faster. He didn't have it in him to deny her and draw it out. Not this time.

Curling his tongue around that taut peak, he skated his hands down her torso, worshipping the lush curves of her breasts, past the trim nip of her waist, down to the flare of her hips and the waiting heat below. He gloried in the familiar feel of her beneath his hands, in her purrs of pleasure. Her legs parted, welcoming the intimacy of his touch. She was drenched when he drew his fingers through her folds. He wanted to bury his face there, taste her sweetness, and send her flying, but she was too far gone for that just now.

Later. He promised himself. There had to be a later.

Her breath exploded out on a curse as he slipped one finger inside her. "More."

"Your wish."

He worked another finger into her tight, wet heat, shifting so she could more easily ride him and take her pleasure. He'd always loved her willingness to do exactly that. Never afraid to tell him or show him what she wanted. Her body was an instrument he still knew, could still play. Curling his fingers in exactly the right way, he felt her tighten around him and watched those golden cheeks flush a gorgeous rose gold, her head falling back as the first wave of pleasure broke over her.

Brax kissed her again, coaxing the orgasm out until she lay gasping beneath him. He'd no sooner slipped his hand free than she was rearing up, wrapping around him, rolling until her knees straddled either side of his hips and his cock nestled in the wetness between her thighs.

Clinging to one last shred of sanity, he gripped her hips, held her in place. "Wait. Slow down." There was some reason for that, he was sure of it.

But her breath sobbed out. "Please. Don't stop." And he was powerless to resist her plea. He'd always been powerless against Mia.

He thrust up, and she sank down until he was buried inside her. Their mingled moans echoed through the room as her body adjusted to his. How had he gone ten years without this perfection? Without her? Everything good in the world was right here. With her.

Mia took his mouth in one long, lingering kiss. And that, too, was a homecoming. Rising up, she braced her hands on his chest and began to rock, her beautiful breasts swaying to the rhythm she set. Those deep espresso eyes stayed locked on his, the brown all but swallowed by the black of her irises. She was gorgeous. Intoxicating. A goddess. His—for the moment. His hands tightened on her hips, wanting more than the moment, more than she might want to give.

The electric current gathered low in his spine, and Brax

fought to hold on. Now was not the time to blow early. He wanted to claim her. To remind her of how good they were together. How no one could know her like he could. Rolling to reverse their positions, he shifted so he could thrust deeper, harder, dragging the base of his cock against her clit, exactly the way he knew she liked. Her breath grew short and ragged, her hips pistoning with his in a rhythm they both knew, no matter how long they'd been apart.

Mine. Mine. Mine.

It was a drumbeat in his chest. Primal. Necessary. With every thrust, he thought it. With every slap of flesh against flesh, he imagined imprinting it on her. And when her long cry of release echoed through the room, he let himself go, emptying everything he didn't know how to say inside her.

MIA FELT WRECKED on every level. She wasn't wearing a stitch of clothing. Just the necklace with their wedding rings. The bands dug into her sternum, pressed between her body and the hardness of his where she lay draped over him on the blanket on the floor. She wasn't entirely sure how they'd gotten here. Maybe his legs had given out. She didn't really care. She just didn't want to move from this spot, preferring to soak up the warmth and feel of him, like a cat curled up in a spot of sunshine.

One of Brax's big, muscled arms was hooked around her shoulders, the other draped comfortably over her ass. "Did we kill each other?" The rasp of his voice had her long-neglected lady parts waving a checkered flag to start proceedings all over again. Too bad the rest of her muscles were jelly.

"Maybe. I'm okay with it if we did." Stupendous reunion sex seemed like a reasonably awesome way to go, all things considered.

"I'm not."

Mia froze, her lovely afterglow fading. She tried to pull away, but Brax only tightened his grip.

"If we're dead, we can't do it again."

Her heart lurched. There was that instant craving for *more*. Knowing she had to face it sometime, she propped herself up enough to look down into his face, carefully blanking hers. "Do you want to do it again?"

He pressed two fingers to the pulse in his throat. "I'm still breathing, so yes."

It was such a *her* Brax thing for him to say. Playful. Teasing. But he was no longer hers. "Be serious."

"I am." He sobered, fixing his gaze on her face. "Unless this was some kind of closure for you."

That was exactly what she'd intended. But it hadn't felt like any kind of closure, and her romantic heart was too willing to see it as a new beginning. She couldn't afford to go down that road. "I don't know what it is." That much honesty she could give him.

"Good. Because the lack of condom could've been a problem on that front."

Mia buried her face against his shoulder to keep him from seeing the reaction she couldn't quite hide. "Birth control isn't a problem."

"Good to know." The rough pads of his fingers traced patterns on her bare back. "Do we have to know the answer to what we are yet? Look, I don't know what any of this means. My entire worldview got shattered last night. I found out I'm the world's biggest asshole, and I'm not entirely sure what you're doing here with me right now."

She kissed him with a lingering sweetness meant to show him she wasn't holding on to a grudge. "You're not. Your actions made sense with the information you had."

He brushed the hair back from her face, eyes full of regret. "I hurt you."

He'd devastated her. But she'd long ago made her peace with that. "We hurt each other. None of it was on purpose."

His fingers curved around her nape, stroking at the sensitive point there. Shuddering faintly, she closed her eyes, pressing into the touch.

"I don't want to hurt you anymore. I just... want to make you feel good. We can figure out the rest later. Will you let me do that?"

Her knee-jerk response was hell yes. But years of disappointment had her erring on the side of caution. What was he proposing? An affair? Dating? A new relationship? Had he forgotten they'd filed for divorce a few weeks ago?

Did she really care? She loved him. Was she really going to turn down the opportunity to be with him in any way she could, for as long as she could?

No.

That was one thing she couldn't do.

Aiming for a lighter tone, she kissed him again. "Okay. But we should probably see about a change in venue."

Brax laced his hands at the small of her back, holding her in place. "What? You don't want to stay right here on this extremely special shag carpet to shag again after refueling with birthday pastry?"

At his reminder of her dessert, Mia's stomach growled. "I am starving. Let me up."

He complied, letting her get only far enough to snag the Danish before tugging her back into his lap. His very naked lap. Well, from this position, she knew she'd have a front-row seat to when they could start on round two.

"How did it turn out?"

"Exquisite. You didn't try any?"

"There wasn't anywhere I could sneak a pinch without ruining the overall look."

Mia broke off a piece, feigning seriousness. "This pastry is a contract. I don't share naked birthday pastry with just anyone."

"Oh yeah? What am I contractually bound to do in exchange for a taste?"

"I have quite a few ideas."

"Yeah? So do I." He reeled off a few in graphic enough detail that she was wriggling in his lap by the time he was through.

"Yes, to all of that." Mia held out the Danish. Brax nipped it neatly out of her hand with a kiss to her fingers.

"Mmm. It would've been better warm, but pretty damned good, considering ingredient and time limitations. If I'd thought about it sooner, I'd have been able to do a true puff pastry with better lamination. This was kind of short-cut cheat."

She tore off another piece for herself. "Can I ask how it is you got into this? I never in a million years would have pegged you for getting into baking."

"None of us did. We were part of the first class of students to go through a special baking therapy program, in conjunction with the VA hospital in Syracuse."

"Baking as therapy?"

"Yeah. Dr. Graham—she's the sociologist behind it— teamed up with her fiancé's cousin, Rachel, who's a professional baker, to develop the program. Turns out it's a really solid treatment for anxiety, depression, and PTSD. I mean, it's not like we just stayed in the kitchen. There was actual therapy, too. And for those of us who've fully separated from the military, it gave us a whole other professional certification so we could find jobs that wouldn't be as likely to trigger us again."

"Wow. And you're... okay now?" She looked down at the pastry. "I'm sorry. I don't have a right to ask that."

Brax tipped her chin up. "You can ask because you care. And yeah. I struggled with some PTSD and anxiety when I got out.

Eight years and multiple tours in some of the worst war zones, it wasn't surprising. I saw a lot of shit. Did a lot of shit. It's under control now. All three of us are gold-star graduates of the program."

Mia had deliberately avoided thinking too hard about what he'd been doing all those years he'd been deployed. How he could've been hurt. What he'd had to do to survive. Needing to turn her brain to something less frightening, she handed him another piece of Danish. "You met Jonah and Holt in the program?"

"Yeah. We hadn't originally planned to go into business together, but Jonah inherited the bar and pitched the idea. It seemed like a good one."

"Even though I'm here?"

His arms tightened around her. "Especially now since you're here. If Jonah hadn't dragged me down here, if I hadn't run into you, I'd never have known, and I'd have kept walking around with this huge piece of me just missing. I know everything's all up in the air, but I need you to know that I'm glad we cleared the air. I'm glad we're here, right now."

For the moment, that was probably as good a statement of intention as she was going to get.

"I'm glad we're here right now, too." Mia leaned in, brushing her lips softly over his. "Now put on your pants so we can relocate to somewhere with water and a bed. I don't relish the idea of having carpet burn on my ass."

His grin spread wide and wicked. "How about beard burn on your thighs?"

11

Brax lifted his head from the pillow, squinting at the colorful wash of sky beyond Mia's bedroom window. "Is that sun rising or setting?"

Mia nuzzled sleepily into his shoulder. "Setting. We haven't lost so many hours that it's tomorrow yet."

"Full disclosure. Keeping you naked in this bed at least until then is entirely my plan. Is that a problem for you?"

"Only if you don't feed me. Orgasms require fuel." Her stomach punctuated the statement by letting out a ferocious growl.

With a rumbling laugh, Brax rolled her beneath him. "Bet I can distract you from being hungry."

"It wouldn't be the first time you've tried that tactic. But in this case, we aren't down to the last pack of ramen with no paycheck until the end of the week." She poked him in the shoulder. "I require sustenance."

"Then foraging, we will go." With a smacking kiss, he released her and looked around the room for his pants.

"I think you lost your jeans in the hall somewhere." She slid out of bed and opened the door.

Leno leapt up from where he'd evidently been moping on the floor and made a beeline for the bed, bounding onto the end with a bark. Brax scuttled out of the way before enthusiastic paws could trample his crotch.

"Poor baby," Mia crooned, scruffing the pup's ears. "I've been neglecting you."

The dog pressed his massive head into her palm before turning three circles and plopping down on the rumpled blankets hard enough to shake the whole bed.

Brax snorted a laugh. "I guess he's declaring this is his spot."

"To be fair, it technically *is* his spot. He's not used to being shut out or having to share me."

He'll have to get used to it. Brax bit back the words. He'd seen her hesitance earlier when he'd pushed for something more without defining things. She wasn't ready to go all in. He couldn't blame her for that after what she'd been through. He shouldn't be this gung ho after just a couple of days. So much had changed. And yet... the fundamental way he'd always felt for her hadn't. Earning her trust again would take time. He was committed to rising to that challenge.

"I need to walk him. Why don't you figure out something for food while I do that?"

"I could go with you."

"You could. But I'm not ready to explain who you are to any of my well-intentioned neighbors." She pulled clothes out of the dresser and began tugging them on. "You go out there with me, and Cayla will show up on my doorstep, to ply me with a bottle of wine while her daughter has a playdate with Leno, the moment your truck leaves the driveway."

"She won't do that, anyway?" It wasn't like his truck was hidden as it was.

"Probably. But if she hasn't *seen* you, it'll take her longer to work around to it." Rising to her toes, Mia brushed a kiss over his lips. "Just go with me on this, okay?"

"Fair enough."

"We'll be back in a bit. C'mon, Leno."

The dog took a flying leap off the bed, paws skidding on the hardwood floor as he scrambled after his mistress.

Brax followed at a more leisurely pace, scooping up his jeans where he found them at the entrance to the living room. Deciding they were good enough, he pulled them on and went to investigate the contents of Mia's kitchen.

Neither of them had been much of a cook back when they'd first gotten married. With both a limited budget and microscopic kitchen space, their options had been few. He hadn't been able to look at a rice and bean burrito for years after he'd joined the Marines.

Her freezer was stuffed with frozen meat and vegetables, and a half-eaten pint of cookies and cream ice cream. Nothing that lent itself to her demand for food in a hurry. The fridge was better, with a partial carton of eggs, some cold cuts, cheese, butter, a bell pepper that had started to wrinkle, and the last of a half-gallon of milk that had started to turn. The pantry gave up an assortment of canned soups, jarred sauces, and an array of pastas and rice. She didn't have much in the way of baking ingredients. A small bag of flour, some baking powder, baking soda, and sugar. But he could work with that.

Switching the oven on to preheat, he pulled out the milk, butter, flour, sugar, baking powder and some salt. Sour milk biscuits would be just the thing with some loaded scrambled eggs. Digging out a mixing bowl and baking sheet, he lost himself in the familiar rhythm of combining ingredients. The predictability of the process appealed to him. The reliability of the results was comforting in a world where so much was uncertain.

The biscuits were in the oven and half the ingredients were chopped for the eggs when the knock sounded on the front door. Had Mia forgotten her key?

Wiping off his hands, Brax went to answer. "Hey, did you—" He cut himself off as he spotted Luca standing on the front stoop.

The other man's eyes widened at Brax's shirtless state, eyes immediately zeroing in on the love bite Mia had left on his shoulder.

As his mouth flattened into a furious line, Brax couldn't quite stop himself from crossing his arms and flexing. "Can I help you?"

Luca's hands curled into slow fists. "Where's Mia?"

"Out walking the dog. Is this a social call or were you coming to update her about the results of today's supply run?"

"Brick already sent the update when we left Knoxville."

"All right then. Well, it's not a great time for a visit. Mia and I have a lot of catching up to do." Brax didn't bother to hold back the cocky smirk. Did that make him a dick? Probably. But he couldn't shake the idea that this guy was a threat.

Luca's nostrils flared, his brown eyes going hard as he visibly struggled to hold on to his temper. "What the hell are you really doing here, Whitmore?"

"That's between me and my *wife*."

A muscle jumped in Luca's jaw. "Mia is my friend, and I don't want to see her hurt again."

On that, they could agree. "Neither do I." Brax dropped the posturing. "Look, man, I appreciate your loyalty to her. But if you're hanging around hoping to swoop in when I get out, then you're gonna be waiting until hell freezes over."

Luca snorted in disgust and shook his head. "We'll see."

Without another word, he stalked back down the drive to where he'd parked by the curb. Brax stayed in the doorway, watching until he drove away. He suspected that was gonna be a problem at some point.

The biscuits were coming out of the oven by the time Mia got back with Leno.

"Sorry. That took longer than I planned. Maddie—that's Cayla's daughter—had to come out for her nightly love fest." She stripped off the dog's harness and sniffed the air, much like her pup. "Whatever that is smells amazing."

"Breakfast for dinner. Fresh biscuits. I'll just put on the eggs now that you're back. They'll only take a minute."

He dumped the diced vegetables into a skillet with some melted butter.

"You're concentrating really hard on those onions. Is something wrong?"

Brax sighed. "I don't know. Luca stopped by."

Mia arched her brows, her gaze raking over his bare chest. "And you answered the door like that?"

He nodded. "I wasn't going to bring it up and ruin the mood, because I really want to talk you back into bed. But given his reaction to finding me here, maybe we need to address it. What's the deal with you two?"

"We're friends."

"Just friends?"

Unperturbed by the question, she slid onto one of the bar stools at the kitchen island. "Yes, just friends. He's always known I was married, even if we were estranged."

"That doesn't matter to some people."

Her gaze was level. "It does to me. Luca's always respected that."

"He was pissed to see me here."

"Yeah, I knew he would be. He'll think my getting involved with you on any level is a mistake. That you'll hurt me again. Given he's the one who dealt with the aftermath the first time, that's not surprising."

Realizing the onions were just a shade too far past caramelized, Brax removed the skillet from the heat before dumping in the ham, cheese, and eggs.

"How do you two know each other, anyway?"

"When I finally made it back from Seattle, my job was gone. The first one I got was as a receptionist for a construction company. Luca was just starting out as a laborer there, after a failed run at college. He sort of befriended me against my will. Doing a lot of the stuff you used to. Walking me to and from the bus stop. Making sure I got home safe. Making sure I ate."

Brax closed his eyes, his hand fisting on the spatula. "I didn't think about the financial position I left you in."

She jerked her shoulders in a dismissive shrug. "I mean, that wasn't great, but I was so depressed it hardly mattered. He understood I needed something to distract me in my off-work hours, so he talked me into helping him with this house flip he was doing. The damned thing was two steps away from condemned, but we took it on. He taught me the basics, kept me busy so I couldn't wallow too much, and then gave me a chunk of the profit when he sold it. Then we did it all over again. Several times. I loved it. Ultimately, he talked the company into letting me help out in places besides just the office. I learned all the ins and outs of the business, everything anybody would teach me. I was good at it. And Luca stayed with me every step of the way. He's a good guy."

Brax began dividing the scrambled eggs between two plates. "He followed you here from Washington?"

"Not immediately. He got engaged about six months after I left. They were supposed to be married last month, but she broke it off in October. Left him for some suit who could give her a more refined lifestyle. I figured he could use a change, and it's long past time for me to return the favor and take care of him, so I invited him to come to Tennessee."

"Are you sure the suit is why she broke it off?"

Mia's fork paused above the plate he'd slid in front of her. "What are you suggesting?"

"That it's possible his feelings for you go deeper than just friends." Possible his ass. Brax had seen how the guy looked at her. And that "We'll see" hadn't been a denial.

"There never has been, and never will be, more between Luca and me than friendship. We have a lot of history. That's it. He's just protective of me."

Brax wasn't convinced, but if Mia was being willfully blind to how Luca felt, pointing it out wasn't going to get him anywhere but sent home or to the couch. As that wasn't his end game, he let it drop. "All right. What are you going to tell him?"

"I don't know yet. I'm hoping that'll be clearer by the time I see him again. But either way, he's my best friend, and I'll handle him."

As far as Brax was concerned, that meant he had the weekend to convince her to give them a true second chance. He was going to make the most of it.

MIA WOKE TO A DREAM, full of languid pleasure and heat. Her body hummed and sang, played by its favorite master. He worked her up a slow and ruthless rise until her core wept to be filled. His name came out as a sigh and a plea. And as he slipped inside her, she opened her eyes to his, dark and determined in the pre-dawn light.

Her heart slammed against her ribs as she came fully awake. He was real. He was here. Still with her.

"God!" The word shuddered out as he began to move.

"Good morning to you, too."

"I thought... I was... dreaming." She gasped as he stroked deeper.

"Good dream?"

She huffed a laugh. "Great dream. Mmm."

Brax grinned, maintaining his relentlessly patient rhythm. "Like that, huh?"

"I'm never letting you leave my bed."

"Good thing. I'm really happy here." On a contented hum, Brax kissed her, lingering, seducing, as he took his time driving them both toward the cliff.

He loved her slowly, as if they had all the time in the world. As if they'd never been apart and never would be again. For the moment, Mia gave herself over to it. To him. Choosing to embrace the fantasy that all could be right between them. And when she flew, she wrapped herself around him and carried him with her.

Later, as sweat slicked skin began to cool, she lay loose-limbed and sated across his chest.

"I'm onto your nefarious plan, you know." She kept her tone conversational, as much because she was blissed out on endorphins as to keep from putting his back up.

"What nefarious plan is that?"

"You clearly intend to keep me in an orgasmic stupor to stop me from asking hard questions." And, for the most part, it had worked. But their weekend was drawing to an end, and reality lay outside her door.

"In fact, I'm working on making up for several years of missed orgasms. By my count, we're up to one for every year I was gone."

"Oh, you missed a couple. We passed that mark sometime last night. And don't get me wrong, I'm not complaining."

"But?"

She couldn't make herself look at him. She was too afraid of what she'd see. "What are we doing here, Brax?"

"I'd say enjoying each other, but that's not what you're asking, is it?"

"No." She shifted to look into his face. "If that's all this is for you... I just... I need to know. And maybe it's not fair of me to ask you what it is, when you're having to adjust to so many changes at once. But Brax, I've waited ten years for a second chance with you. When I saw you again, it became rapidly apparent that wasn't going to happen. I filed for divorce—at your request. And now... you're apparently moving here and opening a business, and you're back in my bed, and I just... need to know where we stand."

It was probably far too late to rein in her expectations. She couldn't be with him like this, make love with him as she had, without wanting more. For the sake of what was left of her bruised and battered heart, she had to prepare herself for the worst. That this was just somehow scratching an itch or falling back into old habits.

His dark brows pulled together. "I'm working really hard not to be offended by the fact that you think I can make love to you like I just did and still think I have any intention of walking away."

She wanted so much to take him at his word. But she didn't know him as she used to. "We were always good in bed. Real life is more complicated than that. Our lives, in particular."

"Fair point." Scowling, he laid his head back on the pillow, staring at the ceiling. But when she would've put some distance between them, his arms tightened around her. "I got shot in Afghanistan."

Mia automatically reached out to trace the puckered scars along his ribs and his shoulder, so much like hers.

"Got caught in a firefight with insurgents. Went down. The rib shot punctured a lung. Thought that was it. I was laying there, slowly drowning in my own blood from the inside. I didn't have my whole life flash before my eyes like some people say you do. I just had you. A thousand different moments from the day we met until that last morning when I kissed you good-bye, not knowing it was the last time I'd see you. And all I could think about, as I was about to die, was that I wished I'd opened one of those fucking letters."

The hot burn of tears spilled down Mia's face, and she

could barely swallow past the knot in her throat. She'd been grateful not to have the details of what he'd faced all these years. She'd have worried more, and she had worried enough as it was. But to know that he'd nearly died in the field opened up a whole new hole in her heart.

"You didn't die."

"Thanks to the stubbornness of Master Sergeant Griff Powell. He carried me two miles, at night, under fire, to get me to the extraction point. Had to keep me conscious while we waited for the evac chopper, so he basically brow beat me about what I had to live for." Brax turned to look at her. "I told him about you."

"About how I'd left?"

"About how you loved. Turns out he also had an ex-wife he was still hung up on. And when I came out the other side, laid up in the hospital for longer than I care to remember, he came to see me. We bonded. I'd already started my transition to getting out at that point. It was gonna take me months to heal, and I wasn't gonna be combat ready again before the end of my contract. Griff asked me what I was gonna do about you. And I said, 'Nothing', because by that point I'd chalked the whole thing up to blood loss and trauma, and I'd worked myself up to a good mad again. He just nodded, said he was about to get out, too, and if I wanted to be a dumbass, that was absolutely my right, but that he was going after his woman."

Not entirely sure where he was going with this, Mia found herself invested, nonetheless. "Did he win her back?"

"I was best man in their second Vegas wedding a few months ago. He's Jonah's brother-in-law now."

"Wow. That's a small world."

"You have no idea. Anyway, my point in telling you all of this is that after I got shot, I had to work—*really* work—to stay angry with you. To convince myself not to look you up. Because deep down, I couldn't handle seeing you with somebody else, and I had no reason not to think you'd moved on with your life. It was easier to hang on to all my assumptions. Getting here, seeing you again, finding out the divorce never went through, finding out why you really left. It changes everything." He rolled to face her, stroking a finger along her cheek. "I know it's not reasonable to expect we can just pick back up where we left off. We've both lived a lot of life in the past decade, and we're not the kids we used to be. But I miss you. I miss us. And I think we should do something we've never done before."

Mia swallowed. "What's that?"

"Date."

She blinked at him. "Date?"

"Yeah. We went from friends to married with basically nothing in between. I know you need to learn to trust me again, and I'm fine giving you as much time as you need. So, I think we should date."

All the knots of fear and worry began to unravel. He still wanted to try. This wasn't a continuation of what they'd been before. It was truly a chance to build something new between who they were now. There were no guarantees. She understood that. But this was so much more than she'd ever expected to get.

"Okay. So, we're... dating now." The word felt strange in her mouth. She'd never actually dated anyone before. "What does that even look like?"

"I don't know. Going out for dinner. Taking in a movie. Spending time together. Getting to know each other again."

"That all sounds really good," she admitted.

"Good." Brax kissed the tip of her nose and stroked a hand down her spine. "This plan does, of course, require that we eventually leave this bed."

Mia gave it some consideration. "It can wait until tomorrow."

Rolling on top of him, she lowered her mouth to his.

12

Brax woke wrapped around Mia. He'd lost track of how many times they'd turned to each other over the weekend. The ache in his balls said he might do permanent damage if he kept up this pace, but it seemed worth it to him. So many years to make up for. A glance at the clock told him it would be time to get up soon. They had to actually leave the house today and get to the job site. Back to the real world instead of the cocoon of her bed. More was the pity. He wished he could just lie here and watch her sleep. Beyond the sexual coma they'd been slipping in and out of all weekend, she'd finally relaxed into the unguarded deep sleep that only came with trust.

He pressed a soft kiss to her shoulder, over the pink camelia blossom she'd had tattooed there. She hadn't had any ink when he'd last seen her, and he was curious about the things she'd chosen to commemorate. Something to talk about on one of those dates he planned to take her on. Trailing his lips up the back of her neck, he caught sight of a tiny semi-colon tattoo behind her ear. He'd missed that one in his inventory. It was so small and would ordinarily be hidden by her thick mass of hair. He wondered what it was for.

The alarm clock blared. On a curse, Mia's arm shot out, slapping it off. "Why is it morning?"

"Because, sadly, day inevitably comes after night." He dragged her back against him, wrapping his arms around her waist and snuggling against her back as big spoon. "I can make up for the insult."

She stretched long and languid against him with a groan of regret. "We can't possibly. We're due at the job site in an hour, and I have to shower so I smell like something other than sex and you. I'm gonna be walking funny as it is." She scooted away from him, and he grinned as he spotted the pin-up-style Rosie the Riveter tattoo on her ass. "I'm digging your ink."

She glanced back at him, lips curved. "I like yours, too." Something he knew after she'd paid special attention to the Saint George tattoo he'd gotten on his biceps during a stint in Germany.

"What do they mean?"

"Those are stories for another day. We've got to get to work."

Rolling out of bed, he started to follow her into the bathroom.

Mia spun, poking him in the chest. "No. You should go home to shower and change."

"But water conservation."

"We've never conserved water during a joint shower in our lives. You are not showing up to the site wearing the same thing you had on Friday." She rose to her toes and kissed him. "Shoo. I'll see you at work."

To settle the matter, she shut the bathroom door in his face.

He'd been dismissed. Chuckling to himself, he began gathering his clothes. Dressing quickly, he opened the bedroom door to find Leno dancing in the hall.

"I'm gonna let the dog out!"

"Thank you!" she called back.

As Leno bolted around the backyard to do his business, Brax set up the coffee. Mia had never been a morning person, and it wasn't like she'd stuck to her normal bedtime routine with him here for the weekend. They'd have to see how he fit into her everyday moving forward. Moving in basically violated the whole giving her time thing he'd promised her. Not that she'd asked him to. And there was the matter of the short-term lease he'd signed with Holt and Jonah on a furnished house in town. They were due to move in this week.

Best go deal with that.

After letting Leno back inside, Brax strode out to his truck in the early morning sun. A blonde woman was driving by as he tugged open the door. Her jaw dropped, her eyes going wide. He didn't look that bad, did he? Then again, with the bedhead and the untucked shirt, he probably looked exactly like what he was. A guy who'd just rolled out of Mia's bed. He spotted a child in the backseat and presumed this must be Mia's neighbor Cayla. He wiggled his fingers in a friendly wave. The woman waved back before continuing down the street. He wondered how long she'd wait before showing up with the wine to interrogate Mia.

On the drive across town to Jonah's mom's place, it occurred to him he probably should've texted or something. Not that he thought his friends would worry. They'd known he was going after Mia, and they were smart enough to put two and two together. But Rebecca had been feeding them since they'd arrived, so it probably would've been polite to let her know he wouldn't be around. Then again, she was also more than smart enough to come to the same conclusion about where he'd been.

Feeling a little weird about that, he made an effort to flatten down his hair before he walked inside.

Holt turned from the stove, where he was making over-easy eggs. "Well, well. The prodigal returns."

"Back in the same clothes he was wearing to work on Friday." Jonah toasted him with his mug of coffee.

Brax caught himself hunching his shoulders and straightened. He was a grown-ass man who'd just spent the weekend with his wife. He had nothing to be ashamed of.

"Didn't expect him to be doing the walk of shame while we were here."

"Is it the walk of shame when he's been gone for nearly three days?" Jonah angled his head in consideration. "That might be the walk of pride."

"Do you need some frozen peas for your junk? That's a long dry spell you just ended."

Brax flipped them off. "You're both assholes."

Holt slid eggs onto two plates. "In all seriousness, I'm guessing you and Mia finally talked? Cleared the air? You want eggs?"

"Sure. If you're cooking." He crossed the room to grab his own cup of coffee. "We answered a lot of questions. Things were... a lot more complicated back then than I realized. She didn't leave me. Not like I thought. I can't really say more about it. It's not my story to tell." That was something else they ought to discuss. With her father dead, was she still in any kind of danger?

"Fair enough." Jonah took his plate to the table. "So, after all that, y'all are—what? You look too damned relaxed for things to have gone badly."

"We're... dating. I'm dating my wife. We're figuring the rest out as we go."

Holt cracked two more eggs into the skillet. "That seems like the mature and responsible thing to do after all this time. You're happy?"

"Yeah. Yeah, I am." It had been so long he hardly recognized the feeling.

Jonah stretched his arms in an expansive gesture. "You can thank me for dragging your ass down here when you get a free minute. Cured meat products are highly encouraged. As is good booze."

Brax fixed him with a side eye. "You didn't know she was here."

"Nope. But fact remains, if I hadn't dragged you down here, you'd never have sorted things out. So, I'm taking at least partial credit."

"Leave it to the SEAL to act like it was all his idea."

Holt smirked and dumped the eggs onto another plate. "Take the gift horse, man."

They sat down with their breakfast and dug in.

"There's just one more thing. Stuff at work might get a little... awkward."

"Just don't bang on the job and we're good."

Brax threw a piece of toast at Jonah. "Perv. No. I mean socially awkward. Luca's not happy about this."

"He got some kind of claim on her?" Holt asked.

"Mia says they're just long-term friends. I think he wants to be more."

Jonah spread butter over the toast he'd caught. "He's had a hate on for you from the get-go. Kept it mostly to simmering glares up to now. You think he's gonna cause problems?"

"I don't know. Mia says she'll handle it, and I've got to trust her to do that. Just thought y'all should be aware."

Jonah clapped a hand to his shoulder. "We've got your back, brother. Always."

~

"This all looks good." Mia climbed down from the back of the truck. "Let's get these replacements unloaded first thing. Brick will go over the security measures we're taking to ensure we don't have a repeat of last week's theft. Once that's done, we're hitting it hard this week to make up for that lost day. There's beer in it for all of you if we can get caught up by Wednesday."

"We'll catch up by tomorrow if you'll promise to sing at the next karaoke night!" Brandon shouted.

Mia winced. "You better be buying me more than beer if you expect me to sing. I still haven't gotten over 'Love Shack'." As they laughed at her expense, she shuddered. "Get on to work. You have your assignments."

Brax strolled over, trailed by Jonah and Holt. One corner of his mouth twitched. "I feel like there's a story there. You hate karaoke."

"I do. Which is why they had to get me two steps from wasted to get me up there in the first place. It turns out, I only know the boy part to 'Love Shack'. It wasn't pretty."

She cast a wary eye between his friends as they circled up, unsure what they thought about her and Brax being back together. They couldn't possibly *not* know.

"You want somebody to kill it at karaoke, you get Holt up there." Jonah jerked a thumb in his direction. "His nickname in the Army was Broadway."

"You're into show tunes?" Mia wouldn't have expected that of a guy who was doing more than a half-decent impression of a Viking.

"Show tunes. Disney. Lotta old movie classics. I used to sing them to my baby sister when she was little." He jerked a shoulder. "The lyrics stuck."

"That's really sweet."

"Yeah, but you kept watching all those Disney movies even after Hadley wasn't a kid anymore."

Holt pinned Jonah with a flat stare. "They're good movies, and I'm secure enough in my manhood to admit that."

"He does a killer impression of the demigod dude from *Moana*," Brax added.

"My neighbor's daughter is five, and that is her current favorite movie. Her mom's just glad she's moved on from *Frozen*."

"Yeah, a lot of people were really happy to let it go," Holt deadpanned.

Jonah shook his head. "Dude, that is terrible."

"What? It was *right* there. I couldn't *not* say it."

Mia laughed. Whatever opinions they had about her and Brax, they were keeping it light. She'd take it. Relaxing, she shoved a hand into the pocket of her fleece vest and sipped at the coffee Brax had so thoughtfully made before he'd left this morning. "Look, I wanted to talk to the three of you. I ran a bunch of numbers on Friday. Replacing the materials that were stolen put a pretty solid dent in the budget. But I had some notions about where we can make up for some of it."

"We're listening. Whatcha got?" Jonah asked.

"If we shifted to using some reclaimed materials, you'd get both character and a cost savings. In keeping with that kind of rustic industrial vibe we discussed, we could do walls in shiplap out of pallet boards. Either as an accent wall or for all the walls, if you're really into it. There's the labor cost of tearing the pallets apart and planing them, but the pallets themselves we can nab for free. I've got sources for that. In the end, it saves on the cost of materials, and avoids the extra time and labor for putting up sheetrock, mudding it, sanding it, painting it."

"I dig it," Brax said. "All that wood feels manly, but not in an animal-heads-hanging-on-the-wall kind of way."

"I'm for the savings, for sure," Holt added.

"It'd change the look of the place. And be sturdier than sheetrock. Not that I expect there to be brawls breaking out here like they did when it was a bar. I like it," Jonah declared. "Let's do it."

"Great. I'll put in a call to my source. We've got some high school kids working hourly who can do the tearing apart. That'll be an additional savings on labor."

The bad-tempered crash of pipe clattering to the concrete floor had them all turning around. Mia spotted Luca, swearing as he picked up and repositioned the materials on the stack. The process was hampered somewhat by the glares he kept shooting in their direction.

"Somebody's having a tantrum," Brax murmured.

Mia shot her own glare at him. "I'll deal with it. You'll only make it worse."

He lifted his hands in surrender. "Your friend, your rules."

"Excuse me, gentlemen."

She strode directly over to Luca. "Take a walk with me."

Without a word, he stalked out the front door and kept going, out past the myriad of work trucks filling the gravel parking lot. Understanding he needed to move to work off some of the frustration, she didn't comment, just kept walking until he stopped and rounded on her.

"What the fuck are you doing, Mia?"

She sighed, reaching deep for some patience to try to take the whole situation down several notches. "I know you're upset."

"Upset? You think I'm upset?" Hands on hips, he paced a tight circle. "Right. The guy who completely left you behind, with no word, no income, no place to live. Nothing. Who broke your heart, trampled all over it for multiple years running when you tried to reach out. *That guy* just happens to show back up, and you decide to take him back into your bed. Because that's a smart decision."

Understanding that he was operating on an incomplete

picture of the situation, Mia bit back her own temper at his interpretation. "It's not like that."

"Really? And what is it like?"

God. Was she ever going to be able to live her life in more than just pieces? Luca didn't know about her past, either. He'd always known there were parts of her life that she couldn't or wouldn't talk about. He'd never pushed, and she'd been grateful. But how could she explain things with Brax without those details?

"It's complicated. There were things he didn't know when he left."

"Like the fact that you were pregnant?"

The blood drained out of her face, and she lunged for him, hissing "Shhh!" even as she looked around for anyone who could overhear.

"Didn't tell him that, did you?"

"I'm regretting ever getting drunk enough to tell you. Don't you dare throw that in my face."

Luca squeezed his eyes shut, his expression softening. "I'm sorry. I didn't mean it like that."

She had to count to ten before she was calm enough to speak again. "Look, there are things you don't know—that you can't know—that impacted what happened between Brax and me back then. I finally got a chance to tell him and correct the world's most monumental misunderstanding. I deserved the right to do that."

"Yeah, you did. And he denied you that for ten years. What makes now different?"

"He's my husband, Luca."

"He walked away from that role years ago. Why does he deserve the chance to get close enough to hurt you again? What's to stop him from doing that?"

Leave it to her best friend to cut right to the heart of her fears.

She met his gaze without flinching. "Nothing. Except his word. I know you think I'm a fool to trust him. But I need you to trust me. And that when I say the situation is more complicated, and has more pieces than you're aware of, that I know what I'm talking about. I know what I'm doing."

He made a visible effort to reel in his frustration, reaching out to skim his hands down her arms. "Honey, I just... don't want to see you get hurt again. You almost didn't survive it last time."

That was the God's honest truth. And she wouldn't have survived if not for him. Because she understood that his temper tantrum all came down to concern, she cut him some slack. "I get that. And I appreciate you're worried about me. But I've wondered for ten years if we could make things work after how things ended. We finally cleared the air, and he wants to try again. We both know we're different people now, so we're not just automatically picking things back up where we left off. We're dating." It felt just as ridiculous to say out loud to Luca as it had in her bedroom the day before.

"Dating?" He snorted. "Right. Because that's a normal thing to do with the guy you're in the process of divorcing. Or did you forget that part?"

Impatient now and itching to get back to work, she crossed her arms. "Luca, I have to do this. I *need* to do this, or I'll wonder for the rest of my life, 'what if?' I need you to be supportive—if not of him, then of me. Can you do that?"

He sucked in a long breath and let it out. "Yeah. I can do that. I'll behave. I promise. And when he lets you down—because I don't for a minute think he won't—I'll still be here to help pick up the pieces. Just like last time."

Figuring that was as good as it was gonna get, Mia nodded and turned back toward the job. She could only hope that he was still around when Brax proved him wrong.

13

"Well, what's the verdict?" Cayla bit her lip, waiting for Mia's assessment.

Mia took one last look around the open concept space. The little house was tiny. Only about seven-hundred square feet, with a teeny kitchenette and a single bathroom. It reminded her a little of the first studio apartment she'd shared with Brax. "End of the day, it's not great. It's not terrible. I can confirm it's not gonna fall down around your ears, the roof's sound, and there's no risk of mold. The toilet runs, but that's an easy fix. The hard water stains in the sink may be permanent." She crossed her arms. "It's definitely not gonna be winning any beauty pageants."

"Mr. Thompson said I can paint and do some landscaping around the outside if I want. I figure with some smart flea market shopping, I could make it cute."

Mia thought of the tidy little bungalow Cayla shared with her daughter. It was sweet and homey, with flowers that bloomed in the spring and a cheerful blue front door. The precise opposite of her own house. "That's definitely more your area of expertise than mine. I still look like I moved in last month."

"I can help with that, you know."

It was, Mia supposed, the kind of offer you got from girlfriends. She'd never really had one of those, given that she worked predominantly with men. Her struggles with Luca lately had really highlighted the lack of other women in her life. There was Maggie, of course, but Mia wasn't sure if they'd have become friends at all without Porter in the mix. Cayla had made more than one overture that she hadn't picked up beyond being neighborly. Maybe it was time she took her up on some of those offers.

"That'd be nice." Seeing her face brighten with enthusiasm, Mia started for the door, lest she launch into decorating suggestions on the spot. "Anyway, I don't see any major red flags that mean you should run. If this place suits your needs, I say go for it."

"Well, the price is certainly right. And I can still take client meetings at their homes while I get it sorted out. I'll talk to Mr. Thompson about a lease later this week. I really appreciate you looking the place over."

"I'm sorry it took me so long to get to it. I know you've been wanting to make a decision. Life's been a little crazy lately."

Cayla tugged the door to the little house shut and locked it. "Does that have something to do with the hottie I saw coming out of your house Monday morning?"

Mia laughed. "I'm amazed you took this long to ask about him. Your restraint is impressive."

"You can credit the wedding disaster I'm trying to avert for your reprieve from inquisition. The cake has fallen through, and the wedding is next weekend. I haven't been able to find a replacement yet, which I do not want to tell my client, for obvious reasons."

"Yeesh. Yeah, I can see how that would be problematic."

Cayla waved that away. "I'll get it sorted. Somehow. Even if it means I have to bake one myself. So, the hottie. Was that the friend you were telling me about? Luca? The one who just moved here?"

"No. Definitely not Luca. He's renting his own place." And thank God for that, under the circumstances. Bracing herself for the barrage of questions that would inevitably follow, Mia admitted, "That was my husband, Brax."

Cayla's eyes all but bugged out of her head. "Holy shitake mushrooms, girl! Husband? You're married? What? You've been holding out on me! Did you elope?"

"No. I mean, not recently. We got married when I was eighteen."

"And you've been hiding him where?"

"He's a Marine."

"Oh, so he's been deployed all this time? Why didn't you say so?"

She'd had time to give some thought to an abbreviated version she could share when everyone inevitably asked. "That's complicated. The long and the short of it is that we've been estranged for a long time. But he's retired now, and we're giving things another try." Seeing she wanted to ask about a million more questions, Mia headed her off. "He's one of Jonah's business partners, so you'll get the chance to meet him tonight. You're still coming to the party?"

The guys had moved into their new rental house earlier this week. They'd opted for a cookout and bonfire as a house-warming party and had invited a bunch of Jonah's local friends so they could meet Brax and Holt and welcome them to town. Several members of her crew would also be in attendance, owing to the ass-busting they'd pulled off to not only catch up on the renovation timeline, but get a little bit ahead.

"Yeah. Mama's keeping Maddie for me tonight. So, Brax is one of the bakers?"

"Yep."

Cayla's look turned considering. "Okay, this is way out there, and I know they aren't even open yet, but... what are the chances that he might be willing to pinch hit and take on a last-minute commission for a wedding cake? Or does he even do that kind of baking?"

"I don't know. But if he doesn't, Jonah or Holt might. You can always ask. The worst they can do is say no, and then you're no worse off than you were before."

"Fair point."

Considering this was one of Cayla's rare nights out, Mia decided to make an overture of her own. "Are you going to have to go pick up Maddie when you're through?"

"No. Mama's keeping her overnight. I've got a baby shower I'm running tomorrow, and it's easier than having to roust her out of bed and get her over there first thing."

"You want to drive over to the party together? I've still got to shower off the day, but I could pick you up. You could unwind a little with a drink or two. It sounds like the way your week's going, you could use it."

"Really? It's not an imposition? What about Brax? I don't want to step on y'all's toes."

"He's not living with me right now. And if he decides to come over later, he'll want his own truck, anyway. It's no trouble."

"If you really don't mind, that would make you my hero twice over. I basically never get a night off from being the responsible grown up." She blushed. "Not that I plan to tie one on or anything."

"No, I get it. Being a single mom is hard. Even with your mom's help. Let's get on out of here and go get cleaned up. Doll yourself up, if you feel like it, and we'll get you out for a little adult entertainment." Mia paused, playing the words back in her brain. "That came out wrong."

Cayla laughed. "I haven't had any of that kind of entertainment since I left Maddie's daddy. Not looking for any either, after how that turned out. But every now and then, I really miss non-battery assisted orgasms."

"I completely understand."

Looping an arm through Mia's, Cayla said, "Since you've got your man back, you'll have to make up enough of the real thing for both of us."

"Is that your way of asking for details?"

"If the shoe fits, sugar. It's what friends do."

Well, this was gonna be interesting.

FROM HIS POST in the kitchen prepping burgers for the grill, Brax decided it was a good thing the house had come furnished. They'd only moved in three days ago, and though they'd all sent for the rest of their things, none of them had that much, considering they'd been actively deployed for the bulk of their military careers. Even in the year and change since they'd separated, they hadn't accumulated much stuff. If Porter hadn't been willing to cut them a deal with a longer-term lease on one of his vacation rentals, their party guests would've been stuck with bringing their own seats. As it was, there still wasn't enough seating. Not that anybody seemed to mind.

People milled about in clusters, noshing on the array of chips, dips, and appetizers that filled up the kitchen table, pot-luck style. The sheriff and his wife, Kennedy, were chatting with Porter and Maggie, who was apparently Kennedy's sister. Holt was huddled up, shooting the shit with the trio of other Rangers who lived in town—his friend Harrison, Ty Brooks, and Sebastian Donnelly, the guy who ran the equine therapy program.

Brax wondered how different things would've turned out if

he'd gone to something like that instead of Dr. Graham's program.

The Rangers' wives and a bunch of other women at the party—friends of Jonah's from high school—were all cooing over Harrison's new baby boy, who rode in one of those sling things on his mother's chest. Cute kid, as far as that kind of thing went. Not that anybody could see much but the top of his head, which was covered in a soft blond fuzz.

Various members of the Mountainview Construction crew had trickled in now that they'd had time to go home and clean up from the workday. Luca was, so far, conspicuously absent, which was fine with Brax. He'd dialed down his hostility this week after talking with Mia, but Brax wasn't convinced things were all fine and dandy now. The guy had an agenda, and he was just waiting for Brax to fuck up. He'd be waiting a long, damned time.

Mia herself still hadn't made an appearance. Brax knew she was helping her neighbor, Cayla, with something right after work, and she'd still need to shower. He missed her already. Which made him feel stupid, since he'd seen her literally every day. But she'd had to take point on another job today, and he was feeling a little restless surrounded by this many people. Most of them weren't *his* people. Didn't matter how many years had passed, being thrust into situations where he was the new guy had him reverting to observer, automatically assessing where he fit in the pecking order.

Hauling the tray outside, he loaded burgers on the preheated grill and went back in to set a timer.

"You got landed with KP for this shindig?"

Brax turned and grinned as he spotted Griff coming into the kitchen, his new bride by his side. "Them's the breaks. How you doing, man? I didn't expect to see you here tonight."

They exchanged back-slapping hugs.

"We're good. Had a little time to swing through town for a visit, before setting out for some travel."

Brax turned his attention to Sam. "I understand congratulations are in order. Taking the leap on into parenthood."

Her smile radiated delight. "Thanks."

Griff grinned. "We're due end of July."

Marriage and impending parenthood looked good on them both. "That's awesome, man. Really. I'm happy for you two."

For just a moment, he wondered if this would be him and Mia, eventually. They'd married so young that they hadn't discussed kids. Even getting a dog had been too big an expense when they were trying to keep a roof over their own heads and food in their bellies. But now... Now, they were a long way from happily wedded bliss, so the topic still wasn't on the table. They needed to shore up the foundations of their marriage before considering bringing a tiny human into the dynamic. But he thought maybe he'd dig that. Eventually. And that was getting way ahead of things.

"We're thrilled. Although I might be just as excited about the babymoon," Sam admitted. "I'm on sabbatical for the semester so we can get in some travel. We were actually supposed to leave a couple of weeks ago, but we ended up buying a new house and had to move everything and get settled."

"Well, I, for one, am glad that means you're here tonight. It's great to see you both. Can I get either of you something to drink?"

"Eh, I'll get us some Cokes in a minute." Griff slid his arm around his wife. "How are you liking Eden's Ridge?"

"It's a nice town. Hard to imagine you cutting up here as a kid."

"Oh, I managed."

"How's my brother as a roommate?"

Jonah strode up and slapped Brax on the back. "I barely

count. Not even sure why he's paying rent here since he's warming Mia's bed every night."

Brax fixed him with a flat stare. "Whatever, dude. And can you maybe do something radical and behave yourself while she's over tonight?"

Griff had gone brows up. "Mia? Like your ex-wife, Mia?"

Brax shifted on his feet, wishing their situation was less complicated. "Yeah. Turns out she's less of an ex than I thought." He offered a brief explanation of the botched divorce. "Anyway, we finally talked and are giving things another try."

Griff offered an approving nod. "Nice to see you got your head out of your ass."

Brax was laughing as he spotted Mia stride in. "Speak of the devil." Then he did a double take. She wore jeans that hugged her curves and a form-fitting V-neck sweater in siren red. She'd painted her lips to match. It wasn't like he'd never seen her dress up before, but in the past and on the job site, she certainly didn't draw attention to herself. This was... wowsa.

Jonah squeezed his shoulder. "Roll your tongue back in, pal."

"She's my wife. I'll drool if I want to."

He was so focused on Mia, it took him a bit to notice the blonde trailing her through the room. The neighbor he'd seen the other morning. She was waving at various people as she went. A local, then.

As soon as Mia got near enough, Brax snagged her hand and tugged her close.

"Sorry, I'm late."

"Worth the wait. You look amazing."

Color warmed those golden cheeks.

Cayla nodded in satisfaction. "Told you."

Brax squeezed Mia's hip. "I want to introduce you to some folks. This is Griff Powell and his wife, Sam Ferguson. Guys, this is Mia."

Mia sobered. "Master Sergeant Griff Powell?"

"Yeah."

She let go of Brax to wrap Griff in a tight hug. "Thank you."

After a moment's shocked hesitation, Griff squeezed her back, understanding dawning as he looked over at Brax. "You're welcome. He'd have done the same for me."

"Anytime, brother."

The three of them fell into conversation with Cayla, who'd clearly also gone to high school with them.

Brax pulled Mia in for a less-than-quick hello kiss.

"Missed you today. Did you get everything sorted at that other job?"

She linked her hands at the small of his back. "I did. Unfortunately, now that we're getting further along in your project, I'm turning more over to my subs and will have to do considerably more juggling, so I won't be seeing you on-site every day."

"Well, you wouldn't be there every day once we get the bakery open anyway, so I guess it'll be practice. As long as I get to see you after work, I think I'll survive."

"Oh, speaking of the bakery." Mia turned back to address the group. "Maybe one of you can help Cayla with a problem. The cake for a wedding she's coordinating for next weekend has fallen through, and she's having trouble finding anyone who can take the job. Any of you interested in a last-minute commission?"

Cayla twisted her hands. "I know it's a lot to ask, but it would really mean a lot to me and my business if I can keep this client happy. And I figure we're going to end up doing a lot of work together after you get the bakery open, since I'm the event planner in town, so you can absolutely count on referrals from me. What do you say?"

Brax was about to open his mouth to agree when Holt stepped up behind Cayla.

"I can do it."

It made sense. Of the three of them, Holt was the cake guy. The detail work he pulled off in fondant and icing was beyond compare. But Brax was still surprised he was leaping in like this for someone he didn't know.

Cayla turned and focused in on Holt, her eyes lingering on his broad chest and shoulders for a few beats too long before making it up to his face. Brax would almost swear he could hear her thinking, *Oh my.*

She swallowed. "Um, that would be amazing."

"Cayla, meet Holt Steele. Holt, my friend and neighbor, Cayla Black."

Something flickered in Holt's eyes. "The one with the daughter currently obsessed with *Moana*?"

Cayla blinked. "Yes. Maddie's five. Although this week, we've moved on to *Encanto*."

"We don't talk about Bruno," Holt said seriously.

After a stunned moment, Cayla burst out laughing. "I see you know your Disney movies."

The corners of his mouth twitched up ever so slightly. "Blame my kid sister." He jerked his head toward the kitchen. "You wanna come tell me what you're needing while I go flip the burgers?"

"Sure. I can do that."

They all waited until the two had made it out of earshot before speaking again.

"She married?" Jonah asked.

"Divorced," Sam corrected.

"I don't think she's looking for anything," Mia put in.

"Neither is Holt. But we've all got eyes," Brax added.

"Anybody want to bet?" Jonah asked.

A chorus of "In!" was his answer.

14

"Okay, I've got to get going. I'm due for a consultation in the south end of the county in—" Mia checked her watch. "—forty-five minutes, and I still need to swing by the office to print off extra copies of the elevations."

"Date night tonight," Brax declared. "Maybe a movie. I don't even know what's playing. Or Brandon was telling me about the live music at Jam Night, up at the... what'd he call it? Old Mill?"

"That would be the Old Mill that's now the new Stone County Artisan Guild and Education Center. Which everybody still calls the Old Mill because that's what we renovated," Mia explained. "Welcome to the South. Anyway, that sounds awesome, but I don't know what time I'll be through."

"Dinner then, if nothing else. We can do that whenever. Let me know when you think you'll wrap, and I can come pick you up."

Mia's eyes sparkled as she grinned up at him. "What a novel concept."

She'd been so delighted by his efforts to date her over the past couple of weeks, Brax regretted not finding more ways to do it when they'd first been married, even with their limited budget. He vowed to do things differently this time, now that the lion's share of their focus wasn't on meeting their basic needs.

"I can still surprise you."

"That you can." She rose to her toes, brushing her lips against his in a kiss that had her crew ooooing like the middle school girls she'd accused them of being. And Brax counted that as yet another step toward her being comfortable being a *them* again. Everybody knew they were together, and she wasn't trying to hide it anymore. If they were all curious about the plans for their divorce, nobody was brave enough to bring it up directly.

Rolling her eyes, she cheerfully flipped the crew off. "Get back to work, you ingrates!" But she was smiling. "See you tonight." She blew Brax one more kiss and headed for her truck.

He was still grinning when he turned to catch Luca's familiar glower. Not prepared for the other man to ruin his good mood, Brax opted to handle him point blank. "You got something you want to say?"

"I've got plenty. But out of respect for Mia, I'm keeping it to myself."

"Alright then." Leaving it at that, Brax got back to work himself.

Most of the crew was working outside today, attaching the furring strips to the cinder block walls in preparation for putting up the Hardie board siding. The new roofline was framed, and once the wrap-around porch was framed in, they'd put on a tin roof. He and the guys were still debating paint colors for the exterior, but it was gratifying to see the building really changing and becoming something new.

Brax headed to what would be their new, expanded kitchen. He'd gotten a line on some used commercial ovens down in Nashville, and he needed to do some measuring to see where they'd fit. Some elements of the kitchen, like the prep sinks, simply were where they were. It hadn't been worth the additional expense to reroute the plumbing. But electrical was easier, and he'd volunteered to work up some prospective layouts for them all to go over later.

If he'd thought about it ahead of time, he could've gotten Mia's drawings that already had the dimensions of everything. But he also knew the measurements on the blueprints didn't always exactly match reality, so he set about drawing out the kitchen himself. In the end, they'd rejected the idea of a fully open concept, as none of them had been too keen on being stared at like animals in a zoo while they worked. But they'd also recognized the need to be able to monitor the front if any of them were here working alone, so they'd gone with a large pass-thru with a roll-down door. It hadn't come in yet, but Brax kept it in mind as he considered placement of worktables, racks, and the other tools of their trade.

It was as he bent to measure the range they'd inherited that he caught sight of something that didn't belong. A tiny black dot on the wall outlet where none should have been. If he hadn't been looking closely, he might've assumed it was just a speck of dirt or paint. But it was too symmetrical. He bent lower, scanning the floor below, and found fine plastic shavings. As if someone had drilled a hole in the socket cover. Was that really what he thought it was?

Needing a second opinion, he kept his face neutral and headed outside. Jonah stood admiring the first couple of rows of siding that had been attached to the west wall.

"Gonna make a hell of a difference in how this place looks." When Brax only grunted, Jonah arched his brows. "Something up?"

Brax kept his voice low. "I need you to go take a look at the power outlet beside the range in the kitchen. But don't look like you're looking at it. Pretend like you're helping me measure."

"Well, that's cryptic." But he did as asked.

They stretched out the tape measure, and Jonah hunkered down. Brax knew the moment he spotted the oddity and that he hadn't been wrong about what it was.

Holt wandered in. "Is it that hard to decide where those ovens are gonna go?"

"Lots of things to consider," Jonah said. Nothing in his tone would've alerted anyone who didn't know him. "Like, should we move the range? We'd need to put in another 220 plug here. Take a look."

Brax saw Holt's posture shift as he recognized something was going on. He crossed over, examined the wall. Stood up. "You two wanna skip out to go get some lunch? I'm starved. We can discuss layouts over lunch."

Jonah looked up from his phone, where he'd been simulating texting, while probably taking photos and video. "I could eat. Brax, you coming?"

With little fuss, they piled into Jonah's truck. Via a series of hand signals, they agreed to keep quiet until they made it into town. The Tavern wasn't likely to be bugged. Their vehicles might not be, either, but it was better to be safe than sorry until they could verify that fact.

Fifteen minutes later, they accepted menus from the busty blonde waitress who flirted with any and every guy under the age of forty. As soon as she walked away, Jonah kicked back.

"It's a high-end wireless camera. Digital. Used to be you couldn't get anything that small anywhere but black-market dealers, but these days there's more and more available for regular consumers."

"Which begs multiple questions." Brax ticked them off. "Why the hell would someone be putting a camera in our building? For that matter, there has to be more than one. What the hell would anybody be able to see from that spot between the range and wall? Is it video only or audio, too?"

"We thought the break in was about casing the place prior to the supply theft. But maybe nothing was taken because something else was left behind," Holt suggested.

Trish came back with their drinks. "What can I get you fine gentlemen?"

"Cheeseburgers all around. The works," Jonah said.

"No lettuce on mine," Brax added.

"Skipping out on your vegetables?" Holt asked.

"Salad does not belong on a burger."

"You got it, boys."

After she strolled away again, Holt leaned closer. "We going to bring Xander in on this?"

"That none of us have immediately suggested that we should probably says a lot." Jonah sipped at his sweet tea. "Xander's a good cop, and at the end of the day, we might end up taking it to him. But I feel like we need a bit more information first. Black market surveillance equipment isn't exactly part of his usual wheelhouse."

Holt stroked his beard. "Who the hell in Stone County would be into that kind of shit? And what could they possibly hope to gain by surveilling our renovation?"

Brax thought of what Mia had told him about her past. She'd said nothing had happened in the ten years since her father had been killed. But what if the people who'd done it had somehow found her here? The idea of it made his blood run cold. He'd just found her again. He sure as hell wasn't going to lose her now.

"You think of something?" Jonah prompted.

"Maybe. Do either of you have any contacts you can get up with who might be able to trace the camera to a source? Either to see where the signal's streaming to or where it might've come from?"

Holt nodded. "I know a guy. Cash Grantham. Old Army buddy. He's in private security now, with a heavy interest in cyber security. If you'll send me those photos and the video you took of it, I'll pass it on to him, see if he can get started on it. He'll probably be able to do more if we can actually get him the camera."

"Then tonight, after the crew leaves, we go over the place with a fine-toothed comb." If this did have something to do with Mia, he wanted to get to the bottom of it ASAP. "Pull out anything and everything we can find. It goes without saying, we tell the crew nothing."

"We might want to pick up something to jam their signal, so they don't immediately realize their setup has been compromised," Holt considered. "I think I can borrow something from Ty."

Jonah arched a brow. "He has a signal jammer?"

"His wife was the victim of a stalker, so he's got a justified paranoia. He'd loan it to me without asking too many questions."

"He's a deputy. You think he'll keep quiet about this?" Brax asked.

"Out of respect from one Ranger to another. Yeah."

"Then make whatever calls need making. I want answers."

MIA SPENT the day itching to be done with work. So, of course, the Universe laughed in her face. Her client meeting ran long, with every idea she presented being shot down, and entirely new requests being made that meant going back to the drawing board. From there, she got pulled in on a plumbing disaster on a residential job that required a quick change from her meeting attire into work clothes. Once that hemorrhage had been stopped, she'd gotten stuck on the phone arguing with one of their suppliers, who'd sold the custom-order tile she'd requested weeks ago to some yahoo who'd walked in off the street. She understood mistakes happened, but waiting on a new order was going to throw the entire job off by weeks, which put a monkey wrench in the schedule for all the *other* jobs they were juggling. By the time she'd finished with *that*, she really wasn't in the mood for a date. At least, not one that didn't involve a beer in the shower and a bottle of Excedrin. So, when Brax texted, asking if she could swing by the guys' house instead of him picking her up, she figured it was just par for the course. There'd probably been some kind of problem on *that* job that they wanted to discuss with her directly, away from the crew.

Just perfect.

At least she'd been able to carve out time for that shower beer and a change of clothes first. She was prepared to get through this meeting and make a bid for takeout pizza at home. Then Brax opened the door, and she immediately understood that her night was about to get worse.

"What happened?" she demanded.

"Come on in. We'll talk about it."

Tension lodged between her shoulder blades as she followed him into the living room, where Holt and Jonah were huddled over something on the table.

"Please tell me there wasn't another theft." Surely not. No one had contacted her. And if something else had been stolen, surely they'd be asking her to meet at the site, not here.

"Not a theft." Jonah straightened and gestured to the table.

Multiple outlet covers were piled in the center. Something small and black was attached to the back of each.

Mia frowned. "I don't understand."

"You should sit," Brax urged.

She wanted to run and didn't even know why. Their sober expressions were freaking her out. But she sat.

Jonah picked up one of the little black dots. "We found these hidden all over the building."

Some inner instinct kept her from picking any of them up to examine. "What are they?"

"Surveillance equipment. Wireless cameras. Bugs," Holt explained.

Blinking at him, she played the words over in her head but couldn't make any sense of them. "What the hell? Like... spy shit?"

Holt nodded.

"Why would someone bug the building?"

Brax took her hand. "I think it might be because of you."

Mia's head spun as all the blood drained out of her face. Panic skated down her spine, both at the implication, and the fact that he'd just brought this up in front of his friends. Everything in her recoiled, shouting, *Don't tell! Don't tell! Don't tell!*

She yanked her hand away. "You told them?"

He didn't bat an eye at the accusation in her tone. "No. I was hoping you'd do that."

That he hadn't betrayed her trust mollified some of the outrage. But how could he ask this of her? Didn't he understand what it meant for her to have told *him* after all this time? She was already shaking her head, curling in on herself at one end of the sofa.

Eyes impossibly gentle, Brax knelt in front of her. "Baby, I trust both of them with my life."

Mia swallowed, willing her voice not to shake. "Do you trust them with mine?"

Holt stepped into her line of sight. "He's ours, and you're his, so that makes you ours, too."

"And, for what it's worth," Jonah added, "we've all spent considerable time running covert operations, so we understand discretion and how to keep our mouths shut. Which is why we haven't gone to the police."

She pressed her lips together and surveyed the lot of them. Each looked steady and unruffled. Capable. And they wanted to help. If this really was about her, she couldn't handle it by herself.

"You need to understand that what I'm about to tell you has colored almost my whole life. I've been alone with all of it since I was twelve years old, and continually had it pounded into my head that doing anything but keeping the secret put anyone who knew in danger. That included Brax until a few weeks ago. If I bring you in on this, I don't know what it might mean for you."

"With all due respect, we're in a good position to take care of ourselves, and you, if it comes to any sort of threat," Jonah promised.

"The potential risk is understood," Holt added. "Please, go ahead."

So, she told them. It was a little easier than it had been telling Brax. Not having her marriage on the line helped. By the time she'd finished, even the terminally unruffled Holt had gone brows up.

"Who did your dad work for?"

"I don't know."

"Your mom or the Marshal never said?" Jonah prompted.

"No. The less information I had, the better. You have to understand, I spent my life trained to hide. I've never even googled my real name or that of any of the family I remember, because somebody, somewhere, could have an alert set that could get triggered."

Brax took her hand again, stroking his thumb over the knuckles. "What was your real name?"

She took a breath and let it out slowly. "Maria. Maria Isabella Ramirez." The feel of it in her mouth, spoken like the melodic Spanish she'd been taught from birth, was strange after all these years. "My grandfather had had a stroke, and he couldn't wrap his tongue around the whole thing. He was the one who called me Mia, so when I had to pick something new, I chose that."

"Do you know why your dad wanted to see you?" Jonah asked. "What he wanted to tell you that day?"

"No. We were both shot almost immediately. It wasn't like he'd passed me a jump drive or the key to a safe deposit box or something. As far as I knew, he just wanted to see me, not share some kind of secret."

"We could maybe do a search on your dad. See what comes up around the shooting," Holt mused. "We've got ways to circumvent any kind of alarms set around that."

"Even if an alarm gets triggered, it seems the horse is already out of the barn, as it were, if someone's already been here setting up surveillance," Jonah said. "Somebody already knows you're here."

"The question is how? I've just been living my life since I got shot. It's been ten years. If this is about me, why now?"

"Maybe when I called to check on our marital status in Washington, it triggered something. That's the big thing that's changed lately, right? I came back into your life."

She thought back to the phone call. "It's not the only thing that changed. Curt's dead. Heart attack just before all this started."

"You sure about that?" Jonah asked.

"It's what I was told." She relayed the rest of the brief conversation.

"That seems convenient, is all. He drops dead. You're cut loose by someone you don't know. And suddenly, after all this time, weird shit starts happening?"

"You're suggesting someone took him out? To what end? I'm nobody. I wasn't important enough to actually enroll in WITSEC. Curt stuck his neck out because I could've been used as leverage with my father. But my father's been dead for a decade. Why would anyone bother with me?"

"Somebody who doesn't like loose ends," Holt mused. "If whoever did the drive-by that killed your dad was meant to kill you both, and you weren't just collateral damage, then you represent a job unfinished."

"Then why not just finish it?" she demanded. "They didn't have any trouble just cutting me down before."

Brax growled, hauling her against him. "I really wish you weren't just casually talking about being shot again."

"I'm not saying it to upset you. But there's no dressing this up to be nicer."

Jonah tapped his chin. "Eden's Ridge isn't the kind of place where a homicide would be easily covered up. We haven't had a murder in Stone County in over forty years. Not since Wynette Burton found out her husband was cheating on her and shot him and his mistress in bed."

"Jesus," Brax muttered.

"My point," Jonah continued, "is it would make all kinds of waves, and seems like these people—whoever they are—don't want to do that."

"I think you're missing another possibility. The guy on the phone told her they considered the project closed. What if it's somebody trying to clean up what they perceive as Curt Savage's messes? If he was operating at the fringes of the rules, could be he pissed some people off. Maybe the surveillance is to see what she does on her own," Brax suggested.

Holt folded his arms. "If that's the case, chances are her house is also wired."

"Oh my God." Mia felt whatever blood had returned to her head drain out again.

"We'll sweep it," Brax promised. "Although I'd be willing to guess there's nothing there, courtesy of Leno. You and I know he's a teddy bear, but he's an intimidating dog, and I don't expect he'd just stand by while somebody went all through your house."

A little of the anxiety faded. "That's true. He's not good with strangers unless I introduce them."

"We'll still sweep it," he assured her. "Should probably do your office, too. As for the rest, we don't know when they were planted."

"Had to be after demolition. After the wiring was checked," Mia said. "I don't know where all you found them, but I went over the entire system with a fine-toothed comb. Nothing like this was there then."

"After the theft," Holt said. "We were all off site for nearly three days, waiting on more supplies. Plenty of time for somebody to come in and wire the place up."

"So, the theft could've been a cover-up, rather than tied to the other supply thefts around the county." Jonah nodded. "Gets everybody out of the way and casts suspicion elsewhere."

"Who would've had access to plant all of them?" Brax asked. "Someone on the crew?"

"Why would someone on my crew plant surveillance on *this* job? They see me all the time, all over the place."

"Well, we don't *know* that it's just this job," Brax pointed out. "But for sake of argument, let's assume it is. For the first few weeks, it's where you were spending all your time."

"Somebody new to the crew?" Jonah suggested.

"We don't have anybody new to the crew."

Brax fixed her with a look. "There's Luca."

Mia scowled at him. "Okay, now you're just pissing me off."

"Think about it. He got here just before this job started. He's Italian."

"Oh, for the love of—" She pinched the bridge of her nose and struggled not to throttle her husband. "You're overlooking the very salient fact that we've been best friends for nearly *ten years*. Him being Italian does not automatically mean he has ties to organized crime. The mob did not plant him in my life for that long on some off chance that I knew something. Which

I don't. I know you two don't like each other, but you're both going to have to get the hell over it."

"What does he know about your past?" Holt asked.

"Pieces. He knows I was shot. I was still healing when we met. But so far as he knows, I was just the victim of a random act of violence. Wrong place, wrong time. He doesn't know anything about where I come from, who my father was, or who he might have been working for."

"Okay, kids, let's dial it back." Jonah kicked back in his chair. "It's safe to say, for now, that we really have no idea who might be behind this. It might or might not have something to do with Mia—although there are enough possibilities on that front that it seems a solid theory for consideration. We used a signal jammer while we were pulling everything out, but whoever did plant stuff is going to know it's been found. Chances are, they'll try something else. Until we know more, it seems sensible that Mia not be left alone."

"I'll be moving in."

Mia opened her mouth to protest, but Brax just rolled on.

"I'm spending most nights there, anyway. I don't think you want either of these two jokers as roommates. This makes the most sense."

He wasn't wrong. And it wasn't as if she didn't want Brax there. But she wished this was happening because it was the next logical step in rebuilding their marriage, not because it was a safety issue. Still, she wasn't about to argue.

"I guess you'd better pack your stuff."

"JAMMER IS LIVE," Holt confirmed. "Go ahead and unlock everything."

Body tensed and ready for action, Brax waited, his favorite Glock 19 a familiar weight in his hand. Jonah and Holt, similarly armed, took flanking positions. Overkill? Maybe. But they'd decided it was better to be safe than sorry.

Mia shot an apprehensive look at the three of them before opening the door to the Mountainview Construction offices. The moment she turned off the alarm, Brax and his friends moved inside as a unit. It didn't matter that they'd never run a military op together. They moved in sync, a different kind of team, as they cleared the building with silent efficiency.

"Clear." Brax slid the Glock back into its holster and flipped on the lights for his first proper look at the office. The building wasn't large. A couple of offices, a small conference room, a bathroom, kitchenette, and a little reception area. The whole thing was a quiet showplace of Mountainview's capabilities, with framed elevations lining the walls, and an assortment of plants adding life to the place.

"You have warehouse space out back?" Jonah asked.

"Yes. We keep equipment, tools, and supplies out there. It's fenced and has a separate alarm system."

"We'll check there once we're done in here."

"If you'll point me to your computer, I'll get my buddy started scoping for any sort of spyware on your network." Holt paused, considering. "I should probably check Porter's computer as well. Do you know his login?"

Mia scrubbed a hand down her face and shook her head.

"Eh, no big deal. Cash can crack it either way."

He headed into the office she indicated, trailed by Jonah, who immediately started removing outlet covers in the search for more surveillance equipment.

Hating the strain he saw around Mia's eyes and mouth, Brax crossed over. "Hey, how you holding up?"

She lifted her hands and dropped them again. "I don't even know how to answer that question. The three of you just essentially tossed my house. I'm grateful you didn't find anything, but this is all so overwhelming. I thought I was safe. I've been following the rules. And now…"

Unable to take the worry inspired by all the things she hadn't said, he stepped close, wrapping around her, as much as a shield as for comfort. "You are safe. I'm not letting anybody get to you. Not again. Neither will Holt or Jonah. And we don't know for sure that this is about you." Not that they had any good alternative explanations, but it seemed worth mentioning, if only to put her more at ease.

"Actually…"

They turned to see Jonah, with the handset of one of the office phones opened up.

He plucked something out of the receiver. "Got another one."

"Fuck," Brax muttered.

The front door to the office opened. Without conscious thought, Brax pivoted to put himself between Mia and the threat and whipped out his Glock.

Porter stopped in the doorway, hands raised, eyes wide. "What the actual hell?"

He lowered his weapon immediately, sliding it back into its holster. "Sorry."

"Jesus, Brax." Mia scooted out from behind him. "Sorry, Porter."

A muscle jumped in the other man's jaw. "I'm going to assume you have an excellent reason for pointing a gun in the vicinity of my wife."

Wincing, Brax lifted his empty hands in placation and shifted his gaze to Maggie. "Again, apologies. Truly. It's been a tense few hours. We're a little on edge."

Porter's gaze slid to Mia, then beyond them both to where Jonah and Holt were going through Mia's office. Jonah had the grace to look sheepish at the partly disassembled phone in his hand, but he didn't make any effort to explain. They all looked at Mia. This was her show. Her secret. Brax could see her weighing her options, struggling with the knowledge that there really was no way around bringing them into the circle.

At last, she blew out a shaky breath. "You may as well come in. This prospectively impacts you."

The two of them stepped inside. Brax immediately locked the door to stop anyone else from strolling in.

Maggie laid a hand on Mia's shoulder. "Are you all right?"

A humorless laugh escaped. "Oh, not even a little bit. What are you doing here, anyway?"

Porter closed ranks from the other side. "My phone gave the alert that the alarm had been disabled. We were on our way home from Jam Night, and I wanted to swing by to check on you. I know how you like to work when you can't sleep. What the hell is going on?"

Brax liked seeing how they flanked her, making a protective unit. She'd made connections here. People who cared about her. People who looked out for her. It didn't make up for all the years he hadn't been there, but it made him feel a little better that she hadn't been alone for all of it, and that there was someone other than Luca.

"Holt, is the jammer still up?" Mia called.

"Yup."

"Brax, Jonah, can you clear the conference room?"

Jonah abandoned the phone. "On it."

"Clear the conference room of what? What are they looking for?" Porter asked.

"Just... wait until they're through."

They made quick work of it, finding nothing in the outlets, behind the vents, beneath the conference table, or hidden in any of the myriad of plants. It was possible they missed something, without fully dumping the flora, but so far, none of the equipment had been that thoroughly hidden. Someone who'd known what they were doing had been in and out quickly.

"It's clear." Brax skimmed a hand down Mia's arm to link his fingers with hers. "You want me in there for this?"

She nodded, and the four of them filed into the room, shutting the door while Holt and Jonah continued the search.

Maggie arched one cool blonde brow. "I'm guessing this has something to do with that thing you aren't at liberty to discuss."

"Yeah, well, it seems that thing is rearing up to bite me in the ass, so it's time I let you in on some things."

Mia held tight to his hand as she told the story again. Her words were halting, as if she had to force them out. She'd spent so long hiding, so long keeping the secret. Did this hurt? Or was there relief in finally bringing others into her confidence?

Her eyes glittered with unshed tears by the time she finished. "I'm sorry. If I'd had any idea this would follow me here, I never would've come. I'd never knowingly put anyone in danger."

Maggie shoved up from her chair, circling the table to wrap Mia in a tight hug. "I know what it is to keep a secret from everyone you care about. I can't imagine having to live with this one. Whatever happens, none of this is your fault."

Mia hiccupped once and tucked her head against Maggie's shoulder. "Thanks."

Porter reached out to clasp her other hand. "I knew we were lucky with our foster situation. Anybody who spends any time in the system hears stories. I'm sorry y'all weren't. And I'm sorry that whatever this is has encroached on what you've built here. What can we do to help?"

It wasn't until he saw the stunned disbelief on her face that Brax realized she'd expected to lose everything. And hadn't that been the case for her all along? She'd lost her mother, her name, her father, even him. Why wouldn't she think the friends and the life she'd made here would be the next casualties?

Holt knocked on the door. "We're finished."

"What did you find?" Brax needed to know what they were

up against, so they could figure out a plan of action and make Mia feel safe again.

Holt came in, taking one of the other chairs at the table. "Nothing to the extent we pulled out of the job site. Just the one bug in the phone and some spyware on the computers. Since this isn't where you spend the lion's share of your time, it makes sense they didn't put too much effort in here."

Jonah dropped into the last seat. "What all do you do from the computer here?"

Mia considered the question. "Um, work schedules. Budgets. Email. Contracts. Invoicing. All the stuff we need to run the business."

"Do you handle any personal correspondence from either of these computers?"

Mia shook her head. "No. I mean, who the hell would I correspond with? I've isolated myself most of my life, and the few people I keep up with, I'd just call or text."

Brax squeezed her hand. "Whoever planted this wouldn't know that, though. Do either of you remember noticing anything out of the ordinary around here? The alarm being off, or something not being locked when it should've been?"

Porter straightened. "Yeah. I came in a few weeks back and found the door unlocked and the alarm not set. But it was right after Brax showed up. You kinda had a lot going on, so I just thought it had slipped your mind. I didn't think anything about it because nothing looked disturbed."

Maggie crossed her legs. "Y'all have removed surveillance equipment here and at the job site. Presumably, whoever put it there will want to know what happened and might go check on it. Shouldn't we notify the police so someone's watching the place?"

"We put our own surveillance on the bakery," Jonah explained. "Anybody comes out since we left today, we'll know about it. But we probably should loop Xander in on all this."

Mia whimpered and dropped her head to the table. This whole thing had to be like emotionally going ten rounds with Mike Tyson.

Brax laid a hand on her back. "I think Mia's had enough for the night. I don't see that there's anything the police can do tonight that we haven't already done. If you two want to loop him in tonight to get somebody physically sitting on site, fine, but tomorrow's soon enough for her to have to go through this shit again."

"Works for me," Jonah agreed. "And I think it goes without saying that, even when we do read him in, we keep all of this on the down low. It'll be to our advantage if our guy, whoever he is, doesn't know who knows. Everything needs to be business as usual. Can you do that, Mia?"

She straightened. "I've spent my whole life acting. What's another day?"

15

Mia shaded her eyes, watching Brax tightrope walk along the edge of the roof. "Take it easy up there. You've never installed a tin roof before."

He just flashed her that smile that stopped her heart. "I've got this, Baby. I want to put my stamp on everything in this place. Really make it mine."

She understood the need for that. They'd had little enough that they could truly call theirs over the years. Ownership was a big deal to them both. Still, she didn't like seeing him up there. She'd be glad when the installation was over and he was back on solid ground.

The place was shaping up. With the new siding and roofline, very little remained to remind people that this had once been The Right Attitude. That had been the entire point of the design, and Mia was proud of the work she'd done here, taking the uninspired chunk of cinderblock and concrete and turning it into something with character and style. The building would serve the guys well, and hopefully, despite all the interruptions, Mountainview would pull off completion of the renovation more or less on time.

An engine revved and tires spit gravel. Mia whirled in time to see a black SUV flying up the drive. Time slowed down, stretched out, so she saw the window lower by inches as it had on another street, in another city, in what felt like another lifetime.

No!

But she couldn't run. Couldn't scream as the barrel of the gun emerged. The muzzle flashed, a syncopated rhythm of destruction. Windows shattered. People shouted. And still, she could do nothing.

No, not again!

But the searing pain of bullets didn't rip into her flesh.

With a rubber-band snap, time sped up again. Baffled, she watched the SUV drive away. She was still alive.

Something crashed behind her, and Mia spun to see Brax in a crumpled heap on the new porch. Blood spread beneath him, staining the boards a deep maroon.

Terror propelled her forward.

"No. No. No. No! No!" She skidded to a halt beside him, dropping to her knees, rolling him over. Blood pulsed from multiple wounds. Sobbing, she pressed her hands to two, desperate to stop the bleeding.

"Mia." His voice sounded far away, weak. Blood leaked from the corner of his mouth, and those storm gray eyes she so loved were dim and full of pain.

"You're gonna be okay. Just hang on. You have to be okay. Somebody call an ambulance!"

"Mia."

Beneath her slick hands, his labored breathing slowed.

Her tears fell harder as she bent over him. "No. No, you can't leave me. Don't leave me."

But his chest was no longer moving, and his eyes had gone glassy and still.

Someone pulled her back. "He's gone."

She jerked free. "No!"

Luca took a firmer grip on her arms, tugging her away. "Honey, he's gone."

Mia screamed, letting out all the impotent rage and pain and grief.

He shook her hard. "Mia!"

She came out of the dream still screaming, fighting at the hands holding her.

"Mia! Baby, snap out of it. Wake up."

The sound of Brax's voice had her sobbing again as she dove for him, running her hands over his chest, checking for wounds. But there was no blood. The whole damned thing had been a nightmare. Locking her arms tight around him, she pressed her face into his throat, where she could feel the hammer of his pulse.

His breath shuddered out as he curled around her. "That must've been one hell of a bad dream."

"You were dead, and it was all my fault."

She'd broken the rules. She'd told him the secret. It was the thing she'd been warned of over and over again, how she'd been kept in line for years. And now he was at risk.

"I'm okay. I'm fine. Nothing's gonna happen to me."

"You don't know that. We don't know who this is or what they want or how far they'll go to get it."

He stroked the hair back from her face. "Baby, I know you're scared. But we're going to figure this out. Nobody's gonna get hurt, let alone killed."

The bedroom door flew open, crashing back against the wall, and she screamed again. Leno came charging through, teeth bared as he took a flying leap onto the bed, looking for the threat.

Worried he'd lunge at Brax, she grabbed his collar. "Stand down, Leno. Everything's okay. Everything's fine. It was just a bad dream."

Finding no one to attack, he whined and collapsed across her legs, licking at the tears on her face.

She hooked an arm around the dog and laid back down. "I'm okay, pal. I'm okay."

Brax stretched out behind her, and sandwiched there between him and Leno, she finally settled, letting the last vestiges of the nightmare go. She wanted to cocoon up and stay here the rest of the day. The rest of forever. Here, they were safe. Brax was whole.

But today was supposed to be business as usual. They'd all agreed. So, it didn't matter that she'd barely slept, or that she felt like she'd been hit by a truck. They had to get up and start their day. The day that would inevitably lead to her having to tell her story yet again, to the police this time. The idea of enduring another recitation, plus all the questions they'd inevitably have, had her wanting to pull the covers over her head to hide.

When the actual alarm clock sounded sometime later, she sighed and slapped it off.

Brax pressed a kiss to her shoulder. "Why don't you hop in the shower? I'll let Leno out and start the coffee."

"If I have to."

She stood under the spray for a long time, wishing it would wash the images of blood from her brain. The crew could finish the remaining siding without them. She'd see that Brax worked inside today. Maybe nobody was planning on doing some kind of drive-by, but she wasn't about to take any chances with him.

By the time she made it to the kitchen, Brax had made more than just coffee. He pulled muffins out of the oven, scenting the air with cinnamon and nutmeg. Mia didn't ask where those had come from. Since he'd been spending more time over here, her cabinets had acquired a whole host of additional baking ingredients. As she'd been reaping the benefits, she certainly wasn't going to complain.

"Apple muffins. I know you're probably not hungry, but you should try to eat something."

Knowing he was right, she slid onto a stool at the counter and dug up a smile for him. "Smells great."

He plated up two and poured her a mug of coffee. "Jonah called while you were in the shower."

"Oh?" Everything in her tensed with dread.

"He and Holt got Xander up to speed last night. They did put a deputy on site. Nobody showed up. There was no evidence on our system either. Whoever planted everything may well decide it's not worth trying to get back in, rightly assuming we'll be on the lookout for any additional equipment."

"So, now what? You don't think whoever it is will just walk away."

"I don't know what to think. If this was about monitoring you to make sure you aren't revealing privileged information, could be they're satisfied that you're no threat."

"And if it's about something else?"

He jerked his shoulders. "Right now, no news is good news. We'll take the quiet night for what it was."

She relaxed a little and nibbled at a muffin. "So far, everything has been about observation. If this was somehow connected to the people my father worked for, it doesn't seem like they'd go to this much trouble, over this much time, without some kind of action. There are easier ways to figure out schedules and routines if their true end goal was to target me."

"All true. Which is what makes me lean toward something related to Curt. Or someone who's trying to determine whether he left messes that needed to be cleaned up."

Mia grimaced. "Well, that's a cheery thought."

"You're not a mess. And in that scenario, it seems unlikely they'd target me. So maybe you can chill out enough to really eat that other muffin instead of reducing it to crumbs."

She looked down at the pile of cinnamon apple goodness on her plate. "Sorry."

Once he was satisfied that she'd eaten something, Brax cleared their breakfast dishes into the dishwasher and pulled her in for a hug. "You actually up to today?"

"I'll feel better when I get to work. It's something I can control." Far too many things felt out of her hands. She needed to get hers on something that would produce results.

"Then let's get to it."

They both stepped outside. Her truck looked wrong, somehow, relative to the house. Mia paused on her front walk, blinking, trying to get her sleep-deprived brain to process what was in front of her.

"Son of a bitch," Brax growled.

It wasn't until he'd rushed forward that she realized her front two tires were flat. Hurrying after him, she circled around to the back of the truck, confirming that the two rear tires had suffered the same fate. One tire she could chalk up to a nail or other job-site detritus. God knew, she had that happen often enough. But all four at once? That didn't happen without human intervention.

"They got mine, too."

Which meant that whoever was behind this had been at her house after they got back late last night. They'd violated her safe space.

This wasn't waiting. This wasn't observation. This was action. Violent action. The tires weren't just punctured. They were slashed.

"We need to call the police."

Feeling a headache circling behind her eyes already, Mia reached for her phone. It rang before she even got it out of her pocket. Luca's number. She really wasn't up to dealing with him right now, but she'd put him off long enough. She had to at least answer this time.

"Luca, this isn't—"

"You need to get down here right now."

Mia went cold. "What's wrong?"

"The bakery's been vandalized."

By the time one of the crew swung by to pick them up, the parking lot at the job site was swarming with people. Three Sheriff's Department cruisers were angled in front of the door, and yellow crime scene tape had been stretched across it, the ends fluttering in the breeze. As they drove up, Brax scanned the exterior, looking for damage. But the framing for the roof and porch appeared to be unchanged, and the siding they'd put up yesterday was still intact. A sick feeling set up in his gut. What were they going to find inside?

Various members of the crew milled about the gravel lot, expressions divided between grave and pissed. Several lifted their hands in greeting, but nobody rushed over, seeming to sense that now wasn't the time for delays.

Luca stepped out of the building, ducking under the crime scene tape to meet them. His dark eyes glittered with fury, his jaw set, and for once, it wasn't aimed at Brax.

"How bad?" Mia asked.

"You're gonna need to brace yourself."

She squeezed her eyes shut and nodded, starting to step forward.

But Brax caught her arm. "Before we go in, is it *just* vandalism? No one's hurt?" The last thing she needed was to walk in on a body or something.

Catching his drift, Luca shook his head. "Nobody's hurt. It's just stuff. The police are inside."

Following his lead, they ducked under the crime scene tape and stepped into chaos. In the course of ripping out the ceiling and upgrading the electrical, they'd planned to overhaul the lighting. But the fixtures hadn't yet been installed, so work lights had been hauled in to illuminate the scene. Their harsh glare showed the pallet-board shiplap in the front room, pock-marked with holes. Big ones, presumably from a sledgeham-mer. Others had been pried off and tossed on the floor. Cameras flashed as Investigator Hammond and Deputy Brooks documented the damage.

Xander stood near the door to the kitchen, talking to Holt and Jonah. Luca passed them, gesturing Mia and Brax into the back. The kitchen, still waiting for all the commercial appli-ances—thank God—was ransacked. Debris was piled in the space they'd prepared for the walk-in cooler. The range they'd salvaged had been beat to shit, one side caved in and the controls destroyed. The gas lines were intact. A small mercy. But all of this was a big fucking escalation from observation. Brax wondered what was next and if the perpetrator would be satisfied stopping with inanimate objects.

Mia said nothing as she took in the destruction.

"The worst of it is out here." Luca led them to the newly finished bathrooms.

Mia stepped inside first. Some sound slipped out, some-thing between a sob and a scream that had Brax moving in behind her. All the freshly laid tile was busted. The sinks were cracked in half, the mirror above them shattered. The only thing unmolested were the stall partitions. Their doors hung open to reveal a pool of water around the upgraded toilets—tanks cracked, seats ripped off. The only reason the place hadn't flooded was the drain in the floor. Someone had, at least, thought to shut off the water supply.

"Is the other one as bad?" Brax asked.

"Yeah," Luca replied.

Which meant the bathrooms would have to be redone entirely. Again.

On a shout of rage, Mia drove her fist into the stall partition.

Before Brax could get to her, Luca had slid between her and the partition.

"Hey. Hey." He pulled her in, and this time she didn't fight him. "It'll be okay."

Her voice hitched as she tucked her head against Luca's shoulder. "They destroyed everything."

That gesture, more than anything else, told Brax how much she trusted the other man. And he had no idea what to think about it.

Luca stroked her hair, his tone softening as he spoke. "Not everything. And what's broken can be fixed."

"All that loss. Materials. Money. Time. We were already behind schedule."

"Yeah. I know. But we'll fix it. We know how, and we're really fucking good at what we do." When she didn't respond, Luca pulled back and tipped her chin up. "We'll fix it. Okay?"

Mia swallowed and nodded.

He wiped at the tears streaking her cheeks. "Now pull yourself together to go talk to the cops. The sooner the formalities are sorted, the sooner we can get started setting things to rights."

Brax watched the exchange and wondered how the hell Mia didn't realize Luca was in love with her. Whatever else the man was, Brax would lay money he'd never hurt her. Not on purpose, anyway. And he didn't think the other guy's anger over the vandalism was feigned. His work had been destroyed, too, and he was well and truly pissed. Which meant Mia was probably right, and he wasn't behind any of this.

She stepped back, swiping both hands down her face. "Okay. Let's go do the thing."

Brax didn't ask if she was okay. He knew she wasn't, knew she'd be second guessing and blaming herself. Luca was right. The only way she was likely to feel better would be to take control and rectify the situation. So, he merely followed as she crossed to join Xander and the others.

The sheriff nodded at them both. "Mia. Brax. I understand y'all had some problems at your place, as well?"

"All our tires were slashed," Brax told him.

Xander arched his brows. "Well, I'd say somebody's having a right tantrum over all this. Neither of you heard or saw anything out of the ordinary?"

Mia wrapped her arms around her middle. "No. We didn't get home until after eleven last night, and my dog didn't raise any alarm."

"All right. As soon as we wrap things here, I'll have someone go over to check your house."

It was the next step, but it felt like nothing. Simmering with impatience, Brax folded his arms. "So how the hell did someone get past your deputy and our surveillance to do this?"

"The security feed was spliced with a loop. Cash confirmed it just a bit ago," Holt explained.

"As to my deputy, he was here from about midnight on, as soon as I was informed. He didn't come inside at the time, and the exterior looked fine, so we presume the damage was already done by the time he got here."

"We figure he—or they—were here around about the time we were at the office last night." Jonah shrugged. "So, it looks like we shut the barn door after the horses were already out."

Brax swore. None of them had thought their target would act this fast. What else would that mistake cost them?

Looking sick, Mia scooped a hand through her hair. "I'm sorry."

"Why are you sorry?" Jonah asked. "You didn't do this."

"But I—" She cut herself off, glancing around at the others in the room. "If not for me, this wouldn't be happening."

"Maybe, maybe not. We don't know the whys behind any of this yet," Xander said evenly. "That's just one possibility."

"Either way, nobody's blaming you," Holt added.

Brax could tell by the distant look in her eyes that she wasn't buying it. She needed something constructive to do. "How long until we can start the cleanup process?"

"It'll probably take another couple hours to process the scene here and talk to everybody. Then we'll need to do the same at y'all's house. But I expect y'all can dive in early this afternoon."

"Is there any reason I can't walk around and make notes in the meantime?" Mia asked.

"Nope. Just don't disturb anything."

She nodded. "I'm gonna get started figuring the damage to the budget and timeline."

Brax started to follow her out, but she held up a hand. "Just... I need a minute. Okay?"

"All right."

He watched her go, feeling powerless to do anything to make things better for her.

Luca strode over. "Brax. A word."

Whatever softness he'd had for Mia was gone, replaced by his usual I-want-to-crack-some-heads expression. Brax was low on sleep and tolerance, and the last thing Mia needed was for the two of them to be snarling at each other like a couple of junkyard dogs. But he met the man halfway.

"Look, we really don't have time right now for whatever territorial pissing contest you've got in mind."

Luca's brows drew together for a moment before he nodded. "I deserved that. But that's not what this is about. I'm worried about Mia. She's gonna take this real hard. She shouldn't be left alone, or she'll get too deep in her head. I don't want to see her backslide from this."

What the hell did that mean?

"Has this happened before? One of her work sites being vandalized?"

"Once. We did a lot of flips in crap neighborhoods that were going through gentrification. Had some guy, high on God knows what, break in and trash one of them two days before the open house. She was there by herself. Hid in a closet upstairs until he left. She wasn't hurt, but..." Luca trailed off, his face clouding with self-condemnation. "I should have fucking been there."

Brax could relate. How much more had she been through that he hadn't been around to protect her from? "Was the guy caught?"

"Yeah. That helped. But she was in bad shape mentally for a long while after. I've never left her alone on a job since. Not until she moved here." He shifted on his feet. "Look, man, I don't know how much you know about her past, but she's got some serious trauma. She's never gotten into it with me, and I've never pushed. I admit, I assumed you were to blame for a lot of it, no matter what she said. I can see different now. She trusts you, and I trust her, so I'm going out on a limb to trust you with her. Stick close and fucking take care of her this time. Okay?"

Brax hadn't expected an olive branch. It made him think that somewhere past whatever rivalry they had going on was a man he might be able to respect. "Count on it."

Apparently satisfied, Luca nodded. "I'm gonna go help her with inventorying this mess. She'll do better if she's occupied."

"Okay. Oh, hey. Since you've been around for a long time, do you ever remember seeing anybody following her? Watching her?" Maybe this wasn't the first time.

Luca blinked, taken aback. "Not anybody specific. Not more than the kind of attention any attractive woman gets from assholes out there. Why? Is she in some kind of trouble?"

Mia hadn't brought him into the loop. Hadn't told him about her past. It wasn't Brax's place to do that now. "We don't know for sure. But just... keep an eye out, will you?" They needed all the help they could get.

"You've got it."

After Luca went outside, Brax rejoined his friends.

"You two reach some kind of truce?" Holt asked.

"Something like that. Can you get Cash to run him?"

Holt went brows up. "You still don't trust him?"

"I don't think he's out to hurt Mia. But no, I don't trust him."

"I'll see what Cash can find out."

16

In the three days since they'd been granted access back to the job site, Mia had barely slept. The crew had stayed late every day, working like stevedores to clear out the damage and prep everything for repairs. She'd stayed even later, needing to see more progress and take control of the one thing that was actually in her hands. Luca, God love him, had stuck by her side, working shoulder-to-shoulder with her like the old days. That little piece of normal helped put her back on even keel. But she couldn't forget that there'd been a police presence parked outside since the latest break-in. And there was no overlooking the fact that Brax was in bodyguard mode. He'd worked as well, teaming up with Holt and Jonah to do the necessary manual labor of tearing apart more pallets and planing the boards to repair the shiplap walls. But they were all watchful, and that kept her on edge. Everyone was waiting for the other shoe to drop, wondering when and how their perpetrator would strike next. It was no longer a question of if.

"Sealant's dry," Luca declared. "I think we're ready to put down the uncoupling membrane and get rolling on redoing these tile floors."

The bathrooms, having borne the brunt of the destruction, were the last area that still needed major repairs. New fixtures were on order and were supposed to come in by the end of the week. Mia wanted the tile laid and grouted so they could install new sinks and toilets and be done. Not that she'd forget the enormous cost of labor and replacement materials, but she needed to see it put right sooner rather than later.

"Let's do it." The three of them were the only ones left, and she was appreciating the relative peace and having full control over the radio.

"It's getting pretty late," Brax pointed out. "You need a break. This can wait until tomorrow."

Her stomach chose that moment to issue its protests about the pace she'd been keeping, which generally had her eating only when someone made her. "Okay, yeah, I'm starving, but I really want to finish this piece. The mortar will have to dry under the uncoupling membrane. Why don't you go grab some takeout for dinner and bring it back? We should be finished by then, or close to. Then we'll be in good shape for laying tile tomorrow."

"Mia, I'm not leaving you here alone."

"I won't be alone. The deputy is still outside, and Luca's here. He's not going to let anything happen to me. I have plenty of guard dogs."

Brax's stomach gave its own growl.

"I'm gonna go grab the stuff from the truck." Luca strode out, leaving them alone for the moment.

"I don't like this," Brax insisted.

"I know. But it'll be fine. It'll take you fifteen or twenty minutes—max—to go grab something from the tavern." When he only scowled, Mia stepped into him, laying a hand over his heart. "Please. I need to finish this."

Luca came back with the roll of polyurethane that would provide some cushion and protect the tile from any moisture or cracking and shifting of the concrete foundation. "If you're taking orders, I could absolutely go for a burger."

Brax growled. "Fine. But you stay inside and keep the door locked until I get back."

"Promise." She drew an X over her heart.

He called their orders in before he left with another reminder to lock the door. She did as he'd demanded before rejoining Luca on the floor of the women's bathroom to start cutting the uncoupling membrane.

"I really appreciate you putting in all this extra time."

He shot her a smile. "I've missed working with you like this. I mean, obviously not under these circumstances, but I miss what we used to do together. Those flips that were just us doing everything."

"I've missed working with you, too." And she had. She loved the work she did here and appreciated the variety of projects that Mountainview offered. But there was definitely something to be said for having her hands on all stages of a renovation.

For a couple minutes, they measured and cut. Fully in sync, in the way of a team who'd worked together for years.

"Do you ever regret leaving Washington? I mean, is this whole owning a construction company, and juggling all the headaches and stuff that go along with that, really worth it for you?"

"There are days I miss the simple. I certainly don't have a passion for doing payroll or work schedules. But I like the life I'm building here. Or did, before everything got blown all to hell with whatever's going on with all of this. And if I'd never come here, I never would have had the opportunity to clear the air with Brax."

Mia knew it wasn't what Luca wanted to hear, but for once, he didn't pop off with a snarky remark.

He nodded. "He's very protective of you."

"Yeah. He always was. I know I've never really talked about

him with you, beyond the basics. Before you, he was my best friend. He looked out for me all those years we were in the foster system. And after. He saved me from being sexually assaulted by one of my foster fathers."

Luca's face twisted in pain and realization. "That's why you don't like being touched."

"Yeah."

"I always wondered." His hands fisted. "Did the bastard pay for it?"

"Brax beat the shit out of him. And then he went to jail. So, yeah."

His hands relaxed again. "Good." He hesitated a moment. "Was that... the only time you were in that kind of situation? You don't have to answer that if you don't want."

"No, it's okay. Yeah, that was the only time. And it only happened because Brax had aged out and couldn't be there twenty-four hours a day to watch over me. Those years in the foster system were... hard. I learned to compartmentalize everything about my life. Put up all kinds of walls. It's why I tend to be slow to warm up. But Brax was in it with me from the start. I know you don't agree with the fact that I'm giving him another chance, but you have to understand what a big part of my life he's always been."

Luca pressed his lips together, concentrating very hard on the line he was cutting. "You're happy with him?"

"I am. We're still figuring everything out, but things have been good. Having him back in my life has been really, really good."

It wasn't the answer he wanted. She could see it in the carefully controlled lines of his face, which just confirmed what she'd been afraid of. He had more feelings for her than she could return, and she had no idea what to do about it.

He rose. "I'm gonna go grab the mortar mix while you finish up cutting in here."

Knowing he needed a minute to collect himself, she just nodded, and kept at the work. When he got back, she was going to have to address this. It was the pink elephant she'd been willfully ignoring for a long time. She didn't want to hurt him. He was her friend. He'd been there for her through some of the worst parts of her life. But she was in love with Brax. She wanted to stay married to Brax. Sure, they hadn't actually discussed that part, but everything in his actions suggested he wanted the same. Luca needed to know that was her intention.

Mia cut the last piece of underlayment. What the hell was taking him so long? Maybe he was already mixing up the mortar? They really ought to cut the pieces for the men's room as well before they started attaching it. She stood and headed for the door to say so.

It opened just as she reached it.

"I wondered what the hell you got up to..." But she trailed off because it wasn't Luca in the entryway.

The stranger's face went slack for one instant before he sighed. "Fuck, you weren't supposed to be here. I'm not being paid enough for this."

Then he pulled out a gun.

"Order up."

Brax took the bag of food from the tattooed guy tending bar at Elvira's Tavern. "Thanks, man. And I really appreciate you putting a rush on this."

"No problem. Tell Mia I said hello."

He'd been in Eden's Ridge long enough that such a remark no longer surprised him. Much. Eventually, he'd learn everybody's names and be considered a regular himself. What a concept.

With a nod and a wave, he wove his way through the

surprisingly heavy weeknight crowd and back to the parking lot. He was itching to return to the bakery. Sure, Luca was there, but that posed its own problem. For all that he'd been on his best behavior lately, and was unquestionably watching out for Mia, there was the fact that he was doing it because he was in love with her. That kind of feeling didn't just go away, and Brax was pretty damned sure the guy was still hanging around, waiting for him to fuck up.

He got that Mia considered Luca a close friend. But something had to give here. Brax wanted his marriage back fully, and he wasn't sure that was gonna happen so long as Luca was hanging around. Not that he'd bring it up to Mia until the question of her safety was settled. It was going to royally piss her off, and right now, resolving the current threat was priority one. At the moment, the more people looking out for her, the better. But he had hopes that Cash would dig up information that proved the guy was hiding something.

As he made his way back toward the job site, a Sheriff's Department cruiser came flying over the hill, lights flashing, sirens blaring. It blew past Brax, heading in the opposite direction.

Was that the deputy who'd been on duty at the bakery? Brax knew Stone County had a small department with limited staff. At any given time, there were only two to three deputies on duty for the entire county. Xander had said he was happy to keep one of them on-site, as an additional layer of security while they got to the bottom of things, but he'd warned them that if anything major happened, they'd get pulled to go deal with it.

Uneasy with the prospect, Brax put the pedal to the metal, racing to get back.

Sure enough, the spot the cruiser had occupied beneath the lone sodium vapor light that illuminated the parking lot was empty. Instinct had him cutting his headlights and parking at the far edge of the gravel lot. Nothing looked amiss. The big white work truck with the Mountainview Construction logo on the door was still parked by the front of the building, and light spilled out of the windows. Still, as he slipped out of the driver's seat, Brax unholstered his Glock.

Moving quick and quiet across the gravel, he scanned the parking lot. Something lay on the ground beside the truck. Why the fuck hadn't they gotten the extra exterior lights installed yet? He couldn't see well in the shadows. Were those... boots?

Heart hammering, he circled around to find Luca face-down in the gravel. In the faint moonlight, blood glinted dark on the back his head. *Shit! Shit! Shit!* Terror for Mia exploded through him. He took one moment to feel the wild whip of it before locking the emotion down. He was no good to her panicked.

Crouching, he felt Luca's neck for a pulse. It was weak but there.

Creeping toward the front, he strained to hear anything from inside. The radio was still playing on the classic rock station Mia preferred. Beneath that, he detected voices. One man. One woman. She was still alive.

Carefully, he tested the front door. It was locked. Did that mean the assailant had locked it behind him or had he come in the back?

Brax crept around the side to peer in the windows. His blood ran cold at the sight of the gun pressed to Mia's torso. Her face was ashen, tears streaking down her cheeks. Brax knew she'd had some additional training over the years, but he prayed she didn't try to use it. Not against a gun. He had to get in there.

Keeping low, he hurried around to the delivery entrance, thanking God he had his keys. Banking that the guy wouldn't hear over the sound of his own voice and the radio, Brax unlocked the door and eased into the kitchen. The pass-through window was open, the rolling door not yet installed. He made use of the partial cover, crouching beneath the half-wall.

"—been here all along. Where's the flash drive?"

That accent definitely wasn't from around here. Was it Brooklyn? Bronx? Jersey? Or was it just what Brax imagined any of those sounded like based on what he'd heard in movies?

"I don't... kn... know what you're t... t... talking about." The fear in Mia's voice was palpable and had Brax's grip tightening on the gun.

"The files, woman. Where the fuck are the files?" She cried out as the assailant shook her, and Brax almost broke cover and came over the wall. But he had to play this smart. So long as that gun was near her, she was at risk.

"I don't have anything. I swear. My father never gave me anything."

The assailant snarled in frustration and disgust. "I've been telling him it's not here."

"What are you talking about? What's not here?"

"Shut up! I have to think. This is not what I signed on for. It was just supposed to be retrieving information. This whole thing has been a clusterfuck from the beginning."

Brax eased slowly up, hazarding a look, but he didn't have a clear shot at the guy. One hand was clamped on Mia's nape, the other still holding the gun to her side as he looked around the building, as if that was going to give him the answer he needed.

"Look, just let me go. I don't know who you are or what you want. Just let me go."

With a look of some regret, the guy shook his head at her. "Can't do that, girlie. You're a loose end. I don't leave loose ends. Bad for business."

Muscles coiling for action, Brax frantically ran scenarios

through his mind. How could he distract the guy enough to let go of Mia?

"Get in there." The guy shoved her forward, toward one of the open bathroom doors.

As he did, Brax began to rise... and his cell phone chimed with a text.

The assailant whipped around, leading with the pistol in his hand. Brax didn't hesitate. He did what he'd been trained to do and squeezed the trigger.

The echo of gunshots was deafening. Mia screamed.

Brax vaulted over the pass-through, charging forward. But the assailant stumbled back, letting Mia go. His eyes had gone wide, his olive-complected face pale. He looked down at the spreading stain on his chest and crumpled to the floor. Brax kicked his gun away and turned toward Mia, his heart all but stopping as he saw her curled into a ball on the floor. Had there been a ricochet? Had she been shot?

"Mia! Baby!" He dropped to his knees beside her, terrified of what he might find.

Shaking hard, she uncurled a fraction, peering up at him with wide, panic-stricken eyes. "You sh... shot him."

Shit. Was she afraid of *him?* Realizing he still held the gun, he holstered it. "Yeah. Are you okay?" He reached for her, relieved when she didn't shrink away at his touch. Finding no injuries, he crushed her to him, careful to keep himself between her and the body. "Christ, I thought I'd be too late."

Mia curled into him, holding tight as she trembled. "I thought it would be okay. I thought—" She jerked back. "Oh my God. Luca. Where's Luca? He went out to the truck and then this guy came in."

"Unconscious but breathing when I got here."

She scrambled up, and they hurried outside, skirting the body of the gunman.

Mia dropped to her knees beside her friend. "Oh, God." Her

hands hovered over the wound, falling instead to his shoulders. "Help me roll him over."

As they did, Luca groaned. "Fuck."

"You're alive. Oh, thank God." She wrapped her arms around him.

"Wha... what was in that drink?"

"No drinks, man. Pretty sure you got pistol whipped. I'll call 911." Brax straightened, finally pulling out his phone and noting the text from Holt before dialing.

"911, what is your emergency?"

"This is Brax Whitmore." He reeled off the address. "I'm gonna need an ambulance and the Sheriff's Department. A man's been shot."

17

Mia finally dropped off to sleep near dawn. Brax wished he'd been able to do the same, but his mind wouldn't turn off. Needing to move, he slipped out of bed, leaving her curled up with Leno and heading for the kitchen.

They'd stumbled home well past midnight, after enduring what had felt like an endless parade of county officials. The Sheriff's Department, who'd left the bakery unguarded in response to a domestic violence call down in Hyde's Hills Trailer Park. The fire department EMT, who'd been dispatched ahead of the ambulance that had to come all the way from Johnson City. The county coroner. Because Brax had killed a man tonight.

There'd been questions. So many questions. But ultimately, they'd both been released.

The dead man had been identified as Joe Abruzzi, an ex-con with a rap sheet about half a mile long, though none of the charges had been for violent crimes. He had a talent for electronics and specialized in information retrieval. He was, indeed, originally from Jersey, though he'd headed south after being released from his latest incarceration. According to what Cash had dug up, his services were advertised on the dark web, and he had done work for the mob family Mia's father had been suspected of working for. It proved nothing. The guy had done work for a lot of less-than-reputable people. But the connection seemed too great to be a simple coincidence. What information he'd been looking for and who'd hired him were still questions with no answers. The authorities had impounded the older sedan they'd found on the scene, but Brax had little faith they'd find much when going through it. Abruzzi had been thorough. Careful.

And now he was dead.

Brax didn't feel guilty about it. Despite the lack of violent crimes attached to the man, he would've killed Mia.

No, the guilt came from knowing that if anything had delayed Brax mere minutes in getting back, he would've been too late. Because the man he'd entrusted with Mia's safety had failed to protect her. The guy who'd been lying about his reasons for coming to Tennessee, according to what Cash had ferreted out. Yeah, Luca had been hurt himself. Concussed. But his injuries hadn't been sustained in a fight. He'd been over-powered without even knowing about the fucking threat, leaving Mia to fend for herself.

Exactly how long was this latest trauma going to haunt her? It had taken years before she'd stopped having nightmares about the foster father who'd nearly raped her. Knowing Wayne was behind bars had only helped a little. And then there were all the traumas Brax hadn't been around for. While he'd eliminated this most immediate threat, there was no knowing whether whoever had hired Abruzzi would send someone else. Clearly, whatever he'd been looking for hadn't been found. Would they ever get a clear resolution, or was she doomed to simply live the rest of her life looking over her shoulder?

He'd do almost anything to give his wife a sense of peace and safety. But he didn't know how to achieve that. And he wasn't positive she didn't look at him differently. It was one thing to know he'd killed in the line of duty. What had happened last night was something else entirely.

When Brax realized he'd been standing in front of the open cabinet for nearly five minutes, without even seeing the contents, he shut the door. Much as he might take comfort in baking something right now, he wanted the violence of beating the shit out of some bread dough, and he wasn't sure the noise wouldn't wake Mia. She needed the rest more than he needed to channel his frustrations into cooking.

A soft knock sounded on the front door.

Who the hell was here at this hour?

A glance through the sidelight had his temper spiking. He yanked the door open. "What the hell are you doing here?"

Luca shifted on his feet. "I saw the light and wanted to check on Mia."

"She's sleeping. And you're concussed. You shouldn't be driving."

"Look, can I come in for a minute?"

Maybe he wanted to apologize for dereliction of duty. Brax would accept that and then kick his ass out. He stepped back, and Luca strode inside, looking far worse for wear, with dark circles under his eyes and blood still matted in his blond hair around the stitches. Maybe Brax should've felt some sympathy at that, but he just didn't give a shit. He was far too angry.

Luca didn't sit, prowling around the living room instead. "Is she okay?"

Brax stared. "Are you fucking kidding? A man tried to kill her tonight. Of course, she's not okay." It was a struggle to keep his voice low when he wanted to shout.

"I didn't mean it like that. I just... I thought maybe the shooting would bring some shit up for her, and I was worried."

"I'm sure it has, and will, as she has time to process everything." And Brax would make sure she had whatever support or therapy she needed to get through it.

Luca narrowed his eyes. "Why do I get the feeling you're pissed at me about all this?"

"Oh, I'm pissed at you about a lot of things." And in the aftermath of everything that had happened, Brax just didn't have it in him to play nice anymore. "Heading the list is that I trusted you to protect her, and you didn't."

Luca flushed. "I was knocked fucking unconscious. But this isn't really about that, is it?"

Finally, they were getting all of this out in the open. "No. Let's talk about the fact that you've been lying to her about why you're in Tennessee."

"What are you talking about?"

"You spun up some sob story about your ex leaving you for some high society guy. You conveniently left out the part where she really dumped you because you're in love with Mia."

A muscle jumped in his jaw. "You don't know what you're talking about."

"Oh, I had you checked out. I've got a whole dossier on the life and times of one Luca Andrew Gallo. Haven't had time to read more than the highlights yet, but the only part I really care about is that you're in love with my wife, and I'm not okay with it."

All pretense of civility faded from Luca's expression. "Your *wife*. That's rich, considering you didn't even know you were still married for the last fucking decade." He shook his head. "I will never understand her allegiance to you."

"We have history."

"So do we." Luca snarled. He stalked over, vibrating with fury. "Who do you think picked up the pieces after you left? Who do you think held her when she cried after you sent back every single one of those hundred and thirty-seven letters? Did you even realize she sent one for every week you were together? Of course, you didn't. Because you couldn't be bothered to open and read a single one."

Brax couldn't stop himself from flinching as the verbal blow struck against his own potent regrets. No, he hadn't realized the significance of the number. He hadn't even counted. He'd just been relieved when they'd finally stopped.

"Who the fuck do you think is the one who found her after she downed a fifth of Jack and an entire bottle of sleeping pills, because you sent back her last letter and she couldn't take the pain anymore? Who do you think is the one who convinced her she still had something to live for? Who took her to get that semi-colon tattoo after she got out of the hospital as a commitment to try?"

Suicide. Brax's breath wheezed out as if Luca had sucker punched him. Horror, shame, and guilt hit him like a tidal wave. Before he could even begin to react, the other man was pushing on.

"Who do you think was there when she found out she can't have children because of the damage to her body when she got shot? Who do you think is the only one she told that the only reason she didn't bleed out that day was because she was pregnant? Me. I have been there for her every day, giving her support and encouragement and friendship. What the fuck have you ever given her but pain?"

Brax swayed as all the starch went out of his knees.

A baby. She'd been carrying his child. Their child had *died*. And she hadn't told him.

Luca took a step closer, going in for the kill shot. "You don't deserve another chance with her. You wasted the one you had, and nothing you can do will ever make up for how much you hurt her. So why don't you do the one good thing you can do for her and sign those fucking divorce papers? Cut her loose to finally live her life free of your ghost."

From where she stood in the bedroom doorway, Mia sagged against the door frame, absorbing this utter betrayal from the man she'd considered her best friend. Leno whined, pressing against her legs, and she gripped his ruff, as much for comfort as to keep him in place.

She hadn't meant to eavesdrop. But when she'd woken from a fitful sleep to find the bed empty, she'd gotten up to find Brax. The moment she'd opened the door, she'd heard angry male voices. Exhausted and not at all feeling up to playing referee between the two most important men in her life, she'd hesitated, torn between going back to bed and intervening. Then she'd heard Brax accuse Luca of lying, and she hadn't been able to stop herself from listening.

Was he right? Had Luca lied to her about what had happened with Larissa? He hadn't denied it, instead switching to the offensive and falling back on the bitter fact of Brax's absence from her life for the past decade.

And then he'd done the unthinkable and revealed her deepest, darkest secrets to the person they would hurt the most.

Brax said nothing in response to the onslaught, and Mia couldn't move. How the hell could she walk into the middle of all this? What could she possibly say now about why she hadn't told him? If she hadn't avoided the subject, maybe she could've found some way to soften the blow. But Luca had delivered the news in the most hateful, damaging way possible.

The sound of the front door closing broke her paralysis, and she hurried into the living room with no idea what to say to her husband. But it hadn't been some mic drop moment of hate that Luca had walked out on. He was still standing in the middle of the room, looking smug as he stared at the door.

It was Brax who'd walked out.

Mia ran for the door, pulling it open. But he was already

backing his truck out of the drive. She ran out, waving at him to stop. But if he saw her, he didn't slow. He gunned the engine, racing down the street. Leaving her. Again.

She fell to her knees in the cold grass, barely feeling the damp soaking into her flannel pants as she absorbed the devastation of seeing the man she loved walk away without a word. Her breath hitched on a sob, and she curled over, wrapping her arms around herself. How could she survive this again?

Leno bumped against her, but not even her beloved dog could dim this pain.

Gentle hands cupped her arms. "Honey, come inside."

Mia flung Luca off, only barely restraining herself from striking out with all the hurt and anguish rioting through her. "How could you?"

The smug expression was gone, replaced by something that looked like genuine remorse. "It's not what you think."

"Really?" she demanded. "You didn't just spout off my deepest, most personal secrets in a calculated effort to destroy my marriage?"

He blanched, evidently realizing she'd heard everything. On a swallow, he lifted his hands. "I didn't mean to say it. My temper got the best of me. He had me investigated—"

"Oh, bullshit. You've always hated him. You just let fly everything you've wanted to say from the beginning. How *could you*? I *trusted* you."

At her use of the past tense, something that might've been panic flitted over his face. "Mia, please. Come inside. Let's talk about this."

"Do you really think you're going to be able to talk your way out of this?" There was no excuse, no possible explanation that could fix this.

"Maybe not. But I don't think you want your personal business all over your neighborhood. And it will be if you stay out here."

The appeal to her private nature worked where nothing else would. She staggered to her feet. When he reached out to steady her, she snapped, "Don't you fucking touch me."

Leno inserted himself between them, lifting his lip in a snarl. Mia didn't correct him.

She didn't want to talk. Didn't want to listen to Luca's excuses. But she had some more yelling she wanted to do, so she let him come back inside.

Because her legs simply wouldn't support her, she collapsed onto the sofa. Leno took up position next to her, as much guard as emotional support, as Luca began to pace the living room.

"I'm sorry. You were never supposed to hear that. Certainly not like that."

"Is that the only thing you're sorry for? That you got caught?"

He shoved both hands through his hair. "No! No. I— Damn it, Mia, I couldn't take it anymore. Maybe I went about it entirely wrong, but it's all still true. He doesn't deserve you."

Shocked, she could only stare as he doubled down on his argument.

"I'm the one who was there for all of that. I'm the one you came to. I'm the one who supported you. I'm the one who was *there*. Always. I'm the one who loves you. Doesn't that count for anything?"

She closed her eyes. She'd known. Deep down, somewhere, she'd known, and she'd willfully ignored how he felt, believing that it would fade and that he'd eventually accept that she couldn't give him what he wanted. But it was a whole other thing to have it confirmed by him.

So now they'd get this all out in the open. Like purging some kind of wound.

"Of course, it mattered. You've been my best friend for years. I literally wouldn't be here if not for you. I can't ever repay you for saving my life that night. For getting me to the hospital. For being there for me through all the months and years of therapy after. I appreciate that. But none of it gives you the right to tell my darkest secrets, without my permission, to the one person they'd hurt the most."

Face twisting with regret, he took a step toward her, stopping when Leno growled. "You're right. You're absolutely right. I have no excuse. I honestly didn't realize you hadn't told him any of it. You've been talking about working on your marriage, and I just assumed by now you'd worked around to it."

"We've been kind of busy trying to make sure I'm not a victim of a mob hit."

"What?" His voice rose two octaves. "Is *that* what's been going on the past month? What the hell? How did you—"

She held up a hand. "No. You don't get to ask questions about this right now. And you sure as hell have abdicated your position in my inner circle. Tell me about Larissa."

His head kicked back. At the demotion to his friend status or the sudden subject change, she didn't know. Didn't care.

"I told you—"

"No. You told me what you apparently thought I wanted to hear. Tell me the truth. What really happened with her?"

He stared at her for a long moment before releasing a long breath and dropping into a chair. "I've been in love with you for a long damned time. You'd made it clear that, regardless of the fact that Brax abandoned you, you didn't consider yourself free, so when you moved out here, I made a promise to myself that I was going to make a real effort to get over you. It felt like an insurmountable task. Then I met Larissa."

18

Before he'd even hit the end of the street, Brax had fired off a voice text to Jonah and Holt asking one or both of them to come watch the house. He couldn't be here right now, but neither could he leave Mia alone. Leno was there. Luca was there. But he'd already failed her once. There wasn't a chance in hell Brax could get his head on straight without knowing she was okay.

Less than a mile up the road, the return text came in saying they were en route. Brax let out a shuddering breath. She'd be covered. She'd be safe. That was priority one. Now he could absorb the rest of what had just been thrown at him. Somehow.

But not just yet.

Ten minutes later, he found himself knocking on a familiar door before he could think better of it.

Shit. He shouldn't be here. The sun hadn't even peeked over the horizon. It was beyond rude to bother anyone at this ungodly hour. But before he could retreat to his truck, the door opened.

Rebecca stood there in her long flannel robe, eyes heavy from sleep. "Brax?"

"I'm sorry. I didn't know where else to go."

Face creasing in concern, she tugged him inside and straight into a fierce hug. He wrapped his arms around her, aware he was shaking. He felt as if his world was being ripped apart.

Rebecca stroked his back. "Is this about the shooting?"

Good God. For a little bit, he'd forgotten about that. "No. It's Mia."

"Is she all right? Jonah said she wasn't hurt."

"No... she's okay... I..." He didn't know what to say. Didn't even know why he was here, except that she'd offered him comfort before, and her presence was calming. He needed all the help he could get in that department just now.

On another squeeze, Rebecca eased back. "Come on back to the kitchen and sit. I just put on coffee."

She took his hand and pulled him. He let her nudge him into a chair at the table. Her fussing was the only thing keeping him from flying apart.

Once she'd poured coffee for them both, she settled beside him at the table. "Now. Why don't you start at the beginning?"

Brax wrapped his hands around the mug, letting the warmth soak into his chilled skin. "I have to leave out some bits. They aren't my story to tell."

"Okay. Tell me what you can."

"Mia's got this... friend. Luca." He laid it out for her, explaining what he knew of their relationship and how he and Luca had been at loggerheads from the beginning. She listened patiently as he talked about their reluctant truce in the name of protecting Mia. Then he told her about the fight and everything Luca had spilled out in his tirade. Rebecca laid a hand on his arm in comfort before he'd finished. Her face twisted in sympathy.

"Oh, honey."

He scrubbed a hand down his face. "She tried to commit

suicide because of me. Because I was too fucking angry and selfish to listen. To even give her a chance." His voice broke as he imagined the pain she must've been in to get to that point.

Rebecca's hand tightened on his arm. "You can't take the blame for that. You didn't know."

"How could she not tell me?"

"Well, sweetheart, I imagine to stop you from feeling like you're feeling right now. From everything you've said about her, it sounds like she forgave you a long time ago. She wouldn't have wanted to punish you with something like this."

"What about the baby? We had *a child*. And he... she... died." He didn't even know how to sort through all the layers of shock and grief tied up with that. To find out that they'd made a life and lost it all in one breath was gutting him. "And she *didn't tell me*."

"I'm sure the whole thing was extremely traumatic for her. Probably still is to talk about. I'm not saying she should have kept it from you. I can't even begin to imagine what you're feeling about that. It's a hard thing, losing a child, under any circumstances. To find out like this..." She shook her head. "Had you been trying for a baby?"

"No. No, we weren't in any place financially where that wouldn't have been a major disaster. We were still so young. But I thought, when we got back together, that we'd get around to kids. And now... she can't have them. We'll never have another child." How could he feel such loss at something he didn't even realize he'd wanted?

"There are options if you both really want to be parents. Surrogacy if you're set on a child of your blood. Adoption if you're not. With both of you having been foster kids yourselves, I expect you'd both make wonderful parents for a child in need. You know what they're coming from. But that's rather getting ahead of things. Have you talked to Mia about any of this?"

"No. She was sleeping when I left." Or was she? They'd

been shouting by the end. What if she'd woken up and heard? The idea of it left him feeling even sicker.

"I don't know how to talk to her about this. I thought she'd told me everything. But if she left out stuff this big, what else is she keeping from me?" What did he have to do in order to be let inside all those carefully constructed compartments she'd made of her life?

"The only way to find that out is to go back and ask." Sitting back, Rebecca took up her coffee, studying him over the rim of the mug. "The question you need to answer right now is whether you want to fight for the chance to go back and ask. Or is there a part of you that thinks Luca is right, and you don't deserve her?"

Brax sat with that for a minute. "He's not entirely wrong. I've hurt her so badly."

Rebecca inclined her head in acknowledgment. "But she took you back. She wanted to try again. It seems to me that whatever hurts you dealt her, she's made peace with. You have to decide if you can make peace with the hurts she's dealt you."

Could he get past this? He was tired of secrets. Tired of having all these hidden pieces of her past rearing up to stab him when he least expected it. If they were going to make their marriage work, he needed all of her. Full disclosure. And that was going to take a conversation.

"I have to go back."

"Good man. Whatever happens, running is seldom the answer."

"Thank you for listening. I... didn't have a good mother. I'd really like it if I could maybe adopt you as an honorary one."

Rebecca smiled and leaned over to press a smacking kiss to his cheek. "I'd be insulted if you didn't. Now, go fix things with your wife, my boy."

Brax shoved back from the table. "Can I borrow your printer?"

"I TRIED. I really did. But in the end, she knew I wasn't in love with her. Not the way I should have been. So, she left me."

Mia shook her head. "Why didn't you tell me the truth?"

"I didn't lie. She did turn around within a week and go out with the investment banker, so I'm not entirely sure she hadn't been looking before she ended things." Luca jerked his shoulders. "The fact that I wasn't more upset about it was a pretty clear sign. As for the rest, I wasn't going to dump that on you. Certainly not over the phone or in a text. Then you invited me to come out here, and I thought, maybe, you'd finally reached a place where you wanted to move on with your life."

She thought back over all their interactions. Had she misled him somehow? Done something to give him false hope? Or had he just seen what he wanted to see? And why the hell was she feeling guilty about this when he'd just betrayed her?

"I meant exactly what I said when I asked you out here. I thought you could use a change, and I *did* miss you. We've been friends for a long time. But nothing had changed. I was still married to Brax."

Luca snorted. "Right. The absentee husband who thought you were already divorced. Suddenly, he's back in your life, and you just welcomed him with open arms and pushed me away." There was no disguising the bitterness in his voice.

She had done that. Knowing how much antagonism Luca held toward even the idea of Brax, she'd kept her distance, not having the bandwidth to handle them both at once. "I'm sorry if I haven't made time for you since Brax and I found each other again. And I'm sorry I pulled the boss card to do it. That was a shitty way for me to handle it. But I won't apologize for putting my focus on my relationship with him. I've been waiting for ten years for a second chance to save my marriage."

"The marriage he just walked away from again?"

Mia gasped as the barb slid home. Leno jerked his head up, woofing softly, as if to show his own objection.

Luca's voice was soft. "I'm not saying that to hurt you. Truly. Hurting you is the last thing I've ever wanted to do. But I want you to take a good hard look at what you've been clinging to so stubbornly all this time. Whatever history you have with Brax, at the first sign of trouble between you, he walks away. You deserve better than that. You deserve someone who stays. Who will stick it out, no matter what. I've stuck. I've always stuck. And I know you're upset. I know I've fucked up. But I love you, and I just wish you'd give me a chance to show you."

Mia swallowed. She'd brought this on herself, in a way. If she hadn't been so conflict averse, hadn't been so afraid of losing him as a friend, she would have addressed this years ago. And even though she understood it likely meant losing him entirely, she was going to address it now.

"You aren't entitled to me, Luca. I'm not some prize that can be won if you just stick around long enough. Your friendship doesn't earn you anything more than my friendship and loyalty in return. And that's certainly not what you showed me today."

He opened his mouth to protest but she just held up a hand to stop him.

"I know this isn't what you want to hear. Despite everything you've said and done lately, I do love you. But as a friend. A brother. I'm not *in* love with you. And that's never going to change because I'm in love with Brax. I always have been. Always will be."

"And if he doesn't come back?"

She closed her eyes, accepting the very real possibility of that.

"Except I did."

Mia whipped her head toward the voice to find Brax standing in the doorway from the kitchen. Her battered heart began to drum with hope, and she shoved to her feet. Then she spotted the sheaf of papers in his hand.

"Are those the divorce papers?" Oh God. Were the last pieces of herself she'd kept from him going to be the thing that truly broke them?

"Yes."

She struggled to keep standing as she absorbed that.

He stepped into the room. "I wanted to print off a copy for this conversation. My preference is that we burn them, but that'll be your choice. Because I need the truth from you. All of it. Everything you've been holding back. I understand why you've had to live your life with everybody in different boxes and nobody knowing everything. But I need to know. I need to be in that box with you." With every word, he closed the distance between them, finally stopping within arm's reach.

Mia understood that this was truly her last chance with him. She had to lay everything bare or risk losing him for good. Swallowing against the thickness in her throat, she nodded.

Brax tucked her hair behind her ear, his fingers lingering over the tiny semi-colon tattoo there. "Were you ever going to tell me?"

She took much-needed strength from the touch. "I didn't know how. You already blamed yourself for so much, and I know you. I knew no matter what I said, you'd take that on, too. What good would that do?" She reached up, skimming her fingers over his cheek. "It wasn't your fault. You didn't drive me to that point of desperation. I did that to myself with *my* poor choices."

His face spasmed. "And the baby?"

"That's... harder." Her breath shuddered out. "I had no idea I was pregnant when I left that day. I want to say it would have made a difference, but I honestly don't know. I didn't see going to meet him as the risk it truly was." That was so hard to admit. But she'd promised him honesty.

"I should have bled out at the scene, the same as my father. The only reason I survived was because my body had more blood to lose. Even with that, it was a very near thing. I had so many transfusions."

Taking another breath, she pushed herself to finish. "I didn't even know there'd been a baby until I woke up days later and the doctor was apologizing. And everything that happened with you after felt like my punishment for being careless and making the wrong choice."

"Mia." Brax cupped her nape, pulling her close, his own eyes wet.

"I destroyed everything because I couldn't let go of the past. I lost you and our baby, and I…" Her voice hitched as fresh tears spilled over. "I didn't know how to tell you so you wouldn't hate me."

He wrapped his arms tight around her. "Oh Baby, I don't hate you. And I'm so fucking sorry you had to deal with that alone. It wasn't your fault. None of it was your fault."

She'd been told the same by therapists over the years. But none of them had been in a position to grant her absolution. The long-awaited relief of it washed over her, and she pressed her face against his chest, soaking his shirt.

"Is there anything else?" Brax murmured.

"I can't have children." It came out as a whisper, though it was no longer a secret. Luca had blurted that, too. But it still felt like some kind of failure.

With gentle fingers, Brax wiped the tears from her face. "It's you I want. You I love. If you want kids, we can adopt or get a surrogate. There are options."

She'd given up on the idea of a family when she'd believed she'd lost him for good, and she hadn't allowed herself to even consider the possibility since he'd come back into her life. For the first time in more years than she cared to count, she had hope that she might truly get back the life she wanted.

"That's everything. All the broken and ugly pieces of me. No one but you has ever held all of them."

He lowered his brow to hers. "I love you, Mia. There's nothing about you that's broken or ugly to me."

And this was why he'd always been her person. Why she hoped he always would be. Taking a breath, she tipped her head back to look up at him. "Do you still want to burn the divorce agreement?"

His stormy eyes burned into hers. "Hell yes. You're my wife. I don't ever want to let you go again."

"Thank God."

He kissed her long and deep. A renewal. A claiming. A new beginning. And as her heart soared with fresh joy, she heard the quiet click of a door closing and knew it was an end as well.

19

Brax shut the door to the truck and eyed the bakery building with some apprehension. "Are you sure you're up to this? It's only been a few days. Nobody would blame you for taking more time."

"I'm going completely stir crazy at home. I need to get back to work and get your renovation back on schedule." Without hesitation, Mia strode toward the front door.

He couldn't decide if she was amazingly resilient or just stubborn. But he followed her, wanting to be there in case she had a bigger reaction to being back in the place where she'd been held at gunpoint.

The body had been removed and police had finished processing the scene, clearing them to get back inside. It occurred to him, as she unlocked the door, that he didn't know whether processing the scene involved cleaning up the blood. He should check. She sure as hell didn't need to see that.

"Mia, wait a minute."

But she was already tugging the door open and stepping inside.

The interior was dim, with little of the early morning light filtering in through the windows. It smelled of sawdust, with a faint underlying odor of bleach. But there was no lingering scent of blood or gunpowder. No hint of death in the air.

Brax switched on one of the work lights in the corner. The concrete floor was free of bloodstains. Though whatever had been used to get it up had left the concrete where the body had lain paler than the rest. Maybe the Sheriff's Department had brought in someone to clean up after all. Or maybe Jonah and Holt had been in?

Mia stood staring at the spot. Remembering?

He laced his fingers with hers. "How you feeling? Are you gonna be okay to work here?"

"I'm... okay. I don't know if I'll ever be all right being alone here again, and I certainly won't be bucking to stay late. But it's not as bad as it might be. It helps to know that Abruzzi isn't going to come after me."

They'd talked about so many things in the past few days, but this hadn't been one of them. "Is that a problem for you? That I killed a man to save your life?"

She turned into him, dark eyes searching his face. "No. I've always known you were willing to do anything to protect me. I'm hardly going to criticize you for doing what you've been trained for."

"It doesn't bother you?"

"I'm no stranger to violence, Brax. If you'd hesitated, I might be dead." She took his other hand. "Does it bother you that you had to kill someone outside the line of duty?"

"I've always considered your safety my duty. I'm not losing sleep that there's one less scumbag in the world."

"Good."

There'd been no further developments in the case. No one had been able to track down who Abruzzi had been working for, and so far, there'd been no further disturbances to suggest someone had been hired in his stead. But it would be a long damned time before any of them let their guard down again.

The door swung open, and Jonah strode in with Holt. "Well, you two are here early."

"Somebody's eager to get back to work," Brax explained.

"I hate to break it to you, babe, but you're married to a workaholic."

Holt's mouth curved into the barest of smiles. "Does that mean the divorce is off the table now?"

"Oh, yeah." Brax held up Mia's left hand where she'd put on her wedding band again. "We burned the paperwork. Had a ceremony and everything."

The whole thing had made him think about other ceremonies. His own silver band felt heavier now than it had years ago. He couldn't help remembering how he'd promised her he'd get her something better when they could afford it.

Jonah grinned. "Good to hear it. I feel like we should have drinks or something to celebrate."

"Well, it's not drinks, but I brought sourdough breakfast sandwiches for everybody on the crew this morning. They're in the truck."

"Is there bacon?" Jonah asked, ever hopeful.

"Is the sky blue?"

He did a fist pump.

Mia had gone quiet. "I need to ask all of you something before everyone gets here."

Her serious tone had Brax going alert. "What is it?"

"Much of this renovation has been a disaster because of me. No, I didn't do the damage myself, but the fact remains that you've had theft and vandalism, and a death on the premises that wouldn't have happened if not for me. We don't know if this is over yet. I'll understand if you want someone other than Mountainview to finish up the project. I have some recommendations—"

"Don't be an idiot, Mia." Jonah's tone was mild, but his green eyes were sharp. "We chose your company and your designs because they were the best. So, we've had more than a few hiccups along the way. Shit happens. Doesn't mean the job you're doing is poor. We expect you to finish things out."

"Unless you being here is causing undue anxiety," Holt added. "We understand, if that's the case."

Her eyes were just a little over-bright. "I'm fine. And if you're still okay with it, I'd appreciate the chance to see the job finished."

"Then it's settled." Jonah headed for the door. "Now I want to get my hands on those breakfast sandwiches before the crew gets here and they disappear."

The sandwiches did, indeed, disappear. The Mountainview crew fell on them like a pack of ravening wolves, with a chorus of pleasurable moans that rivaled an adult film.

"Dude, where have these been the whole job?" Brandon demanded.

"I mean, breakfast wasn't part of the contract," Brax pointed out.

"Totally should be," Wally insisted, making no effort to hide it as he peered into the cooler for another.

"Maybe they just wanted to give you guys a taste of what's in store once the bakery's open," Mia suggested. "You *are* going to have something like this on the menu?"

"Don't know yet," Brax admitted. He'd hardly given a single thought to menus the past couple of months. "We're still working on that part. I expect there will be some experimentation to see what people like around here."

"Consider us all one hundred percent on-board with including these breakfast sandwiches." Brick stuffed the last bite into his mouth and brushed off his hands. "Now, where do you want us to start, boss?"

"Bathrooms. I want to get those tile floors in today. The

sooner that's done, the sooner we can install all the new fixtures that came in. Go check to see where we are on the uncoupling membrane."

"You got it."

Brax was cleaning up the parchment paper wrappers from the sandwiches when Brick came back out. "Uh, boss, you need to see this."

Her face went white. "Oh, shit. Now what?"

"I, uh... You should just come."

Brax stayed right on her heels as she hurried inside. Wally stood in the open door to the women's room. He ducked out of the way as they approached, and Brax caught and held the door.

"What the hell?" Mia muttered.

The bathroom was finished. All the tile had been laid. The new toilets were installed. The new sinks and faucets. Even the hand dryer had been hung on the wall. She ducked around him, opening the men's room. It had also been finished.

"How?" Brax muttered.

"Luca," she murmured.

They hadn't heard a word from him since he'd left the house days before. He hadn't responded to Mia's texts, and when she'd gone by to check on him, she'd found that he'd moved out. Brax assumed that meant he'd finally accepted that Mia would never return his feelings, and he was getting the hell out of Dodge. Brax was completely okay with that. He knew Mia had complicated feelings about all of it. She still felt the sting of betrayal over everything Luca had revealed. But he'd been her best friend for ten years, and she'd been worried about him. The lack of contact had unsettled her. And apparently, somewhere, in the midst of all of it, he'd come back to do this work.

"Why?" Brax asked.

She pointed to the post-it note stuck to one of the mirrors. *I'm sorry.* "A peace offering."

Brax didn't know whether Mia would ever be able to fully forgive him. After how things had gone down, he wasn't even sure if she'd ever hear from Luca again. He didn't blame the guy for not being able to face down seeing the woman he loved day after day, happy with someone else. But as gestures went, it wasn't a bad one. It put to rights the last of what had been damaged.

"Hey, where's Luca?" Brandon asked.

"He's gone to pursue other opportunities." She gave one more long look to the sparkling bathroom. "Okay, since this is out of the way, let's get to the lighting. I'm gonna go call the tin roof guys."

And just like that, she was back to being the boss.

"I *KNEW* there were original hardwoods under this carpet," Mia crowed. With fresh enthusiasm, she attacked the hideous shag with her razor knife.

Brax yanked a section free of the carpet tacks, giving her some heavy side eye as he dragged it back. "Remind me never to piss you off. You're a little too practiced with that knife."

She laughed. "I have a great deal of experience hacking up horrible carpet, and I've been dying to get to this part of the house. The sooner we get rid of the carpet, the sooner we can get to work on the fireplace." And she had such big plans for the fireplace.

"Oh, I don't know. I'm kind of gonna miss this carpet." He waggled his eyebrows and shot her a heated look that had her insides turning molten.

She pressed her legs together as all the memories of that day they'd finally come back together scrolled through her brain. "I feel confident we can christen every room in this house without keeping the shag carpet."

He dropped the hunk of torn carpet and reached for her hand. "I vote we start with the kitchen. Those counters are exactly the right height for—"

Mia covered his mouth with her hand. "I know exactly what you're thinking, and I'm entirely on board. Later. Work first." Work had to come first, or they'd never get finished with this house.

He nipped her fingers. "Slave driver."

"You love me."

"Damned straight."

He hauled her in for a kiss that curled her toes inside her work boots and left her swaying.

"Mmm."

"Incentive to work fast," he declared.

"You are a wicked, wicked man, Brax Whitmore."

He flashed her a grin that proved her point. "You love me."

"God, I do."

She was still grinning foolishly after him when he carried out the first roll of carpet.

Over the past month, they'd finally finished the renovation on the bakery, with no further disruptions or delays. All had been quiet, and she was slowly starting to relax. To live normally again. It would still be months or longer before she stopped looking over her shoulder, but maybe she was finally free of the secret that had haunted her for years.

Next week they'd be down to the punch out work at the bakery. The place looked fantastic, if Mia did say so herself. The guys had gone with a deep forest green for the siding, which set off the silver, tin roof and the natural cedar posts of the porch. Inside was exactly the rustic industrial look she'd planned. The pallet-board shiplap was accented with open shelving built from iron pipe and reclaimed wood. She'd convinced them to let her add a narrow counter at bar height along the front walls to provide additional seating beyond the tables that hadn't yet come in because the crew's response to what they'd sampled had proved people were going to be showing up in droves. The guys were still rounding up the rest of the commercial appliances for the kitchen, but the walk-in cooler had been installed, as had the used commercial ovens they'd nabbed from a sandwich shop going out of business in Nashville. She and Brax had left Holt and Jonah to argue over placement of the new stainless steel worktables, and who got what workstation, so they could come out to work on their house.

Their house.

It had a long way to go, but they were enjoying the hell out of the process of turning it into the dream they'd shared so long ago. Mia hoped to get it to the point of being livable by the end of the year. Maybe faster, as Jonah and Holt had expressed a willingness to lend a hand, and she knew Porter would pitch in, if she needed him.

If there was still a faint shadow on her heart over Luca, it couldn't be helped. She'd finally gotten a postcard from him last week.

I just wanted to let you know I'm okay. Or I will be. I need time and space to figure myself out on my own. I'm sorry I hurt you, and I wish you all the happiness in the world.

He hadn't even signed it, but she knew his handwriting.

That was the best she could expect right now. Maybe someday they'd reconnect, but she knew they'd never be the friends they once were. It would take a long time to overcome the grief of that. She hoped he found someone who'd love him the way he deserved to be loved, who'd cherish and appreciate his big, grumpy caretaking heart.

She went back to work on the carpet, ripping up the next piece herself.

"Hey, Mia! You gotta come see this." Brax's voice floated in through the open living room windows.

Abandoning the carpet, she headed outside to find him standing on a massive rock at the edge of the property.

"What is it?"

"Sun's going down. Check out this view."

More than willing to indulge him, she took the hand he offered, letting him pull her up. The rock made for a high point, overlooking the valley housing Eden's Ridge below. To the west, the sun had dipped below the ridge that gave the town its name, painting the sky in a brilliant wash of color. They stood, hand in hand, watching as those colors deepened, edging toward evening.

"It's a helluva view," he murmured.

"Yeah. I thought so when I first saw the house. But it's better with you beside me." Mia tipped her head to his shoulder, comforted by the solid feel of it.

His sigh was contented as he pulled her against him. "I never imagined we'd get here. I wish we hadn't missed all those years. That neither of us had to go through all the hurt. But all of it makes me appreciate finding you again in a way I'm not sure I would have fully done otherwise."

"The lack of something makes it easier to appreciate when you have it. I don't think either of us will take each other for granted again."

"No. And that's had me thinking." He tugged her to face him. "Nothing about our relationship has been normal. We didn't do anything the usual way. I didn't even ask you to marry me. I told you we should. Gave you a boatload of reasons why it was a good idea. But I never asked. You deserved to be asked. To be romanced."

Confused, she looped her arms around his shoulders. "If you're under the impression that I'm upset about that, I'm not. I married you because I loved you. I wasn't fussy about how we got there."

"Still. You missed out on a lot because of our circumstances, and I want to make that up to you."

Loosening her hands, he stepped back.

"What are you..." But she trailed off as he dropped to one knee in the mountain twilight.

The corners of his mouth lifted as he pulled a small box out of his pocket. "I promised you years ago, I'd get you a better one of these when I could. We're still not doing anything the normal way, but as we start out on this new leg of our lives together, I want to do it right." He opened the box to reveal a white gold band with a diamond solitaire in a bezel setting.

Mia covered her mouth to hide the tremble there as he continued.

"So, Maria Isabella Ramirez Whitmore, I'm asking you to marry me. Again. Will you renew your vows with me in the big white wedding I couldn't give you before, in front of all our friends and found family?"

She blinked back tears as she stared down at the tough, protective man with the secretly romantic heart as he knelt before her. "You want to marry me again?"

"I've never loved anyone else the way I love you. I want to build the life with you we always wanted. Make a family, in whatever form that takes. And I want you to know, every day, that you're cherished and the best part of my world. Another wedding seems like a damned fine way to do that. But if you're not into all that, you could just wear the upgraded ring."

Reaching down to frame his face, Mia bent to brush her mouth to his. "I would love to marry you again, with all the bells and whistles."

His lips curved under hers. "Good."

They both watched as he slid the ring onto her finger against her original wedding band.

"A perfect fit," she murmured.

"Just like us." Brax lifted her hand to brush a kiss over her knuckles.

"For the record, I'm really enjoying this secret romantic side."

"Then you're really gonna love this." Without warning, he scooped her up, bride-style, and strode toward the house.

"What are you doing?" she laughed.

"Carrying you over the threshold."

"Isn't that getting ahead of things?"

"We're already married. I figure we can do this part in whatever order we want. Starting with the kitchen."

And she was happy to let him convince her that the horrible shag carpet could, in fact, wait.

EPILOGUE

L ove and marriage looked good on some people.

Holt Steele watched as his buddy and business partner made googly eyes at his wife on the other side of the bakery's freshly kitted out commercial kitchen as they hooked up the new range. Under other circumstances, he might've busted Brax's chops about it. But he and Mia had been through so much to come back to each other, Holt didn't have the heart. They had a right to wallow in whatever happiness they'd found again, without him sharing his own generally negative opinions about matrimony. Some people wanted to be tied down, and that was fine for them. He just wasn't one of them.

"Hey, where's Jonah?" Mia asked. "I figured he'd be in on this installation if for no other reason than so the three of you can inaugurate the kitchen with deliciousness."

"He said he had to make a run down to Knoxville for something this morning." Holt checked his watch. "He ought to be back soon, though."

As if summoned by the statement, the man himself strode

in through the front door they'd left open to let in the spring breeze. "I have returned with a surprise."

A familiar, willowy blonde came in behind him. "And how are my favorite students?"

Holt broke into a smile. "Rachel McCleary. What brings you this far down south?" He pushed out of the kitchen and past the front counter to greet her with a hug.

She squeezed him back. "You guys, of course. Jonah requested my expertise to make sure you think of everything before your opening."

Holt glanced at his other friend. "Did he now?"

"Man, we need all the help we can get. We know how to bake. We didn't exactly cover the business side of things in the program."

"Fear not. I've got your backs. Brax, where are you hiding? Oh, is this the kitchen?"

They trailed her through the swinging door as she went to meet him. "Oh, this is fabulous. I can't believe you ended up with this from that eyesore you started with."

Brax beamed. "That would be because of this woman right here. Rachel, meet my wife, Mia."

In her usual friendly way, Rachel took Mia's offered hand and pulled her in for a hug. "Sorry, I'm a hugger. And I've heard so much about you, I feel like I know you."

Mia shot her husband the side eye. "Have you now?"

"Wasn't me," Brax protested.

"Jonah's been keeping me up-to-date on everybody," Rachel explained.

They all turned to look at Jonah, whose ears had turned red. "What? We're friends. She wanted to know how everyone was doing."

Rachel grinned. "And he's Southern, so he'll gossip more than either of you."

Mia snorted. "So, you're their teacher from Syracuse?"

"Guilty. It's so nice to meet you."

"Likewise."

Rachel hugged Brax, then stepped back to take a long look at him. "You look good. Happy. It's nice to see."

"Nice to feel. How long are you here for?"

"Audrey's second cohort is making solid progress, and we finally found another baker to help, so I get a break for a while. I'm not sure exactly how long I'm staying. As long as you need me, I guess. At least a couple of weeks. It'll do me good to be out of Syracuse for a while. It's my first time in... well, a long time."

Holt didn't miss the shadow that passed over her usually cheerful face. It had been nearly two years since her firefighter husband had died because of injuries sustained on the job, and she'd grieved hard. Dr. Graham's program had been as much therapy for her as it had been for the rest of them.

"Well, we're glad to have you. Where are you staying?" Holt asked.

"I booked a room at The Misfit Inn. I hear their spa is amazing, so I'm planning to avail myself of their services while I'm here."

"I can attest to the truth of that," Mia said. "My business partner is married to one of the sisters who owns it. You'll love it."

Talk turned back to the building itself and they gave her the fifty-cent tour, ending behind the display cases out front.

"Well, I think it's awesome. It's a well-thought-out space from both a retail and kitchen perspective," Rachel declared. "What are you planning to call it?"

Holt exchanged a look with both his partners.

Jonah offered a sheepish smile. "We haven't actually decided yet."

"You need something clever," Rachel declared. "Something hooky that people will remember."

"Bad Boy Bakers."

Everybody but Holt swung toward the new voice. He didn't have to turn to picture its owner. Cayla Black. Curvy, with honey-blonde hair, and far more appealing than she had any right to be. And, as a single mom, very, very off limits. He'd done his time raising a child when he'd taken on his baby sister, Hadley. He wasn't interested in going down that road again. So, it didn't matter how much this woman made him want to smile, because she deserved someone who could be all in.

He had to remind himself of that fact yet again as he turned and caught sight of her pretty blush. She lifted her hand in a self-conscious wave. "Hi, neighbors. Sorry. I didn't mean to interrupt."

Her other hand stayed on the shoulder of a pint-sized version of her, who tucked in close to her mother's side.

"Bad Boy Bakers?" Jonah repeated.

"I mean, not to objectify you, but... look at the three of you." Her gaze skated over all of them before landing on Holt and lingering a beat too long, the color in her cheeks deepening before she looked away again.

Mia laughed. "You're not wrong."

"I think it's kind of genius," Rachel agreed.

Brax rubbed a hand on the back of his reddening neck. "Uh... I think we're gonna have to discuss that."

Yeah, Holt wasn't touching that with a ten-foot pole. He turned to Cayla. "What are you doing here? Do you have another cake emergency?" He chose not to think about how often in the past few weeks he'd wished for her to pop up with one. Creating that cake on a ridiculous deadline had been some of the most fun he'd had in months.

"Actually, no. Mia asked me to pop over. Something about a job?" Her gaze tracked behind his shoulder to where the woman in question stood with Brax.

"Yeah, I wanted to talk to you in your formal event planner capacity." She lifted her left hand to show off a shiny new diamond. "We're getting married again, and we'd like you to plan our vow renewal ceremony."

"Oh my God! That's wonderful!" Cayla released her daughter to rush behind the counter and wrap Mia in a massive hug. "I'd *love* to plan your vow renewal!"

Seeing the little girl shrink back in the face of all the grownups, Holt skirted around the counter and hunkered down to her level. "Hi, there."

It wasn't until those big Disney princess eyes fixed on his feet and got even bigger that he realized he was wearing his running blade instead of his normal prosthetic with a shoe.

"Are you a Transformer?" she whispered.

"Maddie!" Cayla choked out.

Preferring the kid's direct approach to the way adults tended to go out of the way to avoid the topic, Holt shook his head. "Nope."

"What happened to your foot?"

He wasn't entirely sure what was an appropriate way to explain amputation to a five-year-old. Straightening, he went with the simplest explanation he could think of. "I got hurt, so they had to give me a new one."

Maddie nodded very seriously. Then she bent, wrapping her arms around his leg, and pressed a kiss to his knee where the prosthetic attached.

Everybody froze, including Holt.

Maddie looked up with those big brown eyes that were just like her mother's. "Mama says we should always kiss the booboos to make them better."

In that moment, Holt felt his tough, guarded warrior's heart fall straight at the little girl's feet.

He was so completely screwed.

I HOPE you enjoyed reading Brax and Mia's second chance! As you may have guessed Holt and Cayla are up next in *Wrapped Up with a Ranger*. Stay tuned!

OTHER BOOKS BY KAIT NOLAN

A complete and up-to-date list of all my books can be found at https://kaitnolan.com.

THE MISFIT INN SERIES
SMALL TOWN FAMILY ROMANCE

- *When You Got A Good Thing* (Kennedy and Xander)
- *Til There Was You* (Misty and Denver)
- *Those Sweet Words* (Pru and Flynn)
- *Stay A Little Longer* (Athena and Logan)
- *Bring It On Home* (Maggie and Porter)

RESCUE MY HEART SERIES
SMALL TOWN MILITARY ROMANCE

- *Baby It's Cold Outside* (Ivy and Harrison)
- *What I Like About You* (Laurel and Sebastian)
- *Bad Case of Loving You* (Paisley and Ty prequel)

- *Made For Loving You* (Paisley and Ty)

MEN OF THE MISFIT INN
SMALL TOWN SOUTHERN ROMANCE

- *Let It Be Me* (Emerson and Caleb)
- *Our Kind of Love* (Abbey and Kyle)
- *Don't You Wanna Stay* (Deanna and Wyatt)
- *Until We Meet Again* (Samantha and Griffin prequel)
- *Come A Little Closer* (Samantha and Griffin)

BAD BOY BAKERS
SMALL TOWN MILITARY ROMANCE

- *Rescued By a Bad Boy* (Brax and Mia prequel)
- *Mixed Up With a Marine* (Brax and Mia)
- *Wrapped Up with a Ranger* (Holt and Cayla)
- *Stirred Up by a SEAL* (Jonah and Rachel)

WISHFUL ROMANCE SERIES
SMALL TOWN SOUTHERN ROMANCE

- *Once Upon A Coffee* (Avery and Dillon)
- *To Get Me To You* (Cam and Norah)
- *Know Me Well* (Liam and Riley)
- *Be Careful, It's My Heart* (Brody and Tyler)
- *Just For This Moment* (Myles and Piper)
- *Wish I Might* (Reed and Cecily)
- *Turn My World Around* (Tucker and Corinne)
- *Dance Me A Dream* (Jace and Tara)
- *See You Again* (Trey and Sandy)
- *The Christmas Fountain* (Chad and Mary Alice)
- *You Were Meant For Me* (Mitch and Tess)
- *A Lot Like Christmas* (Ryan and Hannah)

- *Dancing Away With My Heart* (Zach and Lexi)

WISHING FOR A HERO SERIES (A WISHFUL SPINOFF SERIES)
SMALL TOWN ROMANTIC SUSPENSE

- *Make You Feel My Love* (Judd and Autumn)
- *Watch Over Me* (Nash and Rowan)
- *Can't Take My Eyes Off You* (Ethan and Miranda)
- *Burn For You* (Sean and Delaney)

MEET CUTE ROMANCE
SMALL TOWN SHORT ROMANCE

- *Once Upon A Snow Day*
- *Once Upon A New Year's Eve*
- *Once Upon An Heirloom*
- *Once Upon A Coffee*
- *Once Upon A Campfire*
- *Once Upon A Rescue*

SUMMER CAMP
CONTEMPORARY ROMANCE

- *Once Upon A Campfire*
- *Second Chance Summer*

ABOUT KAIT

Kait is a Mississippi native, who often swears like a sailor, calls everyone sugar, honey, or darlin', and can wield a bless your heart like a saber or a Snuggie, depending on requirements.

You can find more information on this RITA ® Award-winning author and her books on her website http://kaitnolan.com.

Do you need more small town sass and spark? Sign up for her newsletter to hear about new releases, book deals, and exclusive content!

CPSIA information can be obtained
at www.ICGtesting.com
Printed in the USA
BVHW030312310722
643401BV00002B/5

9 781648 350351